RED MOON RISING

Margaret Bailey

ISBN: 0986243515
ISBN- 9780986243516

CHAPTER 1

RIVER WILLOW

River Willow busied herself looping hand-dyed wool into skeins, trying not to hear the message of the wind howling about her lonely hogan. It was the great-great-grandchild of the wind she herself had been born into, the late-summer wind that uprooted and scattered. Now, when the pains of her own motherhood had begun, the wind that hurled sand through the barrel lid in the roof also cast fear into her heart. She did not want her child tossed about like tumbleweed.

She hung the skeins according to color in the eight corners of the hogan, lay down on her bed of sheepskins, and fanned herself against the heat pressing in from the adobe walls.

As evening fell, the gusts rushed away to the east, leaving a dome of heat in their wake. In the scoured stillness of the New Mexico desert, only her labor reminded her that the wind had not swept all of life before it.

Faster the waves of pain came, and the faces of her mother and grandmother hovered in them like light shimmering in the distance. They had driven her away; she would not have the age-old comfort of woman helping woman through the birthing. Still, she was thankful her child would not be born into the howling wind.

Her pains close together now, River Willow rolled off the skins, opened the barrel lid to vent the smoke, and lit a fire in the pit to heat water. Groaning, she dragged the sheep skins out into the cooler air that still smelled of dust. She spread the skins next to the southeast wall and placed a hand-woven cloth on them to receive her baby. In the deepening dusk, she brought a pan of hot water and lowered herself into a birthing position against the wall.

When she looked up, dread clamped her heart. Behind the Sangre de Cristos Mountains to the east, a dim red light outlined the stark peaks. The time for birth was wrong, but it would not be put off.

The eerie light grew brighter, more baleful than the wind. The full moon climbed the peaks to glare down on her through the red dust. It clutched at her heart and she tried not to push. But the signs were too strong, and the child answered the pull as if it knew Mother Earth's call. River Willow's eyes brimmed. Mother Earth would want too much of this child, and give little in return.

And then, as one last gust of wind rushed past, blowing more sand to redden the moon, two people lay on the skins where there had been one. River Willow held her daughter to her breast to shield her from the moon. She kissed the tiny forehead, her joy for the end of loneliness mixed with fear for her baby's future.

The moon shone fiercely. Father Sky was showing her what she must call the child. River Willow frowned back, but in the end she bowed her head. She must name the child now, though it was the custom of her people to wait. "You are born in the rising moon," she said in her native Navajo, smiling at the child and shading the face with her hand. "You will live long. But the moon is red. I fear..." No, she would not say the fears aloud. "Mother Earth needs something special from you."

After a minute she went on, a catch in her voice, "You will be Blood Moon Rising." The name swirled from her breath like vultures through the desert air. "No, it is too much. Your name will be Red Moon Rising." She caressed her daughter's head and rocked side to side, leaning against the hogan. She glared back at the moon but lowered her eyes again and whispered, "I will keep you safe even if it brings the anger of Father Sky."

A jagged, stabbing pain struck her right temple and threw her head against the wall. Breathing hard, she waited for it to pass. Perhaps his anger would pass, too.

She curled over to become one again with the baby and the joy she brought. Slowly, the dust settled and the moon bathed the desert in silver and gray. Unwillingly, River Willow cut the cord that bound them and washed her child with a clean old shirt sleeve. She put a pinch of pollen she'd collected from cactus flowers on the infant's tongue. From the mountains the cool of night descended across the vast sage desert.

The brief winter after Red Moon's birth eased into spring. On a day of warming wind, River Willow forced herself awake quickly, trying to keep a dream from following her into the predawn light. It was the old dream—her mother standing in front of the white trader's store in Shiprock where they'd sold their blankets, her arms folded across her chest, eyes angry and forbidding.

The remembered anger tracked down her spine like a cactus thorn. She turned on her side and looked at her daughter. Red Moon's big, serious eyes were looking back. The wisps of hair that had grown in lighter at the corners of her forehead stood out like little tufts of down. River Willow stroked one with her thumb, feeling the melting sadness in her heart. That was what Brad had left her, a bit of his hair color. He'd brought her with him from Shiprock, helped her build the hogan, and then left without knowing he had a child.

"Good morning, little one." She smiled away dreams and memories and shoved herself up to lean against the wall. As soon as she freed her right breast, Red Moon's mouth opened, ready to feed.

"Come, hungry child," River Willow said, laughing. She drew the baby to her and pulled the woven blanket back over both of them.

Afterwards she laid the child back on the skins and tickled her. Red Moon answered with her big open-mouthed smile. River Willow knelt over the baby. She picked up a seed pod and rattled it. The baby's breath caught. It was almost a laugh. It caught again. "Yes," said River Willow. She blew on Red Moon's stomach, fanning the little flame of joy. Her laughter blended with Red Moon's in the warming hogan.

River Willow sat up on her knees. "Well, child," she said, "It is the day for the First Laugh gifts." She got up from the sheep skins and took a small paper sack from the shelf by the window. "May you always walk in laughter," she chanted.

Her voice caught on the memory of the red moon. How much laughter would there be for this Red Moon? The question haunted her as she played with the baby.

She rattled the sack and set it down on the skins. Red Moon rolled on her stomach and slapped at the noisy paper, laughing. When she tired of playing with the sound, she sat up and picked up the sack at the bottom. Two little dolls fell out, the one from the white trader in Taos and the one River Willow had made. Mr. Koenig's doll had come from his store with blond hair and frills and bright colors. The other, made of scraps and stuffed with left-over yarn, wore the black velvet skirt of Navajo women and a tiny squash blossom necklace embroidered across the dark blue blouse.

Red moon laughed at the dolls. She picked each one up by its foot and tried to put them both in her mouth.

River Willow smiled sadly. "You cannot eat both the white and the Navajo, child," she said. "It makes you choke." She gathered her daughter and the dolls up and went out to greet the morning sun.

River Willow was weaving on the south side of her hogan, working faster than she liked. If she didn't finish this blanket today, she wouldn't have enough to trade in Taos tomorrow for salt and flour. There would be little to feed her child. Red Moon was growing so fast, tall as the tallest sage bushes now, and there never seemed to be quite enough for them both.

She heard scratching in the dirt behind her. The child, five summers now, was tracing the shadow of the mule's lean-to in the sand. River Willow smiled and went back to her design. The scratching went on for a while and then Red Moon was standing behind her.

"That game is no fun anymore." the child complained. "Let's go to Taos, Mother."

Taos. River Willow went there only when she had to trade. Red Moon had become so curious about everything she saw there, about the whites who looked at them like scorpions. The child was safer at home.

"We have to go tomorrow, child, after I finish this. Come now, sing with me." River Willow smiled and began to chant the weaving song she'd learned from her Tewa grandmother. Red Moon sang the parts she knew. A light desert wind playing around the hogan caught up the words and danced them away toward mountain and sky.

O Mother Earth, O Father Sky,
Your children are we, and with tired backs
We bring to you the gifts you love.
Then weave for us a garment of brightness;
May the warp be the white light of morning,
May the weft be the red light of evening,
May the fringes be the falling rain,
May the border be the standing rainbow.
Thus weave for us a garment of brightness,
That we may walk fittingly where birds sing,
That we may walk fittingly where grass is green,
O Mother Earth, O Father Sky.

Red Moon watched her open the warp with the flat stick, thread the colored yarn through the pattern with her fingers, beat twice with the comb-like beater, and pull on the rod above the weaving line. It was the first time she'd concentrated on the loom.

"Why do you have those sticks in the strings, Mother?" she asked in Navajo. "Why so many strings hanging out?"

River Willow motioned for Red Moon to climb onto her lap. "Come, child. I think it's time for you to learn to weave." She knew if she stopped now she'd have to work later in poor light, but passing her family's tradition on to her daughter was important. She kissed the back of Red Moon's head. "You see how the colors make a pattern? You see I need more gray in it here? I'll open these strings for you to put the yarn through." She slid her smooth, flat stick into a section of the warp and turned it to open a shed. "Now you put the gray yarn through there."

Red Moon obeyed and let out a shriek of delight. "Look at me, Mother, I weave, just like you."

Red Moon couldn't get the teeth of the beater through the warp and the yarn remained loose.

"Never mind. Now I pull on the long stick up here. You see how it's tied to every other string? When I pull it forward and open the strings, you can thread the gray yarn from the other end. See what happens?"

Red Moon was all concentration. "Yes, now it's behind the strings." She pulled it through and then wove a few more lines in her mother's pattern before she lost interest and began to wiggle. River Willow gave her a push.

"You go get water and we'll have supper soon, child. When I finish this I'll make a small loom for you and you can weave your own."

She watched her daughter skip toward the cistern. The strands of light hair, the color of Brad's, flitted in the sun like two insect wings. If it were safe, she would leave the child here tomorrow, but...

Pain stabbed at her temple, as it sometimes did, jerking her head to the side. She put her hand over it and let it fade. Perhaps it was only the setting sun piercing her eyes. She turned back to the loom and undid Red Moon's loose weaving in the reddening light.

The following summer, River Willow helped Red Moon cut her first weaving from the loom, a small blanket the color of sage inset with a diamond in the red-brown of the desert sand. She showed her how to tie off the ends.

Red Moon held it as high as her small arms would reach. "I really finished it, Mother, look."

With the blanket blocking Red Moon's face, River Willow allowed herself a smile. The blanket was unevenly woven with loops hanging out of it, and the diamond was so crooked it was nearly round. "I'm very proud of you, child."

Red Moon looked at it and then at the one on the larger loom. Her face fell. "It's not really good. Look at the diamond."

River Willow tried to comfort her. "Things made by people are not supposed to be perfect. If they're perfect, the spirits can't pass through them."

Red Moon looked at it again and traced the lopsided diamond with her finger. "It has my name in it, see?"

River Willow squinted at the irregular pattern. "Yes, it does." Her name. How much should she tell her? She pulled her lips between her teeth and looked up at the mountains. So far she'd kept her child safe. Father Sky hadn't shown any anger. Perhaps he'd forgotten Red Moon's birth.

"I gave you that name because Father Sky showed it to me when you were born. It's a special name because Mother Earth has a special thing for you to do."

Red Moon puffed up with importance. "What thing?"

"I don't know. She'll give you a sign. But that's why Red Moon Rising will always be your most important name, even if you take others. When you feel very strongly about something, you can take it as a name."

"Can I be First Blanket?"

"Of course. But don't use it too much. Names are special things and it takes the spirit out of them if you use them all the time."

"Do I have to trade this at Mr. Koenig's?"

"No. It's yours to keep. But it will help when you can weave blankets we can sell."

"Help what?"

"Help us keep going, child. Now, come, let's hang it in the hogan."

Her child grew as tall as her shoulders, and River Willow knew that in a few summers her body would reach womanhood. There was still so much to teach her. She took her, as she did every summer, to the mountains to collect edible plants, herbs, and dyes. They camped by a stream, glad of the clear running water after the scant water that collected in their cistern.

River Willow watched her daughter. Happiness and pride welled up from her heart. In other years Red Moon had spent her time playing in the water and chattering at the busy squirrels. But this year she listened to the explanations of drying the bitter bind weed milk for stomach sickness or making yarrow tea for the head. All afternoon she helped with the gathering and washing, and by evening the plants that needed boiling before drying hung over the branches that walled the clearing.

River Willow sent Red Moon to the stream for water while she fashioned a spit and skewered a rabbit she'd snared. When Red Moon didn't return, River Willow found her squatted at the stream's edge in the dying light, listening to the ceaseless babble of the water. She looked up and asked, "Mother, why does the water just run and run. Why doesn't someone up there turn it off?"

River Willow laughed. She knelt on the bed of dead needles and drew Red Moon close. "I don't know where you get your questions,

child," she said, the laughter still in her voice. "This water is not like in the rest room in Mr. Koenig's store. It comes from all the snow higher up that's melting. You know how the snow makes little streams around the hogan when the sun melts it? Well, a lot more snow is up there and it runs off in streams like this."

Red Moon looked upstream, still pondering. The rushing murmur of the water went on as before.

Her mother turned her so they could look at each other and stroked her cheek. "This water is life," she said. "The snow is what makes the mountains like the breasts of Mother Earth so she can feed us. You don't remember, but I used to feed you milk from my breasts."

Red Moon cocked her head to her left. "I don't know 'breast.'"

River Willow bared her breasts. "I had milk in there for you when you were a baby. You will have breasts, too, in a few summers. And one day you will have babies to feed with them." Her breath stopped. That was not what Father Sky had showed her. The words had popped out as a bubble of hope, and maybe if she kept her safe from... What? The white world?

Red Moon giggled as she stared at the rise and shadow of her mother's skin in the firelight. "You fed me from there? Funny breast mountains, hanging on sideways like that." She pulled up her rabbit skin shirt and looked at her flat nipples. "Do streams run down breasts when you feed babies?"

River Willow laughed. "No, the baby drinks the milk before it can run down. Maybe that's why you think the water shouldn't run like this. Anyway, when the baby can eat other things, the milk dries up."

Red Moon dipped a handful of water from the stream and let it run through her fingers. "Is this water going to dry up?"

"It could, I suppose." She listened to the stream now, and felt a wave of fear. The water that fed her spring came from the mountains, too. "There isn't much water this year, is there?" she said.

Later they piled pine twigs up to make mattresses then spread the sheepskins to buffer the needles.

In the darkness Red Moon asked, "Did you have a mother who fed you?"

"Yes, of course. And a grandmother. They're weavers, too. My grandmother was from one of the Tewa pueblos over near Santa Fe, and she taught me the weaving song and the patterns of her people."

Red Moon breathed out sharply. "There are people who belong to you? Where are they now?"

"A long way from here, near the place called Rock with Wings."

Out of the dark came the skittering of an animal. Red Moon moved closer as she asked, "Why don't they live here?"

"Because they live there. On a place for Indians."

"Are there other people who belong to you?"

"My father and brothers."

Again a minute passed. Red Moon's voice dropped to a confused whisper. "Do I have a father?"

River Willow reached out to touch the face she could barely see in the dark. "Yes, everybody has a father."

"Who is he? Why isn't he with us?"

Now it was River Willow's time for silence while she gathered the story she'd never told her daughter. "Your father's name was Brad. He was a white man. When I met him he was working for the white trader who bought our blankets. Your father was a laughing man and he made me feel good."

Red Moon's sleeping roll rustled in the dark and River Willow knew she'd sat up, too stunned to lie still. "My father. Tell me more."

River Willow threw off the sleeping roll and sat up cross-legged. She reached across and took her hand. "I suppose you should know, and I hope you're old enough now. It happened like this: I'd been in the white school, and I thought I wanted to live in the white world then. But after a while I knew I couldn't, and Brad couldn't live in the Indian world, either. He never promised me he would stay. He was a nice man, very kind and hard-working, but sometimes he could get very angry. And he was a drifter, my child. When I knew you were in my belly, I didn't tell him, because I didn't want him to feel bad when he left. And I knew he would." She took a heavy breath. "When there was no more work for him around Taos, he went away."

Red Moon's voice quavered. "Is he coming back?"

"No, child, he's not."

Red Moon's breath went ragged with sadness. "I want to know my father. Someday I'll go find him." She got up and settled in River Willow's lap with her arms around her neck. "Did it make you sad when he left?"

River Willow hugged the child who was almost as big as she. "For a while. He left me the mule. He probably thought I'd go back to Rock with Wings on it."

"What did my father look like?"

"He was taller than Mr. Koenig and he had brown hair exactly the color of yours where it's lighter. He had laughing brown eyes and a mustache."

Red Moon shook her head. "I try to see a face, but all I see is the brown eyes. How did you know him?"

"One day he came down to the river from the trading post where he was building another room. I was watching the Navajo willow trees. I loved to watch them. They looked like they were dancing under the footsteps of the wind."

She stopped, but Red Moon seemed to know she was looking back and would go on in a minute. She hugged her tighter. "He stood next to me for a while before he asked my name. I didn't feel right about telling it to him. White people use names too much. When I didn't say anything, he said he would just call me River Willow. I kept the name for the white people."

"Why didn't you go back to your mother when Brad left?"

River Willow rocked herself and the child.

"My mother and father were angry with me. And I knew they couldn't afford the Enemy Way."

Red Moon twisted around to look at her.

"That's a ceremony to help people who have taken on too many ways not of The People."

"Are the whites our enemies?"

"Not so much anymore. But there are many things whites do that The People shouldn't do."

"What?"

"Well, the People believe it's bad to kill rattlesnakes. Brad told me that was just an old story and didn't make sense any more. He taught me how to shoot and gave me the rifle. But whenever I shoot a rattler, I feel bad. I wouldn't do it any more, if we didn't need the money we get for the skins. Still, every time I shoot one, I apologize and thank it for helping us. That's why I taught you to respect the things you have to kill."

"Why didn't you and Brad go to Taos to live?"

"When we first came we found the spring. The water just dripped out of the rocks, so we camped there for a while. Brad made the cistern and covered it so the water wouldn't dry out. Then we found an old buckboard in the gulch that goes down to the river, you know the one where we nearly always get a snake or two?"

Red Moon nodded and turned to lean back on River Willow's breast.

"We used the wood to build a little house. That's where I got the chains for the loom, too. But the house was too cold in the winter and in the spring we used the rocks from the desert to make the walls thicker and the house bigger. Brad laughed at me for wanting eight walls. But then he helped me."

She paused again, and Red Moon waited. "I think he already knew he would leave. After he left I went to the pueblo near Taos and learned how to make adobe and used that to cover the rocks."

"Do you know where my father went?"

"No." The story had brought back all the pain of Brad's leaving, and it made tears well. "Time for bed now." She lifted her and Red Moon scrambled into her bedroll again.

"Mother,..."

"Go to sleep now, child. We have much to do tomorrow."

The following morning Red Moon looked pale and tired.

River Willow placed her hand on the child's forehead. "Are you sick, child?"

Red Moon looked up and her eyes were very sad. "No, I dreamed someone turned the water off up there and then a white man came and took me away on the mule. He had brown eyes, but he didn't have anything else on his face. Is that my sign, Mother?"

River Willow led her to the stream. "No, child. See? The water's still running. And I will not let anyone take you away from me." But she stared at the water again and felt the dread.

They gathered red bugler, blue lupine, Indian paint brush, purple larkspur, and wild onions for making wool dyes. They stripped bark from Douglas firs for tannic acid to cure rabbit and snake skins, and River Willow gathered herbs and roots she used for making teas.

On the way back down the mountain they stopped at the open place where they could see the whole desert below them. River Willow traced with her eyes the endless, branched, dark scar that was the Rio Grande Canyon, the mountains on her left that stretched away to the southwest with the slender mesa just before the edge of the world. She could see Taos and the pueblo.

Standing next to her, Red Moon raised her arms straight out. "I like it up here. I feel like an eagle in the sky. Why don't we stay here?"

"Someone would come and tell us to leave." River Willow looked toward the northwest.

Red Moon tugged at her skirt. "What are you looking at? There's nothing there."

"Rock with Wings is there, but too far away to see."

In a few minutes they led the mule on down the slope.

In the last summer of Red Moon's childhood, they stood outside the hogan, watching the sun release its hold on the peaks above Taos. Only a few patches of snow dotted the north sides of the peaks.

River Willow's eyes narrowed and she shook her head. "Remember when you asked why no one turned off the water in the stream up there? Perhaps Father Sky is doing it."

Red Moon, as tall as she was now, asked, "What would happen if all the snow dried up?"

"We'd have no more water. We'd have to leave."

Red Moon took a step backwards. "Leave? But this is our home."

"I know but we have no paper that says this land belongs to us, and the white men think they own it all. They could make us leave."

Stunned, Red Moon asked, "Where would we go?"

"I don't know. Back to my family, maybe. They were very angry when I left with Brad, but maybe not so angry now. And maybe they'd forgive me if they met their wonderful granddaughter."

Red Moon turned and started into the hogan. "Let's go there now."

"Not now, child. Maybe someday."

"But I want to see the trees that dance in the wind and the Rock with Wings."

When River Willow didn't answer, Red Moon looked at the cistern and back at her. "Mother, your family made you more afraid of them than you are of Father Sky. I don't like this family."

River Willow put both hands on her face, reached up to kiss her forehead, and went into the hogan to light the lantern.

In the second summer after her daughter became a woman, River Willow was hunting rattlesnakes far from home, in one of the gulches that lead down to the Rio Grande. She was not thinking about the hunt. Her friend from the pueblo had visited her, as he sometimes did, and afterwards, Red Moon had asked about lying with men. She'd been asking questions since she'd started the cycle of her womanhood, which always came with the full moon. She'd soon be old enough to marry. Perhaps there would a kind man, a few good years.

River Willow saw the fierce red moon again. She'd explained the reason for the name, but not the bad timing. She fought back the fear. Hadn't she kept Red Moon free and safe all this time? She would put off the bad times as long as she could.

She stopped to aim at a big snake on a rock ledge down the gulch. Suddenly, under a sage bush just to her left, she heard a rattle. She froze; then she saw the stunned mouse at her foot, saw the snake prepare to strike. She lunged to the right, lost her footing, and fell. Her head struck a jagged rock and the pain shot into her right temple. The rifle went off as it hit the ground. An echo ricocheted through the canyon and died, leaving the desert still again; and out of the silence of the end of her time, pictures rushed in. Her mother and grandmother. Red Moon's baby smile, her first blanket, her need for a father. Brad. Red Moon as she'd left her this morning, weaving and chanting the song, waiting for the sign. And Father Sky above, dimming now long before evening fell. The snake struck her leg, slithered across it, and sidled away, rattling furiously.

CHAPTER 2

RED MOON

At sundown, Red Moon walked to the north, fighting fear and straining to see her mother coming toward her. She stopped at the last rise where she could still see the hogan. The wide sage floor of the world lay before her, and it was empty. She waited, her eyes roving the desert and the ends of the dark gulches where River Willow might climb up.

She went back for the lantern, and when the stars came out, she returned to the high spot through sage that appeared from the dark and faded into it again, like ghost bushes. She held the light up to guide her mother. From every side and from above, darkness pressed through the tiny bubble of light into her shaking heart. The desert stretched into the black—silent, endless, and forbidding.

When her arms would no longer hold the lantern, Red Moon went back and crawled into a corner of the hogan. Her mother must be hurt, but she'd never find her in the dark. She sat facing the door, shaking, alone for the first time in a silent world. Where was rustle of her mother's clothes? The whisper of her breath? During the deepest dark, she fell asleep with her knees drawn up to her chin.

Morning came on a howling wind. At first light she was on her way through sand blowing up to meet the sky, making the sunrise dull and red. She tried the closest gulch where the snakes coiled on the ledges, then the next. From the third she saw a flock of vultures riding the wind and flapping into a gulch far away. With a cry of horror she ran toward them, hoping they'd found a dead coyote, screaming to scatter them as she scrambled down the rocks.

Her mother lay with her head resting on a rock, her blood dark around it, her hair waving in the lighter wind of the gulch. One leg was swollen and purple around two black dots. The vultures had hacked at her arms and the other leg.

Collapsing on her knees next to River Willow, Red Moon pulled the head from the rock, and held it in her lap, sobbing. She pulled the hair back and bent to kiss the cold face robbed of smile, of spirit, of love. She did not speak her mother's name, knowing the spirit was gone. Instead, she pressed her fists against her mouth to hold in her own spirit.

The vultures returned, inching closer, sitting a few feet away on the sage and the ledges of rock.

She grabbed the rifle, still kneeling. "Get away," she screamed.

The vultures wheeled into the sky.

She shot one. It flopped into the gulch and she shot it again.

The others reeled away.

She put a third bullet in the vulture and looked around with the rifle still ready, wanting to see the snake, any snake that she could shoot.

Her mother's voice spoke in the wind, "The snake only did what a snake must do."

Red Moon stared at the face in her lap, but the lips were still. She shuddered and lowered the rifle.

She needed to tend to the body. She didn't have the shovel to bury her mother here in the sand. If she went to get it, the vultures would come back. She tore out part of her mother's skirt to cover the face.

She tried dragging the stiff body but had to walk backwards through sage and rocks. She pulled her mother to a big rock, laid her face down over it, stooped under the shoulders, and managed to get the body on her back. Bent under the weight and sinking into sand that threw her off balance, she walked the whole way without stopping. If she put the body down she wouldn't have the strength to lift it again.

She reached home, washed the body, and dug a grave in loose sand some distance from the hogan. When she'd laid River Willow in the hole, she lay down next to her with her head over the silent heart that had been her whole world. "Mother, I don't know how to be without you." She looked up from the grave. "Mother Earth, let me die with her. Father Sky, blow the sand over both of us," she begged, but Earth and Sky were still now, and the new moon rode above like a small red smile.

She kissed River Willow's face and got up. Covering the face, she shoveled the sand back into the hole and smoothed the mound over. Then she took handful after handful of sand and let it run on the top of the mound in the shape of a woman. At the foot of the grave she drew the form of a snake and then stamped it out with her feet.

It was dark by the time she finished. She went into the house, took her mother's black velvet blouse and skirt out of their box and crawled onto the sheep skins. She hugged the clothes close to breathe in her mother's spirit with her smell, a mixture of the open wind, sage, and a bit of smoke. All night, she rocked herself, too devastated for tears and too frightened for sleep.

The next morning Red Moon went to the loom, cut off the rug that was in progress and set up a new warp. For a week she did nothing but weave.

The blanket was the white of natural wool. Across the bottom Red Moon wove the hogan in the middle of the reddish sand with spots of sage. Above that and to the left River Willow sat at the loom. On the right, she stood on the Taos square, a blanket over her arm. Above these were three trees, a cottonwood like the ones in Taos, Red Moon's guess at the Navajo willows her mother had loved, and an evergreen from the mountains. At the top, on the northwest corner, were a rock that looked like a sitting bird and a Navajo woman with her arms stretched out, as if in welcome.

When she finished, Red Moon laid the blanket on the grave and placed rocks around the edges to keep it from blowing away.

All around the blanket there were tear drops in the sand.

Loneliness haunted her through the winter when the snow made the little streams around the hogan, and through the spring when her mother would have set up a new warp.

On a morning bright with sun, Red Moon stepped out of the hogan and tossed the last water from breakfast onto the squash plant. She bowed a little to the sun, pressed a pinch of corn meal to her forehead, and scattered it on the ground. It still made her cry, this thing she'd always done with her mother to bless the day.

For a few minutes she stood there and tried to give her day shape and purpose. She couldn't go to the mountains, though it was time. Her happy memories would turn to ash. No need to hunt today; there was enough rattlesnake stew left from last night. She looked over at the pile of firewood from the Rio Grande Canyon. Enough for two days before she'd have to burden the old mule with another trip for driftwood.

She walked to the corral, avoiding the loom, and checked the supply of oats. The mule looked indifferently at her as she stepped through the gap where the bare sage bushes that marked off his area had blown away during the winter. She hadn't bothered to replace them. The mule stayed in the sagging shelter out of habit. He'd been with them ever since she could remember and was so old the hairs above his nose had gone gray. She touched her forehead to the top of his long face. "Don't you leave me, too," she said. He pulled his head free, stretched his neck to the ground, and ran his tongue over the salt lick.

She walked to the cistern and took off the lid. The water was low, hardly a hand's depth. She turned, tucked a strand of the light hair into her headband, and shaded her eyes against the sun. Only a few patches of snow dotted the north sides of the peaks behind Taos, less than last spring and the spring before that. Her mother's voice whispered on the breeze, worried, as she'd been when they'd talked about the dry spell. Her mother's hands had cupped her face then, but now Red Moon's cheeks were cold and her hands cold and empty with no one to touch.

Red Moon gazed at the packed dirt and dragged her foot over it, trying to blot out her mother's smile and the feel of her hands, so real and so absent. They made her heart hurt. She thought of her mother's family somewhere to the northwest, and anger burned her heart for her mother's fear of them and for her own fear that kept her here alone.

At last she approached the loom on the south side of the hogan. She didn't want to weave any more. Every stroke of the beater would remind her of the white blanket on her mother's grave. But she couldn't put it off forever. She would always have to trade her weaving for supplies. Today she'd tie up a warp for a small blanket, one she could do quickly.

She went into the hogan, flipped through the wool hanging in the corners, and found only one skein of white. When this one was gone she'd have to go to Taos. Her heart beat heavily and tears welled. She'd never been to Taos alone.

She took several skeins out, sat in front of the loom, and reached for the upper beam. The sun was warm on her back, like the feel of her mother when Red Moon had sat on her lap for the first weaving lesson. She glanced at the little loom she'd used as a child. Its upper beam was hanging by one rope. There hadn't been a warp on it since she'd gotten big enough to use her mother's. She smiled sadly, remembering the first blanket.

Gazing past the loom, Red Moon watched the child she had been, playing with wind, clouds, and cactus flowers, always safe in her mother's love. The emptiness of the desert around her returned, and the winter and spring of not knowing what to do, of waiting for the sign from Mother Earth.

Her hands heavy, she began tying up her warp, and immediately tears blurred her vision. The death blanket on the grave beyond the corral enveloped her. Her shoulders drooped under its dark weight and she stopped weaving. She went back into the hogan, took her rifle and the last three bullets, and went out to hunt rattlesnakes.

It was early afternoon when she came back with one bullet and a single snake. She skinned it and laid the skin in a pan of water, bark, and ashes. She sliced off the meager meat, soaked it in brine, and hung it on a strand of wire under the eaves to dry. She was on her way to the cistern to wash her hands when she noticed a boy on a horse coming from the southwest, not the direction of Taos like her mother's friend. She frowned. There was nothing in that direction.

She washed her hands quickly, tucked away a strand of the brown hair that never grew long enough to stay in her braids, and shaded her eyes. Even from a distance, the horse looked huge.

Not until the boy climbed down from the horse did she realize he was actually a young man. Only half a head taller than she even in his cowboy boots, he had light brown eyes, thin brown hair growing down his chin and under his nose, and brown hair that kept the shape it had been forced into by a hat big enough to shade his whole body. His skin did not have the tanned, leathery look of the men from the pueblo, but it was very dirty.

"Good evenin', *madame*," he said, smiling, holding his hat in one hand and the reins in the other. "Is this your place?"

He continued, but Red Moon could barely understand. His drawn-out words didn't sound like the English her mother had taught her. The one question she understood scared her and made her ask, "You take this place, make me leave this land?"

He blinked and drew his head back. "*Mais, non, cher.* I just want some water, me. I'll give you some Texas jerky if you could spare me and my horse a drink."

"Oh." Her mother's friend had often left jerky or some corn-meal. Once there'd been a bar of chocolate. Maybe this was the good man her mother had wanted for her.

"You come inside," she said to the small man with the long words.

The stranger tied his horse to the post of her covered entry. Inside, he stared at everything in the hogan, the yarn hanging in the corners, the fire pit, and the old barrel lid in the roof. He showed no interest in the sheep skins on the floor to his right.

"What you want me to do?" Red Moon asked.

"*Mais*, give me a drink, like I said."

"You only want drink?"

He backed away a little and squinted. "*Mais*, yeah. Listen, *cher*, maybe I should talk to your folks. Where are they?" He looked toward the door.

Red Moon deduced the meaning of "folks." "My mother died in the summer."

"Oh, I'm sorry to hear that. And your father, is he here?"

"No, just I live here now."

He gave her a sideways look. "You live here all alone, you? You're a child. How you manage that?"

"Winter was not hard because we had enough for two before my mother died." Her breath caught and it was a minute before she could go on. She shoved the dipper into the bucket of water to hide the sadness. "Now I prepare for next winter like I did with her. Hunt and weave and trade blankets in Taos." She turned back to him and straightened to her full height. "I am woman now."

The man scratched his head. "Maybe we better introduce ourselves. They call me Rattlesnake. Rattlesnake Jackson."

Red Moon dropped the dipper, and water splashed into the fire pit. She breathed out hard to dispel the vision of the dots on her mother's swollen leg. "Why you take snake name? Rattlesnake bite you?"

"Well, *cher*, I'm a small man, me, in a world of big men, and a name like that helps, yeah. It makes people think you're tough and dangerous and they leave you alone. At least until they get to know you, and by then the name is stuck, see?"

"But why 'Rattlesnake'? You could take Bear. Or Eagle." She dipped a mug into the water and handed it to him.

He took it with a smile. "I got it in Texas. See, I was working on a ranch. There was this big fellow who teased me a lot 'cause I didn't know much about ranching. He was real fond of killing rattlers and used to keep all the rattles on a string tied to his belt. One night all us hands were in a bar in Cross Plains, drinkin' a few beers and eatin' popcorn. He waited till I was talking to a girl and then scattered a few broken rattles in my popcorn. It made me throw up when they told me what I was eating, and they called me Rattlesnake all evening. After that I let the name stick."

Red Moon hadn't understood half of his story. "You have other name?"

"Yeah, *cher*, but I don't think you'll like it any better. It's pretty biblical. Ezekiel."

Red Moon let "biblical" pass, not knowing what it meant. He was right, it was not a good name. He should use it a lot until it had no spirit left. "What does 'Ezeekier' mean?" The corners of her eyes crinkled in concentration as she tried to pronounce it.

He gave her a funny look. "I don't know."

"I will say 'Rattlesnake.'"

"And what's your name?"

She hesitated. Her mother hadn't wanted to tell her name to a white man. "Red Moon," she whispered.

He leaned toward her. "Well now, that's real pretty. Red Moon. I see why you wanted to know what my name meant. Do they call you 'Red,' or is there more to your name?"

"Rising. My mother called me 'child.' But I have other names."

"Red Moon Rising. A real Indian name, yeah." He glanced at her hair. "Are you full blooded Indian?"

Red Moon pulled a strand of the brown hair behind her ear. "Only half. I had white father but never saw him."

"Well, Red Moon, I'm not full blooded Cajun, either. And I'm on my way from Louisiana to Montana, or maybe even Alaska. So I'm just passing through."

She looked away from him. "I don't know these places." He'd used her name three times already. Her mother had been right about these white people, they wore names out. Mother Earth might not be able to send a sign if her name got too weak. Or maybe—the thought rushed into the world as a gust of summer wind—the man was her sign.

No. He couldn't be. He'd said he was leaving.

He handed her back the cup. "Well, look, soon as I water my horse, I'll get a map out of my saddlebag."

Red Moon showed him where the cistern was, and watched him fill a bucket to water the horse. His walk was too heavy for his size and made her smile at his back. He carried his arms out from his body as if his muscles needed room. He splashed her water about without even glancing at the drying mountains.

No. Not the sign. If Mother Earth were going to send a man, she'd send an Indian, not a dirty white man. Even one who was friendly like this one.

1911

CHAPTER 3
RATTLESNAKE

Marie Jackson went into labor on Easter Sunday as the sun was setting behind the cypress trees outside her window. The Spanish moss, swaying like gold feathers in the breeze, brought back Father Landry's sermon that morning. He'd read from the Old Testament, the book of Ezekiel, describing the wheel of light in the sky and the angels with four wings. It was a strange sermon for Easter, but Marie knew God had prompted him to speak directly to her.

As night fell, the full moon turned the graceful angel-feather moss into the dry, white bones that came to life at God's bidding. Ezekiel's message of the power of God over sinners settled like a black stone in her soul and turned the groans of birth into moans of guilt. Of course, she was married now, but they had sinned greatly.

When her ordeal ended, she took the fruit of her sin from the midwife without smiling. She looked at the father. "We'll call him Ezekiel," she said.

Joe-Don started to protest the ugly name.

"The sins of the father shall be visited on the son," she explained, and Joe-Don knew there was no changing it.

Joe-Don Jackson, escaping the certainty of a shotgun wedding in Mississippi in the spring of 1910, had headed "out West," where he'd always been drawn. He made it as far as the Atchafalaya in the middle of Louisiana. Local Cajuns explained about the swamp and the river that ran through it, both with the same name meaning "treacherous waters." Joe-Don decided to cross the swamp when he knew it better.

By September, however, he'd fallen in love and married a petite swamp girl, Marie LeBlanc, who was two months pregnant by him. He converted to a lip-service Catholicism and built her a cabin on a small and tenuous scrap of dry land near Petite Tete, a settlement between the Atchafalaya River levee and the levee several miles to the east that controlled its flood plain and the swamp. He made an equally small and tenuous living by catching and selling crawfish. And if he sometimes stood watching the sunset with longing in his eyes, he never failed to smile at his family.

Ezekiel grew up on the swamp. He knew the town by the levee, and vaguely, he knew his mother's connections did not make him a proper Cajun, even if the Domengeauxes and Morreaus did speak kindly to the "Jacquesongs" when they met after church. But he lived in his own world on the shallow brown water, and his friends were egrets and coons. At five, he was a happy, independent mite who could avoid alligators and water moccasins in his pirogue or catch a mess of catfish for supper.

When he was six, his life changed. Nothing had prepared him for the first day of school in Petite Tete. He stood with his mother at the classroom door. The nun beckoned him forward, her huge black veil arching out over her shoulders like wings waiting to fly at him. His hand went automatically toward his mother, but she moved her hand out of reach and shoved him from behind.

He started up the aisle. The second graders on his left turned to eye his scuffed shoes, bare ankles, and faded overalls. The first graders sat on his right, barely able see over the tablets, yellow pencils, and brand new boxes of crayons on their desks. The nun led him to a desk in the front row. On it there were no tablets, no crayons. It was completely bare. He looked back at his mother. She was gone. He wanted to run, but when he turned, his nose was an inch from the black folds of the nun's habit.

He sat down and peered around. All the children were dressed in new clothes. He glanced down at the frayed hems and patched knees of his pants, at the mismatched buttons on his shirt. His face flaming, he didn't even hear the nun's command to stand for morning prayer.

All through first grade, Ezekiel thought about this. His mother believed God could do anything. So why had He made him poor and different from everybody else? What was he being punished for?

On his seventh birthday he came to terms with God—his terms. On his way home from school, he pulled his pole up and let the pirogue drift. He looked up at the sky and said in his mixed Cajun and Mississippi English, "You don' play fair, you. I ain' done nothing to you. An' I ain' gonna let you do this to me." He started poling again and stopped. "And I don' believe in you no more neither, no."

He didn't tarry long over his heresy, however. His mother had promised him alligator tail. She'd simmer the meat for hours in the red *sauce piquant*, and he'd smell it all afternoon. Alligators were just coming out of their winter sleep and would be tender. His mouth watered at the thought of the white meat that felt like beef in his mouth and tasted like chicken and fish. It was his favorite, even with the rubbery aftertaste. He took up his pole again and in a few minutes the smell of the red sauce drifted out to guide him home.

Ezekiel's home was a two-room shack with doors from each room opening onto the front and back porches. Three slatted rocking chairs graced the front porch for the few months when mosquitoes weren't biting. On one side, a steep stairway led up to the *garçionniere*, the attic where he slept in the winter. On the back porch stood washtubs, barrels to catch rainwater, and the huge old cypress mortar with the three-foot pestle that his mother used to grind corn for grits. Crab nets, fishing poles, saws, and extra paddles hung from the walls. It was all covered by a rusting tin roof that extended down over both porches. It had never known a coat of paint.

As he headed home, however, the familiar shack barely registered. His mind was busy with other things. Having dispatched God and guilt, he was ready to tackle a more fair distribution of goods in his world.

Three weeks before the end of first grade, Ezekiel hunkered in the dirt behind the school, watching a game of marbles. Recess was nearly over. Excitement drew the boys into a tight circle buzzing with bets on the next shot.

"Looks like I get your last one," Henri Hebert taunted Bobby Landry.

"Bet you don't."

The little crowd jeered at him.

Henri shoved his drawstring bag at Ezekiel, saying, "Hold this."

The bag weighed strangely in Ezekiel's hand. He knew Henri had just put the aggie into it, the crystal clear one with the beautiful red swirl in the center. Henri had so many aggies he could hardly fit them in the blue bag, and anyway, the one Ezekiel had always coveted wasn't even his favorite.

He allowed himself to be elbowed to the edge of the circle. He palmed the red aggie out of the bag and into his pocket. Of course, he couldn't play with it; all he wanted was to own it. His fingers curved happily around the smooth glass, and he saw the red swirl in the shadows of his pocket.

He hid it in the crotch of two cypress knees a few yards from the school's jetty. The next day, not to gloat but to avert suspicion, he asked to borrow the red aggie and then helped Henri search for it. And when, two days before school was out, Bobby Landry found it while untangling his fishing line, Ezekiel helped Henri try to think how the beautiful red aggie could have gotten there.

As he honed his skill over the next years, fewer things found their way back to their owners; and the swamp between Petite Tete and his home concealed pocket knives, erasers, a yoyo, fishing line, a baseball, and an exceptionally fine top, all tucked into hiding places known only to a young swamp rat.

By the beginning of eighth grade, Ezekiel's lamentable performance had earned him the name Eazie. He wanted to be out fishing or teasing alligators, not sitting in school. Except for Mrs. Guidry's geography class. He liked hearing about the other parts of the country—the desert, the Rocky Mountains, the tundra of Alaska.

He didn't like English or the English teacher, Sister Mary Aquilina, the meanest nun in school. She seated the children by size rather than alphabet. Eazie hated her for it. Small for his age, he had to sit in the second row, surrounded by girls.

On a Monday at the end of September, even Sister "Mary Ackie" was sodden with the heat as she instructed Henri Hebert to give his oral book report. The class groaned.

Henri trudged to the front and read from dog-eared papers about *Riders of the Purple Sage*, mumbling as usual. Before he knew it, Eazie was listening, lost in visions of the Old West. His father had often talked about going there. But Eazie knew his father was trapped, even if he found the trap comfortable; he would spend the rest of his life patching up the house, crawfishing, and wishing. He would never go out West.

Eazie let a couple of weeks pass before stealing Henri's book and hiding it in the hollow of a cypress stump between home and Petite Tete. He read it laboriously, stopping day after day on his way home and sitting hunched over it in his pirogue. Though he couldn't visualize the setting Zane Grey described, his own fantasy filled in scenery that beckoned to him.

He made up his mind he would not end like Joe-Don Jackson, tied to a woman and a hungry child. One day he would live like the cowboys, roaming the Old West on horseback. He saw himself making camp, unrolling his bedroll, going to sleep under the stars with the dying fire crackling beside him, his faithful horse nickering gently a few feet away. Now and then he went off alone and camped on a clump of high ground in the swamp to practice. The swamp island became Venters' secret valley of the novel; a huge cypress knee was the balanced rock that would seal it off forever. He flew on the unbelievable horse Wrangler through sage that he imagined as something like the azalea bushes in front of the church.

Near the end of his third year of high school, when he had just turned eighteen, two events came together to change his life. After an hour's detention in a stifling classroom, he passed the history teacher's room on the way out. Her questions for the test the next day were already on the blackboard. Eazie checked up and down the hall, stepped in and began copying them down. They ought to be worth something to...

"Well, I might have known," said Sister Mary Magdalene in her clipped Yankee accent.

Eazie jumped and his pencil flew to the floor. She was standing right at his side, and Eazie had no idea how such a fat nun could've gotten there without making a sound. As usual, the starched wimple under her veil was dark with sweat and wilted against her round face. A few strands of short gray hair had escaped and plastered themselves to her cheeks.

She went to the board and started erasing the questions. "Just like you, Ezekiel Jackson. Sit down."

He eased back into the seat. How had she even known he was getting up?

Without glancing around, she asked, "Did you think these questions would be of use to you? You would have had to *look up the answers*, boy, and if you had the energy to do that, you wouldn't have failed every test I've given you since September." She switched the eraser to her left hand with her back to him. "And even if you'd passed one test, you'd still have failed the class." She turned and looked him in the eyes. "You're not only lazy and ignorant; you committed a sin for nothing. Now, you're under detention for the rest of the week. Report here for one hour at 3:10 every day. You may leave."

Furious, Eazie bided his time and watched for a chance to get even. He found it on Friday, when the nun had a substitute who didn't bother about the detention.

Alone in the room, he held a match to Sister Mary Magdalene's grade book and watched the flames lick through the crimped handwriting and the columns of grades. He was about to drop it into a trashcan full of wadded papers when Jeannette Thibodeaux walked in, a bespectacled, chubby girl who'd once asked him to a church picnic. He'd turned her down, not as gently as he might have. Their eyes met. The flames licked closer to his fingers. He dropped the book to the floor and stamped the fire out. When he looked up again, Jeannette was gone. She'd said nothing, but her look had spoken of triumph and spite, and Eazie knew she wouldn't be charmed into silence.

On the same afternoon he discovered, in Old Man Louvier's yard, the largest horse he'd ever seen, a chestnut mare with a black mane and tail and no other markings at all. The town buzzed with talk of its size—almost big enough to hold Old Man Louvier, who weighed three hundred pounds. But Eazie knew the horse was his, delivered by fate to take him to the cowboy's life.

Well after midnight, taking a lantern and a torn pillow slip stuffed with his belongings, some food, a few fish hooks, and matches for his campfires, he poled back to Petite Tete by full moon. When he reached the landing, he realized he'd have to sink the pirogue so no one would know he'd come back to town. This gave him pause. His chest tightened over his heart, but there was no other choice. Gripping the damp, weathered boards, he balanced himself with one leg on the jetty and the other on the front of the pirogue and shoved it into the water. It filled slowly.

When it was almost full, he shoved it under the jetty and kept the front end under until it sank. But memories floated still: the sunset behind the sweeping Spanish moss, crawfishing with his father, the time he and Bobby Landry convinced Bobby's cousin from New Orleans that alligators loved it if you drove a pirogue up their backs.

He stood for a minute staring back across the swamp, toward home. Marie and Joe-Don. They had so little, but now he knew they'd given him all that mattered. They'd worry. Guilt ripped through him like a fishhook. He should stay. No, he was in too much trouble now. This wasn't fair to his parents. But the pirogue was already under water. A breeze pushed past his face, as if propelling him away from the jetty. Yes, he was supposed to go out West, and the horse was waiting. There'd never be another. With one last look through the spaced boards to the water that filled his pirogue, he turned toward Old Man Louvier's.

The horse, still wearing her bridle, snorted softly as he eased the gate open. Eazie inched forward, fearful she'd wake the Louviers. Very slowly, he put one hand on her nose and ran the other down the side of her head to the reins. At the first tug, she moved toward him. He turned and pulled gently. She followed him through the gate without a sound.

He didn't try to ride her down the one oyster-shell street of Petite Tete, afraid of sudden resistance and thoroughly awed at

the size of the mare. He couldn't even see over the lowest part of her back. The clatter of hooves seemed loud as the approach of a dinosaur, every nicker the roar of a bull elephant, every toss of the head an act of beastly rebellion.

At the rusted drawbridge across the bayou that separated Petite Tete from the levee, the horse put a hoof on the iron grillwork. A dull metallic thud punched the night air; her ears went straight up, and she balked.

"Come on, *cher*," Eazie whispered. He gave a tug, but she backed off the bridge. Eazie scratched his head. If he pulled harder, she might run or rear up and kick him.

At the other end of town, the rich people from Baton Rouge had silted the bayou to make a small cove near their fishing camps. In dry weather they even used the dam as a road. But using their road meant going all the way through town again and coming back on the levee. He tried once more to pull the horse onto the bridge. She laid her ears back and her legs turned to stone. Shaking his head, he led her away. "*Mon dieu, cher*, I don't know what I'm gonna do with you when we get to the river."

When they'd made the circuit and passed the town again, he pulled the horse to a tree stump and tried to climb on. She drew away and waited. Eazie tried again. This time the mare jerked the reins out of his hand and crossed to the other side of the stump so he could mount on the left. She turned and looked down at him. Eazie kicked the dirt, feeling foolish. He grabbed the end of her mane to steady himself, put his left foot on the stump, and swung his right leg over the back of the horse. Then he discovered the reins were still dangling from the bridle and he had to climb down again.

By the time he and the horse had gotten their positions and ropes properly arranged, the stars were fading and the mysterious night sounds of the swamp were giving way to the croaks of frogs and bull alligators. With Eazie bumping about on the horse's back and realizing there was more to this horse business than met the eye, they followed the levee for an hour more. Vaguely, Eazie planned to go north and west around the swamp. He knew it ended somewhere up there. He had no idea where he could cross the Atchafalaya River.

When the sun came up, he led the mare into the swamp and tied her reins around a small cypress. He caught a catfish, speared it on a branch, and set the branch in the ground at an angle. He gathered some leaves and a few twigs to start a fire. "Now this is the life," he said to the horse standing a few feet away. He used half his matches trying to light the damp leaves. After he'd eaten the half-raw fish, he slept until a brief, drenching rain woke him; and as evening fell, he started out again, slapping mosquitoes and hoping the cowboy's life was drier.

Over the next few days he came to love the amiable horse as his friend, his savior, and his companion in destiny. He also realized he didn't know her name. He decided to call her "*Bontemps*" from the Cajun expression *Laissez les bons temps rouler*, "Let the good times roll." He said the new name often, offering her grass, talking to her as he broke camp, stroking her neck as he rode. And the congenial *Bontemps* complied with the wishes of her new, lightweight owner.

By the fourth day he'd worked his way to the end of the swamp. He was in central Louisiana, already three feet above sea level, where swamp gave way to dry land. Passing sugar cane and cotton fields, he cut across to the Atchafalaya, rode up the levee and looked for a place to cross.

He stood on the east bank, kicking at cattails and scratchy sword grasses, shading his eyes from the setting sun. Before him the brown water, swift and full of eddies, sped to the Gulf. A few fishermen floated by in their rowboats among the flotsam of the river, but he couldn't see where they'd put in.

On the west shore trees and grasses grew right down to the water. To his right was a bridge whose rusted arches looked as if they'd been there a hundred years. The road beyond it was the only route through the thick underbrush. Just under the bridge on the other side was a clear spot where he could camp.

He rode *Bontemps* up the embankment and discovered it was a one-lane wooden bridge too narrow to allow the horse to get out of the way if a car or carriage caught them. He got down and walked forward far enough to see that some of the cross planks that supported the wheel tracks where missing. Easy-going as she was, *Bontemps* wasn't going to like the bridge, and he'd have to get her across it before dark.

A few lights came on behind the trees across the river. Hoping to use the last light, he led *Bontemps* forward. She followed warily until her first hoof on the wooden track clopped and echoed off the water. She flattened her ears and backed away.

"Come on *cher*, you can do this," he pleaded, pulling harder. She yanked the reins out of his hand and backed out of reach. Eazie looked at the length of the span and the gathering darkness. "Okay, *cher*, we'll try again in the morning. But sooner or later, we got to cross this river."

He made camp under a sprawling live oak behind the levee and rose at first light the next day. He gathered clover and other things he knew she liked, and led her up to the bridge again. As they approached the wooden planks, he began talking to mask the sound of her hooves. He pulled gently, walking backwards, talking steadily, and holding the clover just before her nose. Very slowly, so the hooves would make as little sound as possible, he drew her forward, trying to keep her feet on the wheel tracks. She was nervous, her eyes rolling constantly from the wooden planks to the rusty metal on her left. A third of the way across, she stopped. Eazie looked around. Two of the cross planks were missing. A leafy branch swirled by beneath them in the muddy water. *Bontemps* snorted and the whites of her eyes showed.

"It's okay, *cher*, we'll be by it in a minute." Eazie moved off the wheel tracks and positioned himself to block her view of the gap. "Come on," he coaxed, drawing her forward with his right arm and shoving along her side with the left.

Talking constantly, giving her all the encouragement he could, he led her across the whole span. When they reached the west end of the bridge, he let out a whoop and patted the side of her face. *Bontemps* stared back at the bridge and looked pleased with herself. The sun was just high enough to hit their backs as they rode boldly along the dirt road into Melville.

From there they headed west through LeBeau, avoiding towns and always camping by water, where he could find food.

A few miles west of LeBeau, Eazie stopped at dusk across the road from a cornfield. At the far end of it a rusty roof and a smoking chimney rose above the new tassels. Even from the distance, he could smell hush puppies frying. Leaving *Bontemps* tied to a sapling pecan tree, he edged through the woods until he could see the Negro dirt farmer and his family. An ancient woman sat in a rocking chair on the porch, watching her great-great-grandchildren romp about the yard. A younger woman was scrubbing clothes in a tin tub set up on saw horses. Two boys were hoeing a vegetable patch near a pig sty.

He watched several generations working and playing about the yard, amazed at the number of people living in the shack, trying to ignore the homesickness that engulfed him. When he got to Texas, he'd write his parents to let them know he was all right.

He went back to *Bontemps* and stroked her nose for a long time before taking her back up the road where his fire wouldn't be visible. In the morning he watched until he knew even the ancient woman had gone into the field. He stole into the house, helped himself to a cooking pot, leftover food that was in the warming oven, a box of matches, and two stubs of candles. He dashed into the garden and picked a handful of string beans and a few small carrots, which he fed to *Bontemps* when he stopped for a lunch of cold hush puppies.

He worked for a few days in the Mamou general store in exchange for some canned food, salt, a Bowie knife, and a can opener. Leaving town in the middle of the night, he also had a saddle bag, some rope, and a tarp that weren't in the bargain. When he had all his possessions hanging in the saddle bag or rolled up in the tarp, they kept sliding down *Bontemps'* rump, crowding him.

He used his knees to shove himself back and patted *Bontemps'* neck. "I guess I ain't all that ready for the cowboy's life," he admitted. "I need a saddle, *cher*. You 'spose they come in different sizes? You so big, you need a large fer sure. Now that's gonna be a real challenge. Not like a yo-yo or a pocket knife." He decided to leave that problem until he reached Texas. They probably knew about such things over there.

Three weeks after leaving home, he crossed the Sabine River and saluted the faded sign that welcomed him to Texas. He reached down and stroked *Bontemps'* long neck.

"Well, *cher*," he said, "our new life is just beginning, yeah! '*Laissez les bon temps rouler!*'"

CHAPTER 4

RED MOON AND RATTLESNAKE

Red Moon watched from her door as the man who called himself Rattlesnake spread a big paper with one burned corner on the dirt. He was cleaner now where he'd washed off the dust, but the sides of his face were streaked with it. He looked younger, and his hair was still dripping. She liked the smiling face now, even with the hair growing all over it.

When he'd smoothed the paper, he looked up at the slatted roof built out from the door and the tumbleweeds wedged in the slats for shade. She followed the gaze of his warm brown eyes but could see nothing wrong.

"Everything's so dry here, *cher*," he said, squinting toward the mule's lean-to and the desert beyond. "Makes me thirsty, yeah. Where I come from we got so much water you have to take a boat to get anywhere."

"What is boat?" she asked, going to stand next to him.

He looked up, his eyes wide. "It's something you ride in across water."

"You live in river?" Red Moon saw the rushing Rio Grande in its canyon and tried not to laugh. Even if he could ride across such a water, he'd have to be an ant to climb the steep rock walls on the other side.

"*Mais, non*, not a river, a swamp." He waited a second, watching her. "A swamp? Hmm, see all the sand here?" He waved his arm to include the whole desert. "By Petite Tete that would all be water. And there would be trees growing right out of it."

Red Moon felt the earth heave beneath her and put an arm around a post for support. "You make fun with me."

"*Mais, non, cher*, that's the truth."

She stared.

"Come on, let me show you my map."

She knelt beside him and looked at the picture that was all marked off in different colors, sizes, and shapes that made no sense at all. A tail stuck out at the bottom right, but there was nothing on the left to balance the pattern. No one would ever weave such a stupid design.

The man didn't think it funny. He ran his hand over the whole picture. "This shows all the States. See, this dot here is Santa Fe. Let's see if Taos is on the map. Yeah, here it is. So you and I must be about here."

Red Moon couldn't hold the laugh any more. "Now I know you make fun. Taos is very big, I am very small. If I sit on this place, I sit on top of Taos."

Rattlesnake laughed back at her. "No, look here, this is the scale. That means that an inch," he held up his fingers with space between them, "is a hundred miles."

"What is hundred miles?"

He frowned. "Hmm. How to explain it. Maybe ten times as far as from here to Taos."

Red Moon understood now; he wasn't making a joke, he was talking about things her mother had never told her. The sky and the earth grew out in all directions until she was smaller than a dot on the paper.

He drew his finger around a blue box near her knee. "See, this much is New Mexico." A top corner flapped up in a puff of wind. "Whoa, there goes New England." He put the mug on it.

She pulled a strand of hair out of her eye, tucked it in her headband. Her arm grazed his shoulder. She jerked it back, embarrassed. He smiled, and the brown eyes drew her in. Her face grew hot and she squinted again at the strange pattern on the paper.

"This map's been through a lot," he said, running his finger along a torn fold. "I burnt Baja California clear off once, *cher*, trying to read it too close to a fire. Hope those Mexicans jumped in the ocean."

He gave a short laugh and turned his head as if waiting for her to answer, but Red Moon kept her eyes down, not knowing what he'd meant. There was a wavy gray line drawn across the bottom part of his map. Before she could ask him about it, he was talking again.

"This is all one country, see? But all the parts of it are different. Way up here is New York. You know about Manhattan and all those beads? *Non?* Well, I'll have to tell you about it."

She put her finger on the paper and moved it along the gray line.

"That's my whole trip," he said. "And see here, where the pencil line begins? That's where I come from." He glanced at her. "These blue lines are rivers and the green stuff is swamp. That means there's lots of water and trees."

Red Moon stared at him.

He waited a minute. "Have you ever seen a map before, *cher?*"

Red Moon shook her head, realizing it was she who was stupid, not the picture.

"Well then, this is too much to take in all at once, yeah. Don't they teach you any geography in school?"

"I don't know school."

Rattlesnake's eyes got very round, but then he looked off in the direction of Taos. "Yeah, *mais,* I can see why. I thought taking my pirogue to Petite Tete for school was a lot of trouble."

She looked hard at him. She didn't want to ask what the new word meant.

He smiled. "A pirogue? That's a kind of boat."

His eyes didn't say he thought her stupid. They were kind. Maybe he was kind like the man her mother wanted to find for her. "You tell me more, please."

"Well, look, *cher,* I could use a rest. Been on the road a couple of months. If you'll let me stay here a few days I'll try to make myself useful and tell you about the few places I've been."

Red Moon heard "stay," and the word danced in her heart like the whirling wind. "Yes, you stay."

"I have my bed roll on my horse and can sleep outside."

The whirlwind died. "You don't want to sleep—inside?" Did this man not want to visit her the way her mother's friend had?

"*Mais, non,* I don't want to impose. But maybe we can share our suppers. I'm real tired of this jerky and would be glad to give you some. You have anything you want to share?"

At least the man would stay and tell her about the world. Laughter bubbled from her throat. "I give you rattlesnake."

He laughed and honored her with a deep bow. "*Merci beaucoup, mademoiselle.* I'm sure your rattlesnake will taste better than mine." He took a mock bite out of his forearm and then offered it to her. She pretended to bite, too, made a face, and spit it out. Laughing, they went into the hogan.

Rattlesnake lay in his bedroll on the east side of the Indian girl's strange eight-sided house. His hands behind his head, he gazed at the desert shapes barely visible in the starlight, feeling the dry, cool breeze from the mountains slide across his face. What a strange girl this was, who could survive alone in the desert but knew noth-ing of the world beyond Taos. Her open-mouthed stare came back to him; her long black braids; her slender, slightly barrel-chested body; her face lit with amazement that reminded him of Eazie Jacquesong in Mrs. Guidry's geography class. He put that thought in the back of his mind to mull over when he left.

He saw Red Moon's full mouth again, and her eyes, so black he couldn't see the pupils. She'd nearly invited him to sleep with her. Who'd have thought she'd be so bold? Or maybe she wasn't bold at all, but simply the kind of person he had come out West to find—free, open, and friendly, even if he was short and had been a misfit all his life. He tossed onto his side, where he could see the deeper darkness behind her open door.

Mon dieu, why had he not taken her up on the invitation? He liked her, could feel himself holding her. His arms vibrated at the thought of her kneeling close to him, fascinated by the map. But there was something about her, something that was child and woman at the same time. Not beautiful, but very attractive. The men he'd worked with in Texas would have taken this Injun's shy invitation without second thought, yeah, and left without a back-ward glance. But they didn't have Marie Jackson for a mother. Or Joe-Don for a father, who'd warned him about the ways a man could get in trouble with a woman. And this was just a girl.

It was a long time before he went to sleep.

Red Moon lay on her bed of skins. She looked through the door eastwards, where her mother had seen the red moon rising, and felt her heart and her head open to the big world of this small man. He would tell her everything. She felt the laughter again, the excitement; and it filled the hogan with warmth.

"Mother," she whispered, "was it like this with your friend? Or my father? Did you have any of these laughing white men besides him?" She heard the rustle of the man's bedroll, the only sound another person had made since her mother died. It whispered into her heart. She moved closer to the edge of the skins, from where she could make out the top of his head by the doorway. "Mother," she thought, "Did they make you want to go where they'd been, see what they'd seen? Did they tell you about trees growing in water? Did they make you happy? Mother." She lay on her back again. A tear rolled down her temple and into her hair, but she was smiling.

It was a long time before she went to sleep and dreamed of a forgotten afternoon.

A pink face with a red beard and blue eyes appeared from the past, a stranger on the square in Taos. The child Red Moon, felt his hands on her arms as he lifted her onto his shoulders. She re-membered the smoothness of his long red hair, but in the dream it became light brown.

As tall as River Willow's waist, Red Moon sat cross-legged under the cottonwood tree in Taos, proudly wearing the new black velvet skirt that was just like her mother's. It was the day of trading the summer's weavings, and her mother had bought her a slice of wa-termelon to celebrate. It was so red and so wet, not like yucca or cactus fruit, and she ate it carefully, trying not to drip on the skirt.

"Mother, can I walk around the square by myself?" she asked when she'd finished.

River Willow brushed at her own skirt and smiled down. "I think you're still too little."

"No, see? I didn't spill any juice on my skirt."

"Child, you're growing up too fast for me. All right, but stay on the square where you can see me."

Red Moon, walking very straight, began her tour of the wood-en store fronts that lined the square. She ducked under ladders in front of a store that the people were changing to look like the pueblo outside of town. When she passed white women, she let her hand brush against their skirts, all in colors stolen from wildflowers. She stared at the displays in Mr. Koenig's window, the snake skins her mother had brought already laid out on a rug in a Two Gray Hills design.

She was halfway around the square when she saw the back of a man as tall as the cottonwoods. He turned toward her and her mouth fell open. He had red hair and it grew all over his face like fire burning his head. Frightened, she stepped backwards so fast she fell into the street.

She scrambled to her feet, not taking her eyes off him.

He smiled down at her. "I bet you never saw a red beard before, huh, little Indian maiden?" he said, waving his chin hair up and down. He stooped to her height. His eyes were bright blue. "You know what? I think the cat's got your tongue." He waited. "Do you have a name?" he asked, touching her chin with his finger.

She clasped her hands behind her back and leaned away from him, speechless.

He put both hands on his knees, and he looked puzzled. "Are you here with your family?"

She stared.

The man smiled again. "Where's your mother?"

Red Moon turned around, but she couldn't see over the machines her mother called "chuggies" that stood in front of the stores or rolled by, snorting smoke. Her lip quivered.

The man stood up now. "You don't see her? Don't be afraid, little Pocahantas, we'll find her. Now, can you tell me your name?"

"Red Moon," she whispered. What would happen to her name if she gave it to a man with fire on his face? Where was her mother?

He bent over her. "Well, little girl with the pretty name Red Moon, I'll help you find her. How about if I pick you up so you can see over everybody?"

"Yes," she said, raising her arms.

The man picked her up as if she were a twig of sage and before she knew it she was straddling his shoulders. "Can you see your mother now?"

"Yes."

River Willow was standing on a corner across the square, looking around, frowning.

"Well, let's get you to her. Point the way."

She pointed toward the end of the square and he bounced her to the corner. Red Moon laughed. At the corner she pointed to the right.

"That way?" cried the man, turning two full circles to the right. Red Moon squealed.

"Or this way?" he laughed, spinning to the left.

Red Moon laughed. "Do more!" She was whirling on top of the huge man like a dust devil in the sand. On the first turn she glimpsed her mother looking around, alarmed; on the next turn River Willow was running across the square, screaming, "That's my child." And then her mother was next to the man.

"You let my child go!" River Willow cried, her face pale.

The man stopped spinning. His laughter died.

Red Moon poked him with her heels. "Do more," she said again. Her mother was reaching for her, but she didn't want to get down. "This man is fun. He put me up here so I could find you."

"I beg your pardon, lady. I guess your little girl never saw a redhead before and it made her forget where you were."

River Willow clapped her hands and kept her arms up, waiting. The funny man bent down and returned Red Moon.

That evening, on the long moonlit ride back to the hogan, Red Moon asked, "Mother, why did that man have red hair?"

"Some white people do, child. Some have brown hair, some yellow, some red. Mr. Koenig's used to be brown and it grew all over his head. I never saw one with so much red hair before either."

"Why do you call him white? That man is not white like clouds or sheep wool. More pink like cactus flower."

"I know, but they call themselves white. They call us Indians and think we're red."

"Is it good to be an Indian?"

It was a minute before her mother answered. "It is good if you are a good Indian. But we call ourselves The People."

Red Moon shook her head as the mule picked its way through the flat gray expanse of sage in the moonlight. "Pink people with red hair. Are there blue ones with blue hair?"

Her mother laughed. Red Moon wiggled around to look at her without waiting for an answer. "Are there green ones, too?"

"No, but I've heard there are black ones and yellow ones."

"Black men and yellow men?!" Red Moon giggled. "I like this pink one. I want to see more rainbow people." But when she remembered later, the thought of black men made her back tingle.

In her dream the rainbow man changed slowly to a small one with light brown hair. His warm brown eyes laughed with her as he showed her two gray lines moving over the paper he called a map. The lines became entwined and then knotted. The knot broke over a place on the map that she had heard of but did not know. From the knot only a single gray line remained and it was bleeding. An angry black face grew out of the blood stain and beckoned her to follow. She woke up feeling choked and frightened. She had moved off the skins in her sleep, and the cold white moon was shining full on her face.

CHAPTER 5

The next morning, Red Moon took a few steps from the hogan, embarrassed to look at the man who'd been in her dream. He was still sleeping. She looked out of the corner of her eye at the bedroll that had come from a store and the slight form in it. His hair was light and fine as an eagle's down and made her want to put her fingers in it. He stirred and she looked away.

She stood facing east until the sun shone on her face, then sprinkled a few grains of corn meal on the sand. She waited a minute to see a sign that this man was her special thing, but nothing happened. She went to the white blanket in the sand and swept away the small new drifts. When she stood up Rattlesnake was standing behind her.

He looked puzzled.

"My mother lies here," she explained, pointing to the figures in the weave. "See, here she is weaving, here selling the blankets, here the trees in Taos and in the mountains, here the mother she was afraid of after she went away with my father."

"Did your mother weave this before she died?"

"No, I made it after I put her here. I didn't know what to do..." her voice trembled, "...with her body."

Rattlesnake squatted on his heels and felt the edge of the blanket. "*Mais,* this is beautiful, Red Moon. Do you have more blankets?"

"Yes, I have to go to Taos soon and sell them, buy corn and salt and bullets. But I don't know how to sell them." The ache that came from the white blanket stabbed at her, and she choked back a sob. "My mother took them to Mr. Koenig, but I don't know how much he gave her. Always I went with her, but so much to see in Taos. I only looked at other things."

"I'll go with you, *cher.* Let's do it today, while I'm here. Maybe I can help."

Red Moon stared at him, feeling the pain of the blanket ease. No one had ever helped her or her mother before. "Thank you," she whispered. It made her heart sing to have him here. Maybe he'd stay a long time.

He was already leading her away from the grave. "Do you have a saddle for the mule?"

"No. We just put a blanket on mule and rode together."

"Well, show me what you want to take and I'll load it on *Bontemps* while you put some breakfast together."

After they'd eaten and Rattlesnake had gone out again, Red Moon took the black skirt and blouse her mother had always worn to Taos from the buckboard chest. She buried her face in the velvet folds and breathed her mother's smell and spirit into herself. Her breath caught in a tearless sob. She dressed in her mother's clothes and joined Rattlesnake for the trip.

"Hey, you look real pretty in your fancy clothes, *cher,*" he said, struggling to toss the saddle over the horse's back.

Red Moon's face went hot and she threw the blanket on the mule.

Rattlesnake tied the stack of blankets on behind the saddle and climbed on the horse, swinging his leg over her neck. He sat much higher than she was on the mule, and he rode with his elbow resting on the blankets. "Okay, you lead the way."

She smoothed the blouse that made her look pretty and prodded the mule into motion with her heels. "Why you have this big horse? Small one better for you."

He looked down at her and shrugged. "This is the one the fates gave me."

Red Moon nodded. *Fates* must mean something like *folks*.

He stroked the horse's neck. "But I wouldn't trade *Bontemps* for anything, no. I'll let you ride her later. She's the most easygoing horse I ever saw, and I worked around a lot coming through Texas." He laughed. "You should see Texas, *cher*. That's one big place, yeah. It just goes on forever. And it's dry like here only with no mountains or anything. And hot? Whooeee, it's some hot, yeah!"

"I like your place with water better. I want to see where trees grow out of river."

Rattlesnake smiled and shrugged. "Maybe you will someday. Who knows?"

As they approached the square in Taos, they heard music and the buzz of voices. More chuggies than Red Moon had ever seen lined the streets and others sputtered by, leaving the choking smell in the air. A man with a paper sign pinned to his chest told them to hitch the animals to a tree and walk the rest of the way.

Rounding the last corner with half the blankets in her arms, Red Moon stopped and stared. Little cloth buildings crowded the center of the square, and more people than she'd ever seen were milling around them. People dressed in colorful clothes were driving funny, tiny chuggies or riding on one wheel or throwing a lot of balls in the air and catching them all. Children skipped after them, laughing and clapping. All around the square, in front of the stores, Indians sat on blankets and sold silver jewelry, pottery, baskets, and blankets. One of the women had even built a loom and was weaving right there.

There was so much noise, she hardly heard Rattlesnake.

Pointing at the long row of women sitting in front of the stores, he asked, "Is this where your mother sold her blankets?"

Red Moon tore her attention from the busy square. "No, she just took them to Mr. Koenig. And snake skins, too. I never saw Taos like this before."

"Let's try selling yours out here. I bet we can get a better price, yeah. If nobody buys them, we can always go to the store later."

The square was crowded, and Red Moon had to take a space behind a hitching post in a corner. As she piled up both loads of blankets, Rattlesnake left. She watched him through the crowd, walking around the square, looking at the other weavings, asking questions. Then he disappeared. No one had even looked at her blankets when he returned, out of breath and carrying the rope he kept on his saddle.

"We have to get your things out where people can see them," he said. "Let's tie one blanket to the post. Which one do you think is best?" She took out one in a thunderstorm pattern, and he tied it up. Then he wandered off again. Red Moon had still not sold a thing when he sauntered back. Next to her an Indian woman was bargaining for a blanket with a white man wearing three turquoise rings on his right hand. "Four fifty?" he said.

Rattlesnake slipped the thunderstorm blanket from the rope, held it up toward the man with the turquoise. Winking at Red Moon, he said loudly, "Three dollars and fifty cents? *Mon dieu*, that's a good price, all right. I can sell this blanket in Santa Fe for twice that. Now you wait right here and I'll go get some money from the bank."

Red Moon stared at him. "Why...?" she started, but he'd already laid the blanket on her stack and left.

The man with the turquoise took it up and felt its weight. "Has nice colors. You use plant dyes?"

"Oh, yes. Sage, onion skin, lupine..."

The man ran his fingers in a small circle at the edge of the weave. "Looks like about twenty threads per square inch. Not bad. I'll pay you three. Right now."

"But..." Red Moon looked in the direction Rattlesnake had gone.

The man glanced around. "He might not come back."

"I know him. He will come."

"I'll give you four."

Did Rattlesnake mean for her to sell her blanket to this man? Confused, she stalled. "Four for this blanket?"

"All right. Make it five."

Through an opening in the crowd she saw Rattlesnake jumping up and down on a bench under the cottonwood tree, waving both arms and nodding.

The man with the turquoise rings was turning to go.

"Yes, five," she said.

Money and blanket changed hands. The man left the square. The woman next to her muttered angrily, refolded her blanket, and laid several silver bracelets on it. Red Moon sat looking at the money in hand, wondering whether she could buy salt, corn, kerosene, and bullets for five dollars.

This man Rattlesnake was amazing. He had gotten the man to buy the blanket, but somehow it didn't feel right. Would her mother have sold it that way? Stuffing the bills into her rabbit skin bag, she pulled out another blanket and tied it to the post.

In a few minutes Rattlesnake came up again, grinning. "Worked pretty good, yeah." He had a piece of paper in hand. It had gray marks on it the color of the line on his map.

"Listen, somebody just left a space on the other side now, right by the hotel. Move your stuff over there. Tie the best one to a post and use something to tack this to the blanket. Put the one you like least on top of the stack. And give me your money."

Across the square there were many more buyers. Red Moon tied up her best blanket, took a splinter out of a post to attach the paper to it, and stacked the others next to it with one woven in browns on the top. Out of the corner of her eye she watched Rattlesnake work his way toward her past the other sellers, picking up a blanket here, a turquoise belt there, looking as if he knew all about them.

As he stood in front of the next seller, his eyes seemed to light by the merest chance on the sign on Red Moon's blanket.

"What?!" he cried, fingering the paper. "'Blankits by Red Moon'? You wouldn't happen to be *the* Red Moon Rising, would you?"

Red Moon was startled. "Yes, but..." Embarrassed, she pushed a wisp of hair behind her ear.

"*Mais, cher,* I've been hearing about you since Texas. They told me you might be from around Taos, but I never thought I'd just run into you like this." He looked around at the other people, as if to share his amazement, and then turned back to her. "My uncle has one of your blankets in his ranch house outside Austin. He's quite a collector. He told me to keep an eye out and let him know if I found any more of your work. Are these all yours?"

"Yes."

Rattlesnake pulled Red Moon's brown blanket off the top of the stack and looked it over. "Yeah," he said, "just the colors and designs that Uncle Bill likes. How much is this one?"

Red Moon had no idea what to ask, but Rattlesnake had her money. "Five dollars."

"Okay, I'll take at least that one for him. I should probably try to get the price down, but I know he expected to pay more. Here's your money. I'm going to come back in a month, and I hope you have some more like it by then."

Several people had come to look at Rattlesnake, among them a woman with black hair streaked with gray, pulled straight back from her face and tied into a bun at the back of her neck. She was wearing a black squaw skirt, a silver belt, and a squash blossom necklace. Her lips were a dark red gash across her sharp face. "Let me see some of the other blankets," she commanded.

Before she left she'd bought two for four dollars each and one for five. A man with a turquoise belt buckle bought one for three fifty and two rattlesnake skins for a dollar.

Only the blanket that Rattlesnake had "bought" remained, and half a dozen snake skins. Red Moon had more money than she'd ever seen and no idea whether it was a lot or a little.

They went to Koenig's. Rattlesnake looked around the store while Red Moon talked to the trader.

"Vell, Red Moon, how are you?" Mr. Koenig asked in his English that was like a fuzzy cactus. He smiled from the top of his head down to the chins that wouldn't go in his collar. The row of white hair that ringed his head was thinner than Red Moon remembered. "Ver iss your muzzer?" he asked.

"A rattlesnake killed my mother before the winter."

His eyes grew sad. "Oh, child, I'm very sorry to hear zat." He stared at the blanket she'd put in his hands. "You know, I remember ze first time I saw her. She came in here and stood a long time at ze door holding her blankets. I had to go to her and ask vat she vanted. She vas a nice lady and my best weaver. She vas very strong and brafe, do you know zat?"

"Yes." Red Moon fought back tears.

"Are you all right wizout her?"

She glanced at Rattlesnake, who was studying a pair of black leather boots. "Yes."

Mr. Koenig bought the last blanket for two dollars and the snake skins for thirty cents each. He sold her two large sacks of spun wool for eight dollars before sending her to Dawson's general store for the other supplies. "Here, this iss for you, in memory of your good muzzer," he said, holding out a kind of tool. He showed her how to make sparks with it for starting a fire.

Outside the store, she joined Rattlesnake, staring at the money she had left and feeling dizzy from the morning's happenings. "You made people buy my blankets," she said. "How did you know what to do?"

Rattlesnake didn't look at her. "Well, *cher*, I figure you just have to even things out in this world."

Red Moon didn't understand the answer but before she could ask any more, Rattlesnake pulled her toward a man with a flute, who was leading people to a big cloth building beyond the square.

"You know what, *cher* Red Moon? You made so much money this morning, you could treat yourself to the circus. You want to go?"

The feel of his hand on her arm made her miss the question.

He took her hand and led her toward the big cloth building. "Did your mother ever take you to a circus, *cher*?" His glowing eyes drew her right into his excitement.

"No, what is circus?"

"Well, it's fun, yeah. Come on, *cher*, you have plenty of money left for a couple of tickets."

He gave a man some of the money, and they joined the crowd. Red Moon watched the men and women in shiny clothes do things she'd never dreamed of. Often, she felt Rattlesnake's eyes on her. When she glanced at him between acts, he smiled, but it was not like the smile of her mother showing her something new, or even like his own smiles this morning. There was something else, something warmer.

She giggled over the funny men. One of them had a great bush of red hair, and for a moment the choking feeling came back from the dream of the blood and the black face, but then he tripped over his own huge foot and made her laugh.

Rattlesnake leaned toward her and said over the loud music, "You like this, *cher?*"

She nodded without taking her eyes off the performers.

A woman with yellow hair sitting in front of them turned and eyed them with a mean frown. Rattlesnake stared back at her. Red Moon barely heard her mutter, "Indian lover," as she turned back. Red Moon didn't understand why she'd said it, but it made Rattlesnake pale before he watched the circus again.

Leaving the tent at dusk, Rattlesnake took her hand. "Don't want to get separated in this crowd," he said, his voice different, deeper than before. His hand in hers made her feel special to him. He didn't let her go until they reached the horse and mule. His hand warmed her in the chill of the evening, but the warmth was in places where she'd never felt anything before.

They left Taos and rode silently through the dim sage. *Bontemps* and the mule walked with their heads down, as if they, too, were going over the events of the day. When night fell, they had to camp at a place where Red Moon and River Willow had sometimes stopped. The moon came over the mountains in a circle of haze and gave them little light.

With no bed rolls in the cold desert night, they gathered a pile of old sage and made a fire, which they'd have to feed all night. They sat side by side for a long time, both with their arms wrapped around their knees. They were not touching.

"I can remember the first time I saw a circus," said Rattlesnake with a dreaminess in his voice. "I must have been eight or nine. My father took me to Baton Rouge to see it. I thought that was all the way to the end of the world. And the circus, *mon dieu*, how I loved the riders doing tricks on horseback. I guess even then I loved horses."

Red Moon took a deep breath for the question she'd been afraid to ask. "Rattlesnake?"

"Yeah, *cher?*"

"The people in the circus, the funny ones, like the man with the red hair. They color their faces like that?" She hunched her shoulders and drew in her head, sure he'd laugh at her.

"Yeah, *cher*, nobody looks like that."

He hadn't laughed.

"My mother told me once about yellow people and black people. You see these men with color?"

"The yellow ones come from way across the ocean that way." He motioned behind them. "But I never saw any either."

"What is *ocean?*"

"Very big water."

"Bigger than the Rio Grande?"

"So big it would take you days and days to cross it. And the water in it is salty." He looked at her face. "That's the truth."

Red Moon could not imagine it and went back to the colored people. "You see black ones?"

"Oh, yeah, they have lots of them in Louisiana. They came from across another ocean."

Red Moon tried to visualize Rattlesnake's face all black with the light brown eyes and the brown hair around it. It sent a chill down her spine, like the black face from the dream. She tried to see herself at the edge of a big salty water, but she could only see the Rio Grande.

She looked at the fire, ashamed of her ignorance. "You know everything," she said. "I am poor in the head. I know nothing."

"Look, *cher*, I don't know much at all. I was terrible in school." He put his hand on her arm. "And you know more than you think, a lot more than I do about the desert. I'll have to learn that from you. So you ask me what you don't know, and I'll do the same and we can help each other along, *bon?*"

"Yes," she answered, but her mind was on his hand. He'd touched her again and without any reason. He must like her.

The moon silver-plated the edge of a cloud and then disap-peared. The desert stayed dark around them. A chill wind sent a few sparks from the fire into the sand and made her draw closer to him.

After a while Rattlesnake asked, "How old are you, Red Moon?"

"I am woman now." She didn't know how to tell him what she meant.

"When did you become a woman?"

"Before two summers."

"I see, then you must be fourteen or fifteen." He paused. "What about the rest of your family. Don't you have a grandfather or aunts and uncles?"

"My mother said her family lived near The Rock with Wings."

Rattlesnake stretched a bit, but when he settled again, he was a farther away.

Why didn't he want to touch her now? What was wrong? She was afraid to ask.

After a long time, Rattlesnake said, "You lie down by the fire now, Red Moon. I'll stay up and feed it."

Choked with confusion, she laid a bundle of wool on the ground for a pillow and lay down facing the fire. He was so near, and the happiness of the exciting day came back. She could see him again, working his way through the crowded square, helping her sell her blankets, laughing with her over the clowns. "Thank you," she said into the fire, too softly for him to hear. She hardly knew she wasn't thanking him for the day, but for the beginning of love.

CHAPTER 6

Morning came without the sun to draw shadows toward the mountains or warm the day. Instead, a layer of gray lowered over the desert, blotting out the endless sky and the endless land but magnifying their burned-out fire to an entire world, cold and dismal. Not a wisp of smoke rose from the ashes.

Red Moon woke with Rattlesnake at her back, his arms around her, one leg thrown over her hip. From sleep to the sensation of him was a single leap of awareness. Her back was the only part of her that was warm, but the cold didn't matter. He was holding her, sheltering her. She lay motionless until she shivered. Heart racing, she moved very slowly closer, hoping not to wake him. Then she knew he was awake. She heard his sudden breath, felt him move his leg just as slowly. He thought she was still asleep. She turned to him.

Rattlesnake froze. His own leap of sensation was the desire to kiss, to move his hands where he knew no hands had ever touched this girl. Her eyes, black velvet in the dull light, gave him adoration and trust. He could do anything he wanted. He'd had his way with a couple of girls in Texas, but this one was so...what? Defenseless.

Open to him. His mother's horrified face flashed in front of Red Moon's for a moment. Chills ran up and down his spine, and for a second he was grateful for the biting cold.

Red Moon's heart was pounding hard enough for him to feel it, too. Was she supposed to do something? Her mother had never told her how to start. If she did something wrong, what would he do? After he lay with her, would he go away like her father? Oh, please, she thought, don't go away. She smiled at him.

Rattlesnake's face turned red and he smiled back. "I guess our cold bodies found each other in the night," he said, his voice husky like last night. "I'm sorry, *cher*, I let the fire go out."

Red Moon hardly heard him. Lying on her right side, she lifted her left hand to his face. His whole body stiffened.

He put his arm around her and held her close, rubbing his hand up and down her back. "Poor *cher* Red Moon, your hand's like ice, and you're shaking." He pulled her head close to his chest and then pushed it away again. "*Mais*, what am I doing? You'll think I'm trying to take advantage of you. Come on, we better get moving so we can warm up." He let her go, saw the confusion on her face and said more gently, "I didn't do that right, did I? Come on, *cher*, let's go back to the house. We'll freeze out here, and we can talk there." He helped her up, tousled her hair, and smiled. "You need to pass some water? Me, too, yeah. I'll go off in the sage that way and you go behind that rock, then let's get back and build a big ol' fire."

The gray cold grew and bit at them as they headed for the hogan. They huddled over their animals for warmth. Rattlesnake told her about the climate where he came from, about the heat and the mild winters.

She could see he was suffering in the icy wind. She wanted to share warmth with him, ride in front of him in the big saddle. She opened her mouth but couldn't bring out the words. By the time they reached the hogan, snow was swirling in the gray. They led the animals into the sagging lean-to, unloaded the supplies and hurried inside. Red Moon made a fire and opened the vent.

She took a wool poncho that had belonged to her mother out of the buckboard box and held it out to Rattlesnake. "You have no coat?"

"No, *cher* when I left home it was June, just before school was out, and I didn't even think about a jacket." He slipped into the poncho, knelt by the fire, and stretched his hands over it. "Not that I ever owned one for this kind of weather. Didn't you...?" He slapped his head with the heel of his hand. "No, of course you didn't look in the newspaper for the weather report. How do you ever know what the weather's going to do?"

Red Moon laughed. "Look west. Sometime north."

"You have this kind of weather all summer?"

"No, just winter. Don't remember snow so late in spring."

Rattlesnake shook his head. "*Mon dieu*, I don't know about Montana." He rubbed his hands up and down his arms, staring into the growing fire, kneeling as close as he could without holding his face in the smoke. "I thought I was going all the way to Alaska."

Red Moon's heart was pounding. "You can—stay here." It came out as a whisper.

He put his hand up to hers and pulled her toward him. "Come down, Red Moon." He turned so that they knelt facing each other and put his hand on her cheek. "You like me, don't you?" He smiled when she nodded. "*Mais*, I like you, too."

Red Moon's face warmed.

"But, listen, *cher*, we can't get to like each other too much. There would be problems, things we would want to do to each other..."

"I know. Man and woman lie together. Feel good, my mother told me."

Rattlesnake looked down, his face sad. "I can't do that with you, Red Moon, much as I might want to. It wouldn't be right. I know I don't think twice about much else, but my mother taught me to respect women. And my father taught me how much trouble you can get into with girls. We got laws, see, and they don't let men lie down like that with a child."

"I am *not* child. I am woman two summers now."

"I know, you told me that, but I'm talking about something else. There are problems when a girl is only fifteen. Her folks might think she was bad, and they would sure think I was bad. They'd want to put me in jail, I guarantee."

"I don't know 'jail.'"

"That's a bad place, *cher*, where you can't see the sun and they don't let you out."

Red Moon was shocked. "Who do that to you?"

"Your father might come back, or an uncle or somebody."

"No, my father not know about me. Nobody care about me." The silent aloneness of the winter pressed against her chest. There was no family to care what happened to her. Now this man who liked her was here. She did not want him to leave.

Rattlesnake was frowning with surprise. "What about the people in Taos? Doesn't anybody come out to check on you from time to time?"

"No, no one ever came here except a man came to see my mother. He was her friend."

He relaxed, but only a little. "Well, anyway, there's always the risk that you could get pregnant—have a baby."

Red Moon's answer was lost in Rattlesnake's sneeze. She put her hand to his head. "You very hot," she said. "You lie down over there, I bring you cold tea--no, tea for cold."

"*Mais*, yeah, I think I have to lie down for a little while. But as soon as the snow lets up, I'd better go."

He was almost asleep by the time she had a cup of sage tea ready.

"Hoooeee," he said with his nose wrinkled after the first swallow. "This all you got in your drug store?"

"No," she said proudly. "My mother teach me many things for body." She tried again with mullein steam and a tea of rose hip and yarrow.

"Now this is some better," he said, sipping and blowing on the tea.

She boiled mint and gave him a cool cloth dipped in it to rub his chest and bring down the fever. He did it quickly and sheepishly. She took the cloth from him and massaged the cooling mint water into his chest and across his forehead. Rattlesnake closed his eyes. "You do that much better than I do, *cher*."

All the next day, Rattlesnake lay feverish and miserable in the hogan, sneezing and coughing. Little by little he abandoned himself to her care as the snow storm raked itself dry against the peaks and spring returned to the high desert.

When night fell, leaving the hogan dark but for the small fire, he said in a stuffy voice, "It's so quiet here at night. Back in the swamp there's a lot of noise, night animals getting their food. Screech owls and frogs. Did you know that a bull frog and a bull alligator sound a lot alike?"

"What is alligator?"

"An alligator? Hmm. You know what a lizard looks like?"

Red Moon nodded, settling on the dirt floor next to him.

"Well, an alligator looks a little like a lizard, only it's huge. A 'gator can get longer than your mule, longer than your whole house. It's sorta gray or black and it has eyes on the top of its head so that when it swims in the water only its eyes show."

Red Moon hid her mouth with her hand and bit her lip to keep from laughing aloud, but he wasn't looking at her any more.

He was lying on his back on the sheepskins with his arm on his forehead.

"It has a great big mouth with no tongue, and it kinda smiles at you, like it's saying, 'come on in.' A big 'gator could get your whole head in his mouth."

Red Moon laughed this time, unable to stop herself.

"No, really, *cher*. It has the meanest, sharpest teeth, yeah, and it can tear your arm off. I'll never forget one time I went fishing way off in the swamp with my pa. We kept hearing this gu-duk sound and I asked my pa if it was a bull frog or a bull alligator. Now any of those swamp Cajuns would've known right off, but my pa was from Mississippi, see, and he had to hear both before he could tell the difference. After a while he got his line caught in a dead tree on the bank of a little island."

Red Moon frowned. "What is this, islan'?"

"An island? That's a little piece of land that's surrounded by water. And my Pa told me to go up in the tree and untangle it. So I did. Then I climbed down and waited on that muddy bank. But he didn't come get me. His line was still tangled and he was set-tin' there in that pirogue working on it. Right behind me I kept hearing this gu-duk, real close. Finally he got the line straight and came back to get me. After I got in the boat we heard both sounds, and my pa's face went white as an egret. 'I declare, son, thet were a bull 'gator fer sure.' *Mais*, I guarantee, I just about wet my pants."

While he got well, Red Moon felt his eyes on her as she moved about the hogan. He ate her meals of cactus fruit and *piñon* nut and rattlesnake meat without asking what they were and always managed to thank her, even when the look on his face said he didn't like it. In his better moments he asked about her life with her mother or told her about the swamp. Sometimes he talked about the places he wanted to go.

Each time he spoke of leaving, Red Moon turned away or busied herself nursing him.

"How you feel this morning?" Red Moon smiled down at him on the fourth morning.

He pulled himself up against the wall. "Oh, *cher*, I feel much better."

"Good, I bring you one more tea."

She returned with two mugs and drank one herself, sitting on the edge of the skins.

He nodded at her mug of tea. "Did you catch cold, too, *cher*?"

"No, this other kind of tea."

When he'd drunk his, she took the blue mug and started to get up. He put his hand on her wrist.

"Stay here, Red Moon."

She reached over, set the cups next to the fire pit, and settled again, her heart banging inside her chest.

It was a moment before he continued and his voice was different, like in Taos. "I guess you really are a woman. I mean, you nursed me like a mother." He took her hand and rubbed the top of it, then wove his fingers with hers and pressed their hands palm to palm. He kept his eyes on her and they were gentle. "Thank you for taking such good care of me, *cher*."

Warmth filled her until she seemed to float just above the floor. She could see there was more, but he stopped speaking. Her hip pressed into his. She wanted to lean over and rest against him, show him she would do anything for him.

Rattlesnake put his hand on her face, smiling now. Huge gusts of love swept through her and filled the hogan, pushing wind and sage, desert and swamp away into another reality and leaving only the heart that filled her entire body. Rattlesnake cared. It was in his eyes. He wouldn't leave her. Not now. She felt the tug of his hand and let him pull her to him.

Her head was to his left just below his chin, the lower part of her right arm came to rest across his groin. He breathed in sharply and she felt a lump grow under her arm. She started to move the arm, but Rattlesnake held it in place then put his hand on her head. "You're wonderful, Red Moon," he said into her ear. She raised her head to look at him, increasing the pressure on her right arm. He gasped again. She felt herself melt into his warm brown eyes and they both smiled. She moved her arm slightly, amazed at the effect it had on him, hardly daring to guess whether it was pleasure or pain.

His voice was soft and seemed half choked. "I want you, Red Moon, but after three days of lying here, I'd like to wash first. Do you have any of that hot water left?"

She sat up and nodded.

He smiled, dispelling her confusion. "I'll only be a minute."

She gave him the wash pan with warm water in it and left the hogan. How could the desert look the same as it had yesterday? Even the thin dusting of snow left on the mountains was no match for the beauty in her heart. The endless openness of Father Sky above and the closed roundness of Mother Earth below—she filled them both with her love. Why was the sage not covered in flowers, why did no clouds ride the sky for her to float on? She walked to her cistern and used a little water to wash herself and rinse out her mouth, then returned to the hogan.

Rattlesnake was standing at the small shelf by the window, naked, trying to reach his back with the rag. Red Moon gasped.

He turned his head. "Can you get my back for me, *cher*?" he asked.

She took the rag and rubbed his back, her hands shaking. She dropped the cloth and started to reach for it. He stopped her, and guided her hands to his chest as he turned to her.

He pulled her face to his and kissed her forehead, her eyes, her nose, her chin. Her lips burned to receive the kiss, but the wait was sweet because she knew it was coming. Then there was a second's pause. His eyes smiled into hers, their breath mingled, and the touch came, sending fire into her body. He opened his mouth, his tongue explored her lips and pushed through. Shock and desire shot through her. She opened herself to him and welcomed his tongue into her body. His full length pressed against her and she wanted his skin next to hers, wanted no boundary of any kind between them.

His hands went to her clothed breasts and she arched back in a wave of new sensation. He pulled her blouse out of her skirt and lifted it over her head, then undid her skirt. She was bare to him, completely exposed. She was his. He touched her breasts, kissed them, and Red Moon heard herself moan in a voice she did not know. He stood erect again and she felt him between her legs. She went limp against him and let him move her toward the sheep skins. They kissed, standing at the edge of the bed, both moaning and exploring with hands, neither wanting to give up the contact to get on the bed. And then he was inside her, making them one body, still standing, but going weak at the knees. She wrapped her legs around him, he sank to his knees, his mouth moving from breast to breast. Red Moon moved on him, and both cried out, she moved again, the rhythm of love took over and both were swept away in the pulsing sea of relief.

Rattlesnake lay back on the bed so that she was stretched out on top of him. He started to turn to the side. "Don't leave me, don't leave me," she whispered. He turned her under him and kissed her. She held her breast for him to kiss. He took both breasts in his hands, pressed them together and put his head between them. They were moving again in the timeless rhythm, each intent on giving to the other. He found her lips again and as they opened themselves they were rocked again by waves of oneness.

He lay next to her for a long time, his brown eyes smiling into hers, his left hand caressing the body she had given him. She put her hand on his to show that she was his. With the other she fingered his down-hair and traced his eyebrows, his nose, his lips. He kissed her fingers. "Thank you," she whispered. "I didn't know it would be like this. My mother only told me it felt good."

"*Ma chere* Red Moon, I'll tell you the truth, I didn't know it could be like this either. I've made love to a few girls, but I didn't have much feeling for them. It's different with you."

His body was beginning to feel cold. She reached behind him and pulled the blanket over them. He tucked it behind her, pulled her close and interlaced his legs with hers. Her last thought before dozing off was that he had said he had feeling for her. Or almost. The rest of his vast world was far, far away, beyond reality. This man, this feeling, they were her life. He was her sign.

CHAPTER 7

After the unseasonable snowstorm, the desert turned to cloudless, baking summer. Rattlesnake stayed. He made no promise, and sometimes Red Moon caught him gazing north with that expression her mother had had when she looked toward Rock with Wings. Each time, she tried to make him laugh and forget north. He stayed, filling her days and her heart.

They trapped and feasted on rabbit grilled over sage. He learned to be sparing in his use of the dwindling water, especially with *Bontemps* needing a share every day, too.

He used half her bullets before he put one anywhere near the target she'd drawn on a cornmeal sack. They hunted rattlers. She taught him how to tan their skins. She learned a few Cajun words while he picked the many tiny bones from their meat before hanging it to dry, but he laughed and told her never to use them.

She took him to the gulch where her mother had died, told him about the vultures.

"What kind of person was your mother?" he asked, looking into the sky from the gulch, as if watching for the black vultures to come back.

Red Moon sat down on a ledge of the gulch and raised her skirt to cool her legs. What kind of person was her mother? With

sudden sadness, she realized she would never know more than she knew now. "She was all I had. She taught me to weave and respect Mother Earth." Red Moon thought a minute. "I don't have good words to explain, but she knew how to be right with Mother Earth."

"Where did she come from?"

"Rock with Wings. She said white people called her place other name. Smaller name. I don't remember it." Red Moon felt herself drift off into the other time, the way her mother had sometimes done.

Rattlesnake squeezed next to her on the ledge and put his arm around her shoulders.

She leaned against him, needing his warmth in spite of the heat. "She liked the trees there."

"What about her family?" he asked, stroking her cheek with the bottom of her braid.

"She never told me much about them. I think they didn't want her any more. Made her sad. But she loved me, and when we went to Taos she always made the day special for me." A dry sob escaped. "I know so little. I'll never know if she saw a circus."

Rattlesnake bent his head to hers and cupped her face in his hand. "She probably did, *cher*. Circuses have been around a long time. But she did have a hard life, didn't she?"

Now the tears fell, and he kissed her.

"It's all right, Red Moon. You can cry. I'm sorry she's gone, too."

She let herself settle into his comfort. Her mother would want this good man to stay. She would want them to happy.

The days grew hotter. In mid-summer they escaped into the mountains. Red Moon took him to the place where she and her mother had camped, next to the stream.

She stopped the mule in the small clearing with its needle covered floor. She loved this spot with the tree tops hanging heavy with cones and the chattering squirrels that snapped them off and dropped them to work the seeds out on the ground.

Rattlesnake caught up with her. "Water!" he shouted, jumping off *Bontemps* and running to the stream. He leapt in with his boots on and started splashing water into the air.

Red Moon watched from the mule. He was so beautiful, and the water sparkled as it flew through the sunlight. She slid off the mule.

By that time he was out again, jumping up and down. *"Mon dieu*, that's cold. Cold, cold!"

Red Moon helped him undress, laughing. "This not hot swamp water," she said as she hung his clothes on fir branches to dry. "This melted snow. You looked so funny in the water, like upside-down rain in the sun."

"You think it's funny, do you, *cher*?" Rattlesnake was laughing now, with the warm sun on his naked body. "Well, let's see *you* make some upside-down rain!" He grabbed her wrist and pulled her toward the water.

She fell to her knees to make herself a dead weight, laughing. Rattlesnake knelt to pick her up, kissed her instead, and suddenly they were both naked in the sun, making love by the laughing water.

Afterwards, Red Moon propped her head on her right arm and looked down at the face she loved. "When I was little, I had to learn about the stream, too," she said, running her hand through his fine hair. "I thought someone up there forgot to turn it off. I still have funny feeling about it, like I should catch water in buckets so not wasted." She sat up and looked more closely at the stream. "The water is less every summer. Almost none left now."

Rattlesnake laughed, tugging gently on a braid. "You thought you should turn it off and I thought it would be warm and endless, like the Mississippi. What a pair we are."

"What is Misipi?"

"Mis-sis-sip-pi. It's a river so long it would take you a year to go from the beginning to the end of it. By the time it goes into the ocean it's as wide as from here to..." Rattlesnake sat up and set her between his legs. "Let's see, how can I explain how far a mile is with all the trees in the way? Well, you know how far it is from the hogan to the Rio Grande? It's almost that wide."

Red Moon turned and stared.

"Only it's muddy and you can't drink it, like the clear water here. You know, *cher*, I think I'll come back here when my trip out West is over. I could stay in the mountains forever."

"I wanted to when I was little, too." The memory that had been pressing at the sides of her mind came into focus. She heard her mother's voice tell about the water as if she there. "Mother told me water was life. Now I know she was right."

Rattlesnake helped her gather firewood, and Red Moon took out the jerky they'd brought and made a stew. Rattlesnake washed his clothes and hung them on the branches again to dry, reveling in the running water. He waited till there was hot water to bathe himself, then bathed her as well.

There seemed to be no end of things they could teach each other. Rattlesnake listened hard when she showed him the plants and animals he could eat. She knew he was thinking it would be useful when he left, but he didn't say so aloud. It made Red Moon feel empty again, like the months after River Willow's death, like the desert that went on and on beyond the hogan. Please, she begged Mother Earth, keep him with me.

They returned from the mountains with both animals loaded. Rattlesnake led them to the corral and unloaded everything.

Red Moon took the bucket from the hogan and went to the cistern. Lifting the boards away, she found only greenish moisture at the bottom. The seepage had stopped.

She put her hands on the rock ledge of the cistern for support, unable to breathe. Her home, her life had dried up while she was gone.

In a moment Rattlesnake was at her side. "What's the matter, Red Moon, are you all right? You look whiter than me. Are you pregnant?"

"No more water. Look."

Rattlesnake stared down and breathed as if he had been struck. "*Mon dieu.* What can we do, *cher*? Even the animals need water."

"Have to get it from the river." She looked around at the last light, just beginning to climb the mountains. "Have to go before dark. Can't wait till morning."

"Let's go, then. I'll saddle up the horse again."

The trip to the river was silent and grim. The black rock of the ancient lava bed released the heat of the late afternoon sun until Red Moon's face felt like seared meat. Only now did she realize how dry everything was, even for the desert. Brittle sage twigs snapped off as the animals brushed past them. She was too numb to think about what would happen now, and Rattlesnake was busy in his own head. Neither had thought beyond the life that Red Moon could eke from the desert.

Reaching the river through the gulch that Red Moon and River Willow had used, they all rushed the water. After a long drink, Red Moon stood and looked upstream. The river was less than half full. Stripes on the exposed rocks showed her that most had been partly under water. She looked for the flat rock with the reedy plants growing around it that she and her mother had knelt on to fill the containers last year. Far from the water's edge, it stood in cracked silt, the reeds small and already gone to seed. Vicious heat bouncing off the canyon walls robbed her of breath.

"Rattlesnake, something wrong. Not just my spring. Not much water anywhere. The river is drying up, and almost no water in the mountains, too."

He slogged toward her, splashing and roiling mud from the bottom. "Do you think your spring will start up again? Maybe it'll rain soon."

Red Moon shook her head. "Here we get rain maybe one time in one moon. But we had no rain since that snow made you sick. My spring won't come back this year."

Rattlesnake reached for the last water can and held it under. "Well, we better get the water and head home. It's going to get dark. We can talk about what to do when we get back."

They stored the water and then sat against the hogan, looking at last light on the peaks that were completely empty of snow. "That's why no water," she said. "See that peak where the sun still shines? The north side should have snow till fall. No more snow to make rivers and streams run. Father Sky turned them off."

Rattlesnake shook his head. "This is a hard country, Red Moon, like a man, somehow. I never thought of Louisiana as being female, but when I think of all that the swamp gives people, it really does seem like a mother. Like your Mother Earth."

Red Moon hardly heard him. Her breath caught and came again as a sob. "We can't stay here. We have to leave."

"Where can you go?"

The question hit her like a slap in the face. He hadn't asked, "Where can *we* go?" He hadn't included himself in her problem or suggested that she go with him. But if he was her sign, Mother Earth must mean for her to leave with him. There was nothing else she could do. She turned away from him. "I don't know."

Rattlesnake drew her back until she rested against him. "I'm sorry I didn't ask that better," he said, holding tight. "Don't worry, *cher*, we'll figure out something together."

Red Moon turned and threw her arms around him. "Oh, Rattlesnake, no place for me. I have nothing but you."

He kissed her hard, but Red Moon knew he was thinking about his future, his trip, the dream that he'd broken when he came to her. She was too shaken to speak of it. She shrank from the void facing her and clung to him as a lizard would cling to a scrap of driftwood awash in a flash flood.

When Red Moon returned from feeding the animals the next morning, Rattlesnake had his map spread out on the packed dirt in front of the hogan. The sun, barely over the mountains, would soon turn the desert into a vast oven.

"Where can we go?" she asked, coming behind him with two mugs of tea.

He took the blue mug from her without taking his eyes off the map. "Well, *cher*, here's a place called Shiprock." He pointed to a dot near the edge of the blue box he called New Mexico. "Do you think that could be where your mother came from?"

"Yes, that's it. I remember now. But you want to go to Mondana. Where is Mondana?"

Rattlesnake pointed at the same spot on the map. Shiprock was west and a little north of Taos. "That would be the right direction, from what your mother said."

"Why you want to go to that rock?"

He looked up at her. "Red Moon, I think the best thing is for me to take you there and see if we can find your family."

His words yanked the ground from beneath her. "You not take me with you?"

Rattlesnake pulled her down until she was kneeling in front of him and held her shoulders.

"It's hard for me to explain, *cher*, but I don't think it's possible. See, you're so young and it's against the law for me to take you away from your home. They call that kidnapping. As soon as anyone saw us, they'd arrest me. I'd never pass for your brother. And I don't even know where I'm gonna end up. I can't take care of another person when I can barely take care of myself."

Red Moon's hope shriveled. "But you said I take good care of you."

"I know, *ma cherie*, and if we could stay here, we could keep on taking care of each other. But we have to go, you said so yourself. I got to be sure you're going to be all right. And I'll try to come back and see you some day."

Red Moon's heart turned to stone and dragged her head down. "I can go somewhere by myself. In the mountains. Don't need you for that."

"Red Moon, you mean too much for me to just go off and leave you. Look at it this way. Somewhere you have a family. Don't you want to find them?"

She shook her head, looking at the dirt beneath her knees.

"*Cher*, trust me. It'll be better this way. Please, let me take you to Shiprock and help you find your family." He put his arms around her and stroked her head.

Slowly she nodded.

"*Ma chere* Red Moon. I will. I'll really come back to see you some day."

But in her heart Red Moon knew that white men drifting through the desert did not return to Indian women. She loved him too much to refuse what he asked, but she would never stay in Shiprock. She would find another place and stay alone just like the past winter. She would never allow herself to love anyone again and hurt so much.

Rattlesnake was already busy making plans.

"...some things for the trip. Let's look in the hogan and see what all you have. Can you sell this place?"

"Sell this? My mother said we have no paper to say this is our place."

"Well, that's simple, then. All we have to do is pick up and leave. Come on, let's see what we'll need." He stopped a moment and lifted her face to his. "We still have some time, *cher*. Let's make the most of it and be happy together." He kissed her, and Red Moon, in a rush of despair, threw her arms around him.

"Rattle..." But his mouth was on hers again and he was hard against her. She made love with him completely and fiercely to block out the emptiness.

CHAPTER 8

As Mother Earth held her breath between the setting moon and the rising sun, Red Moon knelt at River Willow's grave. The dry whisper of her brushing sand from the white blanket trespassed into the hush of the desert. She shuddered, bent down and placed her cheek over the picture of her mother weaving. She stood again and stared silently at the grave until she felt Rattlesnake's arm around her shoulder. "I want to tell her Father Sky turned the water off," she said.

"I know she hears you." Rattlesnake kissed her forehead and drew her away. "Let's look at the map before we go," he said, spreading it out in the first rays of the sun. "Here's the Rio Grande. We have to cross it. Do you know if there's a bridge between here and the Colorado border?"

Red Moon didn't look at the map. "No."

"Well, the map doesn't show any roads." He sighed, took off his hat, and scratched his head. "It sure would be good if we could stay close to the river. But if we did, we'd have to go around a thousand gulches. I guess the only thing to do is stay near the mountains and hope for streams. I just wish I didn't have to cross state lines with you."

"What that mean?"

"It means it's more dangerous, yeah. But I don't see any other way. Come on, *cher*, look at this." He showed her his plan: to cross the Rio Grande in the San Luis Valley of Colorado, go through the San Juan Mountains, then follow the San Juan River to Shiprock.

They ate silently and packed silently. When the horse and the mule were loaded with barely enough room for them to ride, he helped her up and then climbed into his saddle. He started off north and east, toward the foothills.

Red Moon watched him. He was so busy leaving he might not notice if she just rode off in the other direction. She spurred the mule, rode around the hogan, and stopped at the dry cistern, its gray lid lying in the sand now. She looked to the south. There was nothing but more desert in that direction. She couldn't go to the mountain; her mother had said someone would make her leave.

From the south the wind curled up the dust and blew it toward her. Hot air shoved at her, making her turn and head north.

Rattlesnake rode with his back to her in the only direction she could go. He rode into the future like a disappearing star in a sky black and empty. All she could do was find a place to spend her part of that emptiness before they reached Rock with Wings.

She turned the mule and rode after Rattlesnake. He'd stopped far ahead of her and turned in the saddle, waiting.

They headed toward the hills. When they reached the last ridge where Red Moon could see her hogan, she stopped and got off the mule. She took the first blanket she'd woven out of the pack, went to the edge of the overlook, and stood holding the lopsided woven diamond against her, knowing she'd never see her home again.

The sound of *Bontemps'* hooves receded and then came back. The horse stopped behind her, and she heard the creak of the saddle as Rattlesnake dismounted, but he stayed by the horse. After a few minutes he joined her and put his arm around her.

"*Ma chere* Red Moon, I know it's hard," he said gently. "I'll see that you go to a better life now."

Red Moon nodded, her eyes overflowing in despair and home-sickness. He drew her toward the waiting animals. She turned and whispered, "Mother." As she put the old weaving back, she thought, "I am White Blanket in the Sand." But she kept the name to herself.

On their fourth evening in the hills, they sat close together on a rocky ledge, their campsite hidden behind them. Against the setting sun, dust devils moved through the sage like columns of whirling gold light. The wind died and the warmth of the rock rose around them. The heat of the day slowly gave way to a cool breeze that glided down from the peaks. The sun went down, leaving the sky a silvery beige that gradually became night. The lights of a town to the north came out before the stars.

Rattlesnake pointed toward them. "That's probably Fort Garland, which means we're already maybe twenty miles into Colorado. Just think, *cher*, we're in a state we've never been in before."

Red Moon looked at him in the gathering darkness. She didn't know what it meant to be in a different state, but his voice told her it was a thing to be treated with respect. She slipped her hand in his.

"It also means we have to be more careful now. According to the law, I've kidnapped you."

Red Moon heard the nervousness in his voice. "I don't understand."

"I know, and I can't really explain. But if we get caught, I could go to jail and they'd probably put you in a home for bad girls. So we have to stay away from people as much as we can. Remember the way that family looked at us this morning?"

An Indian family gathering piñon nuts had stared at them in wonder and disapproval. Rattlesnake's fear entered her heart, but he put his arm around her and she settled against him. Soon he would leave and be safer without her. She should leave him now, but she couldn't go home, nor to her mother's people. As soon as she found a good place...

Rattlesnake jumped up and held out his hand to help her up. "Come on, *cher*, I'm hungry."

They made their way back to their camp in the dark, treading on brittle pine needles that crackled underfoot and on cones that exploded into sound on the quiet mountainside.

After making love, they lay with their bedrolls together, both with their arms under their heads, her leg thrown over his.

He wiggled his hip the way he did when he was still full of the pleasure, but he said, "Can you stay here tomorrow, *cher*? I'd like to go down to the town and ask what it's like between here and the mountains to the west."

Fear raced through her. Would he come back? He was going to leave soon, and maybe he would go now to be safe. But would he leave without telling her? Red Moon coughed to steady her voice. "Good, I can trap rabbit and make better supper. Wash clothes, too."

Rattlesnake was quiet a minute before he said, "Whooeee, *cher*, look at all those stars. That's one thing I have to say about your part of the country. You can sure see the stars in this thin air."

Red Moon laughed in spite of the fear. "Why you say 'thin'? Air is nothing. How could air be thick?"

He turned in the bedroll and supported his head on his hand. His face was barely a hand's distance away, but all she could see of it was a patch, only slightly less black than the night.

The bedroll swished again and he kissed her. "No, see, the air in Louisiana is thick because it has so much water in it. Real tiny drops, so small you can't even see them."

A squeak of laughter escaped through Red Moon's nose.

He lay back. "Really, *cher*. When you take a hot bath and then try to dry off, you can't really get dry. And you sweat in the summer so much your clothes stick to you."

She looked up at the stars again. She would stay in a place where the air was thin. "Glad Rock with Wings not in Lusana."

Late the following afternoon Red Moon had a small fire going. She was burning cones for a hot fire and little smoke. In the battered old pot she had a stew going with meat and wild greens. She hadn't had any luck with rabbit, but she'd bagged a squirrel. She wouldn't tell Rattlesnake about the chipmunk that was also in the stew. Every place they camped he tried to feed the little striped chipmunks. And she wouldn't tell him how her body had quivered all day in fear that she'd never see him again.

She was taking down the clothes she'd hung about the clearing when she heard the horse. The fear let go and she slumped over the branches before bracing herself and turning to greet him. In spite of the heat he was wearing the jacket that looked like his pants.

"Mmmm, that smells good. But *mon dieu*, Red Moon, this looks like a regular home here. We have to keep the camp simple in case we have to leave fast."

"Why have to leave fast?"

He threw his right leg over the *Bontemps'* neck and slid out of the saddle. "Well, just because. By the way, that's San Luis, not Fort Garland, so we're not as far as I thought. It's still Colorado, though. Here, I brought you something." He pulled a pair of blue pants out of his jacket. "I think these Levi's pants will fit you."

Red Moon gasped and stared at the pants. "I never wear pants. Pants for men."

"I know, but it can't be comfortable for you on the mule with that black skirt, and not just because of the heat. Besides, if you wear pants, people might think you're a boy."

She took the heavy, folded pants and fingered a little bit of paper hanging on a string. "What is that?"

"Oh, stupid of me. I should have taken the price off."

"Price?"

Rattlesnake looked at the tiny paper. "Looks like ninety-five cents," he said.

Red Moon was surprised. "You took money? I thought you left it here."

"I did." Rattlesnake turned to the fire and stirred the stew once. He said without looking at her, "Look, *cher*, you should see all the pants they have there. They aren't going to miss this one pair. I tell you, things aren't passed around fair in the world and you have to balance them out. I don't take much, just what we need. Sometimes you just gotta do that."

Red Moon looked at the pants again, her stomach tight. They were stolen. "One time I saw little boy take a toy axe with feathers on it from Mr. Koenig's store. Mr. Koenig was mad, ran after the boy. Followed him all around the square. My mother said it's not right to take things from store."

He joined her now and bit his lip. He put his hands on her shoulders. "It might not be right, but that doesn't mean you always have a choice."

"Seems to me this makes danger for you, too. Please, you don't steal anymore."

Rattlesnake stared at the ground, his hat blocking his face. Then he took it off and looked her in the eyes. "I promise you I won't take anything unless it's absolutely necessary. Now, come on, try them on."

Red Moon hesitated and then let the pants unfold. She had to hold them above her waist to keep them from dragging the ground. The folds kept most of their shape and there was a bar of dust across the top one. They looked like crooked boards.

Rattlesnake rubbed his chin. "Hmmm, well, put them on. We can roll the legs up. Here, this way." He turned the pants so the buttons were in the front.

She undid her belt and dropped her skirt. "Can't I wear them other way? Don't need open in the front." She giggled as she slipped her left leg in and fell over trying to get the right one in.

Rattlesnake helped her up and she pulled the pants up over her bare bottom.

"Ow!" she cried, getting short, curly hair caught in the first buttonhole.

"*Mon dieu*, I didn't think of that. I'll have to get you a pair of underpants."

While she gingerly did up the remaining buttons, Rattlesnake knelt and rolled the legs up several folds. The waist stood out from her body like a barrel; the legs adjusted with several deep folds around the knees.

Rattlesnake took off his hat and scratched his head. "Well, I don't know. I think they shrink a lot if you wash them in hot water."

Red Moon took a few steps toward the fire, straight-kneed in the stiff new cloth that clutched at her and rubbed noisily against itself between her legs. "Don't think I can do this."

"Let's wash them after we eat and you can wear them tomorrow. They'll be all right after you break them in. And if not, maybe I can wear them."

The next morning Red Moon took her new pants off the dead tree branch. They were even stiffer, and all the seams were wet and cold. She put them on anyway. They weren't quite so big, but they still wouldn't stay around her waist. She took the snake skin she used to keep her skirt up and threaded it through the belt loops. Then she rolled up the bottoms of the pants.

Rattlesnake, watching from his sleeping roll, laughed when the process was finished. "You're quite a sight in a black velvet blouse and braids over your jeans. That's some belt you got there. Where'd you get it?"

"My mother make for me."

He got up and fingered the belt. "Beautiful work. I bet it'll last forever. It's another thing that makes you stand out, though. I think we'll get you a hat and a boy's shirt. Maybe before we get to Shiprock we'll even have a horse and saddle for you. How old's your mule, anyway?"

"Older than me." Red Moon pulled at the cold fabric around her hips. "But how can we get horse?"

"There's lots of ranches down there in the valley. We'll uh... we'll just see what we can do." He slid out of his bedroll. "Well, let's get started. They got fences everywhere down there, *cher*. We're going to have to go close to town to head west. Lots of houses close to the road. We'll walk between the horses till we're past them. The higher we are the more likely someone will see us."

Red Moon pulled at the icy seams between her knees. "Still cold in these pants."

Rattlesnake put his hand on her waist. "*Mon dieu*, they must feel awful. Let's get moving so your body can warm them up."

By the next evening they'd circled the town on foot and reached the Rio Grande bridge. Here the river slipped through shallow, sandy banks instead of the steep canyon farther south.

Rattlesnake stopped and looked east and west along the roadside. "We need to get up river somewhere and spend a day or two where there's grass for the animals and good water. Sure wish this fence wasn't here."

Red Moon was amazed at the three lines of wire that stretched from post to post as far as she could see. "Why they do this? How they get the line so straight?"

Rattlesnake rummaged in his saddlebags while explaining and came up with a wire cutter. Following the fence until it was partly hidden by a large rock, he cut the three strands of barbed wire.

Red Moon looked at his tool, amazed. "Where you get that?"

"I picked it up in Texas. Look, *cher*, I know it's not right to cut a fence. So I try to find a place where the cattle aren't likely to come or where the rancher won't notice the cut too soon. Anyway, the ranchers have people who check the fences every few days, and fixing them is what they get paid for."

They rode north along the river until they found a camping spot under cottonwood trees. Red Moon gave a cry of pain as she got off the mule. She looked down. The seams on the insides of the legs were red. She unbuttoned the pants and inched them down. On both thighs, the lumpy cloth had rubbed blisters that had opened and bled.

"*Mais, cher,* why didn't you say anything? That must've hurt you all day."

"Scared of town. Didn't want to slow down." She threw the pants toward the water. "I don't like pants, hotter than skirt. Skirt always makes air move when I walk. The sun on pants burns my legs."

"Well, we'll have to wash them out again, and you sure can't wear them tomorrow. Do you have something you can use to protect your legs? I'll get some water so you can clean the sores."

Rattlesnake came back from the river looking worried. "The water doesn't look good. Kind of brown. I'll use the water from last night to clean your blisters. Then I'll check upstream for cleaner water." He started a fire while Red Moon put on her skirt and walked down to the river bed, her legs spread and awkward.

She sat down on a rock whose dark water line showed most of it had been underwater in other summers. She looked up at the tops of the giant cottonwoods still catching the last rays of the sun. A breeze fluttered through the leaves and they rustled as if whispering to her. Rattlesnake came down and sat by her, waiting for the water to boil.

"I never knew cottonwoods talked," she said. "There was one in Taos, but always too much noise on the square for me to hear, or too much coming and going for me to listen. But when the leaves moved in the wind, I thought they were waving at me."

Rattlesnake put his hand on hers in her lap. Together they listened to the murmur of the leaves, but now Red Moon heard the voice of the friendly old tree in Taos.

"When I was little, I told my mother on the way back from Taos that I wanted a cottonwood at home. I wanted it to shade the hogan and wave its arms to make the wind."

Rattlesnake laughed. "You thought the trees waved their arms and made the wind. I like that. What'd your mother say?"

"She said it needed too much water and we shouldn't try to force the desert to do what Mother Earth didn't want it to. Before I was born she tried to grow corn to gather the pollen for my birth."

Rattlesnake moved away a little to look at her with his forehead wrinkled. "What did corn pollen have to do with your birth?"

"The People put corn pollen on a baby's tongue for a blessing. But her corn dried up and died. She used flower pollen instead."

Red Moon let her heart slip back to that ride home. River Willow had sung her the growing song she'd sung while Red Moon was still in her belly and while the corn still waved its sharp leaves. She'd walked in it, patting the baby in her belly and singing. Now Red Moon heard it again in the whisper of the cottonwood.

She held onto the chant for a minute, feeling the comfort of Rattlesnake's hand in hers. With the other hand she picked up some sand and let it run through her fingers. "My mother could hear Mother Earth when she spoke, but she didn't teach me how to listen."

Rattlesnake stroked her back. "Well, listen now. What do you think the trees are saying?"

She looked up at the fluttering leaves in the breeze and tried to put all other sounds out of her mind. "I think they share their happiness that the hot day is over and the cool of night will soon come. But maybe they say Mother Earth has a bad time now. I don't know. I never listened before. Maybe if I listen more I will understand better."

"I'm sure you will, *cher*. If there was ever anyone who could understand the earth, it's you."

When the water was hot, he helped her wash her sores and they tied the soft side of two rabbit skins around her thighs to cover them. They ate jerky and drank tea made from river water that Rattlesnake hauled from far upstream.

Red Moon woke in the moonlight doubled up with pain, as if someone were trying to cut her stomach out with a dull knife. She heard Rattlesnake moan. He'd already crawled out of his sleeping roll and was on his knees leaning against a cottonwood. She reached for her supplies. Finding the right herbs, she crawled to the fire. It was nearly dead.

"Bring wood, Rattlesnake, have to make medicine."

He rose and stumbled to the river bottom for driftwood. She waited, bent over on her knees. He came back with a few pieces of wood. Moaning, they built the fire and brewed the bitter tea of bind weed milk and mint, using the last drop of the mountain water.

"Stay out of sleeping roll," said Red Moon. "Tea will clean everything out of you. Feel bad then, but feel better later."

"I'm too sick to care. My stomach's twisted into a knot," said Rattlesnake, taking the cup and downing the tea in one gulp. Soon they separated, Rattlesnake finding a bush upstream, Red Moon a rock downstream. They hid their worst moments from each other, then crawled back to the sleeping bags. Too weak to talk, they lay facing each other. Rattlesnake put his hand across and touched her face.

Now Red Moon wondered whether they would even make it to Rock with Wings.

CHAPTER 9

The sun struck Rattlesnake full force, dry, still, and hostile. He dragged himself up and prodded Red Moon. He watched her bow toward the east, which she did every morning in some kind of ritual she didn't like to talk about. A warm surge of love rose into a smile for the girl who'd cured his stomach and nursed his cold and would follow him off the edge of the world.

Follow him. His smile drooped and he stared at the cottonwood leaves already fallen. He loved her. Now he understood why his father had never left for his trip "out West." But he was not his father; he had no choice but to keep going, and she couldn't follow him when he had no idea how he'd keep himself alive or how to hide an Indian woman. Love or not, he had to leave her, and that stabbed at his gut and his conscience.

Still, that was days away, and there were more immediate problems at hand. If he didn't find clean water within hours, they would die.

He watered *Bontemps* and the mule at the river and helped Red Moon pick up their campsite without taking time to eat. He didn't need words to share the need to find water.

He led her straight west across the rancher's land, toward the mountains on the horizon. At the next fence, which dangled into a gulch, he cut their way into another ranch, leaving the top strand of barbed wire intact. They crossed several small stream beds, all dry. With each one, his lips dried out more.

Late in the morning Rattlesnake sat up straighter in the saddle and pointed toward the road, just visible to their left. There was a bridge about twenty yards long. He turned to Red Moon and smiled tightly with his parched lips. "Look, *cher*, if the creek's big enough to need a bridge that long, it's gotta have water in it," he said, spurring *Bontemps* to a run.

Red Moon caught up with him at the bank of the river.

They stared down at channels between sand islands where yellow grasses clung to life. A few willow bushes dotted the bottom. There was no water.

Rattlesnake's head was pounding with dehydration. "Let's dig around the willows," he said without much hope, the insides of his lips so dry that talking was difficult. "They need a lot of water. Maybe there's some under the sand. You try up there, I'll go downstream."

She nodded, sliding off the mule. When her feet hit the ground, she moaned and rubbed her head.

Rattlesnake slipped her shovel from her pack and handed it to her over the mule.

Red Moon took the shovel and trudged to the willows, working her jaw and tongue to bring a little saliva into her mouth. She knelt in the sand between the bushes and a large cleft rock in the riverbed. Her skirt caught on the rock and covered the gap. Before she could dig into the sand, she heard a rattle behind her. She froze. She turned slowly and glimpsed the head of a huge rattler coming out from under her skirt, its tongue darting at her. It was trying to coil; if she moved it would strike.

Rattlesnake had gone down the riverbed a short way, looking for a better place to dig. "No better down here," he said, turning back. He saw her freeze; he saw the head of the rattler swaying above the rock and the snake's intense concentration on Red

Moon. He raced back, grabbed the rifle from her pack, and aimed. His hands shook so violently he might hit her. He dropped the gun, searched frantically for a big rock to throw at the snake, and found none. In panic he yanked the old enamel kettle free of the thong that held it on Red Moon's pack and hurled it at the snake. It bounced off the rock with a metallic clatter and landed to Red Moon's left. The rattler's head disappeared and a second later the snake slithered away toward the other bank.

Red Moon collapsed in the sand.

Rattlesnake ran to her and held her. His own pulse was racing as fast as the one he could see in her temple. He was shaking as hard as she was. He'd nearly lost her to a painful death. *"Mon dieu, cher,* I thought you were a goner for sure."

Red Moon nodded, her head against his chest. "I almost die like my mother."

"I should've been more careful. I sure saw enough rattlers coming through Texas. Maybe I thought they didn't have any in Colorado."

"Not your fault. I am more careful now, too."

When he'd calmed down he helped her up.

Red Moon beat the dented kettle against the shovel. Another snake glided out of the bushes and up the bank, rattling. Then they began to dig. A foot below the surface they came to damp sand in the willow roots, but no water seeped into the hole.

"Come on, *cher,* this is hopeless."

"Thistles," she said, looking up at the embankment as she stood. "We can eat those. Maybe have water in them."

They dug the greenest ones out and, holding them with the squirrel skin, used Rattlesnake's pocket knife to peel off the thorny skin.

The stringy pulp pulled at her tongue instead of giving any moisture.

Rattlesnake spit his bite into the sand. "Hooeee, this tastes like celery and feels like newspaper. It's not helping."

He led the animals to the stand of willows, but *Bontemps* and the mule went straight for the thistles and cropped them off, thorns and all.

While Rattlesnake repacked the shovel and the kettle, Red Moon climbed back up the bank and studied the horizon. Behind her the Sangre de Cristos and before her the San Juans stretched away, broadening the vast flat valley as they trudged south. Her mother had always seen mountains as breasts of the earth. But these two ranges were dried up, ancient, and demanding, like two old women haggling over a cup of broth, both gray without a patch of the snow that should water them through the summer and nurture all things that lived at their skirts.

She knew now there would be no water in this valley. If they didn't find some in the mountains to the west, they would die. And the mountains were still far away.

CHAPTER 10

Red Moon knelt in the sand and ran her hands over a tuft of dry grass gone to seed too early. She listened with her heart to Mother Earth and drew the weed through her fingers, feeling the tickle of the seed cases against her palms. For the first time she understood the plant's desperate pregnancy. She cupped the seed ends in her hands, shading them from the fierce sun that burned her back.

She closed her eyes and felt the flow from her palms and fingers to the dry stalks, the roots, Mother Earth. The yellow grass tugged on the moisture of her hands, on the water of her body. The dry earth pulled at her until she was buried under the sand. The roots of grasses and willows surrounded her. The finest threads of their roots became one with her veins, and her heart pumped the water of her life into them. Her life flowed into all life and she understood. This was the sign.

Mother Earth could not give now, but must take back. Father Sky was angry and she needed everything to keep herself alive.

Red Moon knew her small scrap of life was nothing against all life. She gazed around at the struggling plants of the vast valley and tried to see the little spot of green that would rise here if she returned to Earth. "I am too small to matter," she whispered. "And I am not ready. Let me keep my body until Rattlesnake leaves. He needs me." She let go of the plant and felt the separateness of her body again. She pulled a hair from her braid and wrapped it around the tuft of grass. Then she made a broad circle around the plant with the flat of her hand and lined the circle with a few reddish brown pebbles. "This from Red Moon," she whispered. "I listen, I understand."

But did she understand? Did Mother Earth want her just for her water? Why would she want her here? Could this really be the sign when her death would make no difference?

She stood and looked for Rattlesnake. He'd gone downstream and was busy pulling up thistles and piling them on a cloth. Love welled in her like a sandstorm coming on the wind. He would leave her because the thing Mother Earth wanted of her she must do alone, but she wanted him to be safe. There was more he need-ed to learn. She rushed to help him.

They packed the half-dry plants on *Bontemps* and continued west. Rattlesnake pulled his hat low to shade his eyes; Red Moon tied the stiff squirrel skin to her head.

She watched the range in front of them. Mother Earth seemed to pull it backwards, as if she were angry now and wanted them to die of thirst because Red Moon had denied the sign.

They reached the end of a ranch, and she waited for Rattlesnake to cut another fence. "Why you don't look for better place to cut?" she asked, watching for ranchers.

Rattlesnake stuck the cutter back in his pack. "Because we can't use the road and have to go as straight as possible."

Toward mid-afternoon Rattlesnake stopped when he'd just climbed out of a gulch. He turned and said, "Don't come up, *cher.* Look, there's a windmill." He guided the horse back down the bank.

"What is 'windmill'?" she said above the panting of the mule.

"It's a thing that pumps water out of the ground for cattle. There's a ranch house pretty close to it, but I think I can get to the tank without being seen. Give me all the skins and anything else that'll hold water. I'll go up the wash and then keep the wind-mill between me and the house. The last fence I cut was probably theirs, so I don't want them to see me. Otherwise I'd just go up to the door and ask. You stay here with the animals."

Red Moon sat against the bank to wait, her head throbbing too hard to worry about whether taking water was stealing. The animals stood head to tail in the stifling heat, barely bothering to flick their tails at flies.

Rattlesnake started up the gulch, checking often for the rancher, until the tower stood between him and the house. Bent at the waist, he darted through cows, most of which had crowded into the little shade thrown by the windmill.

He hadn't quite reached the tank when an old truck sped up the dirt track from the road to the ranch house, raising a cloud of yellow-brown dust. He threw himself flat in the field among the cows, belly-crawled to the tank, and peered over it.

The truck came to a fast stop and the dust blew slowly toward the windmill. A tall gaunt man in faded overalls and a straw hat came out of the barn to meet the visitor. They shook hands and then the driver began talking angrily.

Even from a distance, Rattlesnake could tell the rancher was surprised and angry. The visitor gestured toward the east and enumerated things on the fingers of his left hand. Rattlesnake had no doubt the news was about the breaks in the fences. When the driver sped off again, the rancher ran to the house, brought out a rifle, and whistled at a horse standing under a tree near the barn. He started saddling it.

Rattlesnake filled one skin from the trickle coming from the pump. It seemed to take forever. The rancher cinched the saddle, shoved the rifle into a holder and mounted. To Rattlesnake's relief, he rode out to the highway. No doubt he would turn east to check his line. If Red Moon was moving around, or the animals, the rancher would spot them. Doubled over, Rattlesnake raced back to the gulch, following his own footprints, feeling countless eyes staring out of kitchen and bedroom windows, boring into his back.

Red Moon woke when he prodded her. She rubbed at her head, squinting against the headache of dehydration.

He was kneeling in the sand, pale and tense, and motioned to her to be silent. He slid down next to her, gave her a drink from the skin, and took one himself.

Sighing with pleasure as the liquid eased into her body, she raised the skin again.

Rattlesnake stopped her. "That's all there is. I couldn't get any more. I think the ranchers are looking for us. Did you hear anything from the road?"

Red Moon shook her head, her eyes on the water bag.

Rattlesnake looked toward the road. "There's just enough curve that they probably won't spot us, but we can't take any chances. The rancher's checking his fences now. We have to get out of here. Across the road. Down the gulch." He stood and looked toward the road. "He's past the bridge now, with his back to us. Come on."

They led the *Bontemps* and the mule toward the road, where a short bridge spanned the gulch.

When Rattlesnake saw the space under the bridge, he let out a string of nasal Cajun words, and then said, "I have to unload the horse to get her under here."

"Can't we go over the road?"

"*Non, cher,* there's one rancher in a truck and one on a horse up there." He gave Red Moon the horse's halter while he cut the fence.

The roar of a motor reached them from the left, underscored by a moving cloud of dust. The driver would see them if they didn't get under the bridge.

Fighting panic, Rattlesnake cut the last strand.

"Go under," said Red Moon. Before he could answer she rode the mule through the fence and scrambled up the embankment. She heard Rattlesnake encouraging the horse and shoving at the pack to ease it under the bridge. By the time the truck drew alongside, she was riding slowly along the shoulder, her heart pounding.

The truck skidded to a halt just ahead of her. Patches of tired gray showed under its dust. The driver leapt out, ran around the front of the truck and confronted her as she came alongside it. He put one hand on his waist. With the other he motioned her to stop. "Just hold it right there," he said with his head down, as though intending to ram the mule with it if she refused. He looked up. His face was lined and tanned, as dry and unyielding as the land around him. His green eyes were hard and hostile, even as they registered surprise. "Why, hell, it's a girl, an Injun at that. What you doin' on this road by yourself?"

Red Moon didn't answer. She looked straight ahead and assumed the deaf indifference she'd seen Indians use on unpleasant tourists in Taos.

"You been cutting wires along here?" He motioned her off the mule. "Let me check that pack of yours."

Red Moon slid the rifle out of her pack, opened it to show that it was loaded, and got off the mule.

"Okay, okay, girl." He put both hands up, palms out. "I just want to see whether you got any wire cutters here."

Red Moon waited, the rifle in both hands at waist height, her heart racing. She could put a bullet through the eye of a vulture from a long way off, but she didn't know whether she could even aim at a man, much less wound him. The rancher kept an eye on

95

her as he approached the mule. The mule backed off. There was noise from beneath the bridge, and the man stopped.

"What was that?" He turned toward the bridge.

Red Moon moved the pack to indicate it had shifted.

"Uh-uh, that came from down there. I seen you coming up from the gulch, too. What was you doing down there?" He looked embarrassed for a moment. "Oh. Peeing. Anybody else with you?"

She looked him in the eye and raised the rifle a few inches.

"Probably got the whole damn tribe down there," he muttered, watching her. He untied the thongs of the pack and ran his hand inside. Finally he gave up the search and started back for the truck, saying over his shoulder. "You got no business out here. You get along now. Injuns belong on the reservation." He turned and swept her out of the San Luis Valley and out of all significance with a simple back-handed gesture. He climbed into the truck.

Red Moon heard a click, a growling from the man, and then a roar. The truck made a grinding noise and lurched forward, spinning its wheels, throwing a cloud of dust and grit into her face.

She retied the thongs, climbed back on the mule, and rode slowly after the truck until it disappeared. She went limp. She turned and urged the mule to the far side of bridge, where Rattlesnake was just peering over the embankment. *Bontemps* had lain down in the sand under the low bridge. She seemed to be enjoying the shade.

Rattlesnake pulled her from the mule. "Red Moon, *cher*, you amaze me. You were wonderful," he said, kissing her. "Why, you're shaking." He held her for a moment. "Come on, *ma cherie*, we got to get out of here. He'll be back, and the other rancher will, too. We'll find a place to hide till dark. Wait here."

Rattlesnake climbed cautiously up the embankment, checked the road in both directions, and looked south. "Hey, there's an old cabin down there. And a hill behind it."

He handed Red Moon the reins to both animals and she started down the gulch. He walked behind, checking the road often, still amazed at her courage. Suddenly he saw himself standing on the jetty watching water rush into the pirogue. He'd left his parents then and had felt guilty. He'd missed them. But leaving Red Moon was going to be like sinking his heart.

From a low point in the embankment Red Moon started toward the shack.

"Not there, *cher*, that's the first place anybody'd look. Keep going. We'll hide behind the hill. It won't offer any shelter, but we should be safe there."

They reached the point where they would have to cross open land to reach the knoll. Rattlesnake peered out of the wash.

The rancher was riding slowly back toward his house, rising in the saddle and searching in all directions.

Rattlesnake ducked. "We'll have to wait. Maybe we're just as well off here, anyway. See if you can get the mule to lie down."

He hit *Bontemps* above her back knees, and the tractable horse sat down. After a couple of taps on the front legs, she was lying. The mule would not be tapped or cajoled into following suit.

Rattlesnake took the wilted thistles from Red Moon's pack and spread them in front of the animals. He took down the water bag. "Don't drink much, *cher*, we have to get all the way to the mountains on this tonight."

Red Moon swished a sip water in her mouth as she sat down leaned against the bank. The sun was going down, drawing the worst of the heat with it, and all was quiet.

Rattlesnake sat down and took a sip. His stomach growled just as the water hit. "*Mon dieu*, I'm hungry. I don't suppose you got a nice mess of crawfish *etouffé* packed away someplace."

"I don't know 'crawfish' and that other thing."

"Well, a crawfish is an animal that lives in the swamp. It has two claws like a scorpion, but its tail curls down instead of up and it doesn't sting. It's about this long." He held up his fingers with the length of a lizard between thumb and forefinger. "The tail is what people usually eat. Mmm, my mother could cook up a good mess of crawfish."

When his stomach rumbled in the silence, he leaned his head against the wall of the gulch and sighed. "This sure ain't the cowboy's life I pictured."

Red Moon moved away from him. "I make your life harder."

He put his arm around her. "*Non, cher,* I didn't mean you. I just thought it would be easier. A nice camping place near running water, a warm fire against the chill of night. I didn't think about hiding or feeling guilty or getting anyone else in trouble. After this we'll travel at night so we don't have to cut any fences."

He turned her so that her back rested against his knees. "How are your blisters?" He kissed her, stroked her face and her hair, ran his hand down her braid. He crossed the ends of the braids on his upper lip and said in a deep voice, "Do I look like a villain with this mustache?" He tried to laugh.

Red Moon wrinkled her brow, not knowing what a villain was.

He pulled her close again. "I didn't reckon with you at all, Red Moon, but I'm glad you were in that shack. Hogan. You know what I thought when I saw your place?"

She shook her head.

"I just said to myself, 'No one could possibly live out here, no. It's probably abandoned.' Then I saw you and the mule. I still don't know how you made it there alone for so long."

Red Moon felt a rush of pride, but she said, "Didn't know I could do anything else."

He smiled and took her face in his hands again. "I love you, *cher,* I really mean it. And when I come back, we're going to have a good life."

"Oh, Rattlesnake," she started to say, but his lips were in the way.

In the middle of the night, *Bontemps* snorted. Red Moon woke and jumped up, instantly alert, listening for a rancher's footsteps or a horse's hooves above the gulch. The night was cool, quiet, and very dark. She prodded Rattlesnake. "Something scared the mule," she whispered. "He bumped into the horse."

Rattlesnake rubbed his eyes. "You hear anything?"

She shook her head.

"Well, we're already awake; let's get out of here," Rattlesnake got up and turned the animals toward the road. "I hope we get some moonlight after we pass the ranchers."

"It will come late. Remember last night when we were sick?"

They both shared the last of the water and got on their animals. The mule balked.

Red Moon stroked his neck. "Too dark. The mule can't see."

Rattlesnake backed the horse up to the mule's nose. "Here, let me have the rein." He led the mule, and they started for the road.

When they passed the rancher's gate, barely visible under the stars, she glanced nervously toward the house. There was no light. She plodded on behind him, desperate to reach the mountains before daylight.

The moon lit the peaks long before it shone on the valley, making them deceptively close and giving her hope. When it lit the road she spurred the mule on.

They reached the first rise into the mountains with the moon still at their backs. After they'd climbed a mile or more, *Bontemps* broke into a run and left Red Moon and the mule behind. Rattlesnake tried to rein her in, but she wouldn't be controlled. She rounded a curve and stepped down into the ditch. A little pool of water had collected where a culvert crossed under the road. Rattlesnake jumped down and hugged her around the neck. "*Mais, amie,* you're a lifesaver." *Bontemps* snorted into the water. Rattlesnake ran back down the road. By this time the mule had picked up the smell of the water. Red Moon jumped down to let him have his head and joined Rattlesnake. They passed the animals and walked backwards up the road, watching for a reflection of the moon on water coming down the ditch. They found a trickle and looked for places deep enough to dip their hands in.

"This is grassier than I like to drink out of," Rattlesnake said, water dripping from his chin, "but I guess it's too late to worry about that now."

They drank their fill and started out again, watching for the source.

"When we find where this comes down, we'll follow it up till we find a grassy place to stay for a day. The horses need to eat. I can hear *Bontemps'* stomach growl."

The sun began to lighten the eastern sky before they found a freshet that trickled down the embankment. They separated, looking for a way up through the woods. In a few minutes, Rattlesnake whistled to her and they started up.

By the time the sun cleared the peaks and baked the valley again, they'd found a small clearing that was invisible from the road. The stream, only one-quarter full, glided through on one side. The clearing had been used as a campsite before, but the fire pit was half grown over and there were no tracks through the yellow grass.

Although the sun was already at mid-morning, Red Moon climbed down from the mule and faced east. She stood still for a moment, then pulled some grass seeds and scattered them before making camp. The greeting was personal now, no longer just habit, but a blessing for Mother Earth and Father Sky, mixed with guilt over refusing what might have been the sign.

They stayed three days to give themselves time to trap fresh meat and gain their strength back. Just before dark on the third night they returned to the road and followed it west. Several days later they crossed into the Southern Ute Reservation and camped outside the town of Ignacio.

Rattlesnake visited the town while Red Moon arranged the campsite. He returned with beef jerky and some hard candy he'd paid for, as well as the knowledge that they could take an old wagon road directly to Farmington instead of following the highway.

Feeling safer in an Indian reservation, they traveled by day, reached the San Juan River in Farmington, and followed it west toward Shiprock. Atop the first rise where they could see the Rock, Rattlesnake stopped, turned in his saddle, and waited for Red Moon to catch up. "That has to be the Shiprock," he said.

The land opened out before them in a broad plain of gray sage and rust red sand, cut by a swath of green with an occasional silvery glint of water in it. Beyond a small town that squatted at the river's edge, the Rock rose, more like a cathedral than a ship.

Red Moon looked at it, her heart weeping for the end of her time with Rattlesnake. "I don't know. Doesn't look like bird. My mother's people called it 'Rock with Wings.'" The name brought her mother's face, drawn with longing for the Rock and the trees—and the family she feared.

"Well, it *does* look a little like a ship. This means we'll find your mother's family soon." Even as he said it, Rattlesnake felt something heavy clutch at his heart.

Red Moon didn't answer him, nor did she speak again as she followed him down the river. As night fell, they stopped east of the Rock and made their camp on a sand bar in the shallow river—in silence.

Why do I feel so guilty? Rattlesnake asked himself as he slid bundles from *Bontemps'* back. After all, this is what we planned to do. There was a sick feeling in his stomach that was more than guilt, but he didn't allow himself to examine it.

Red Moon felt her heart slowly being ripped from her breast. In her mind Rattlesnake had already left for the unknown, and the pain of his loss coupled with fear of the future and the aching loneliness of the past crushed her. She didn't want to be here without her mother. She didn't belong here. She didn't belong anywhere.

When he came to her as they settled for the night, his touch was already memory, and she couldn't respond to it.

Rattlesnake, unable to see her in the dark, found her face with his hand and traced her eyes looking for tears. They began to flow. He kissed them away, he kissed her eyes, her forehead, her mouth, believing the tears were for him alone, hoping that a moment's passion would drown the pain.

In a wave of desperation, Red Moon turned to him and kissed him fiercely. They made love wildly and silently. Afterwards, the silence, rather than encompassing them, lay like a canyon between them.

When the glow of passion had ebbed and the trees, sand, river, and breeze came back to her awareness, she said, "I want you to leave in the morning."

Rattlesnake rose on his elbow, and she heard the concern in his voice. "But I want to help you find your family. I can't go off and leave you until I know..."

"And if there's no family left? If we can't find them? Then you'd think you can't leave me." Her mother's face when she talked about her father and brothers glowed out of the darkness, with the look of terrible loneliness. "My mother's family didn't want her any more. Maybe they won't want me. You can't be part of that. I want you to go away now, not follow me to new life I don't want. Please, go before I wake."

Rattlesnake made a strange, breathy noise with his throat. "But what about our things? They're all mixed together in the packs."

"Just leave my things here. Please, Rattlesnake. Make it easier for me."

His face was close to hers again. "But I'm coming back to see you. How will I find you?"

"You won't come back."

Red Moon said this with such dull finality that Rattlesnake knew not to protest further. He reached for her again, found her face, and stroked it. She placed her hand on his for a minute and then turned her back.

CHAPTER 11

RED MOON

Red Moon heard the first rustle of Rattlesnake's bedroll as he stirred before dawn. She knew he was looking at her, hoping she would change her mind, trying to find words that would help. She kept her eyes closed and her back to him. He sighed, got up and started to gather his belongings. She knew every creak and rattle of saddling and packing the horse. It seemed to take forever, but eventually she heard the splash of *Bontemps'* hooves as Rattlesnake rode out of her life.

The humming of her tears starting to flow muffled the last few hoof beats. Slowly she drew her knees up to her chest and bit her lip to stop the pain of love being ripped away.

"Now, Mother Earth," she whispered. She willed herself dead under the sand of the river bed in obedience to the sign Mother Earth had given her. And then she was outside herself but far above the river. As an eagle might, she saw the vast, struggling earth. She saw the Rock with Wings, the desert between Farmington and Shiprock, the mountains they'd crossed, the abandoned adobe hogan, and the huge world she now knew lay beyond, with a lone man riding away into it. She saw the meaningless, tiny, aching woman who lay curled up, alone in the riverbed. "Take me back now," she said, willing the weight of the emptiness to grind her into the sand and crush the pain. Vaguely she saw a black face that faded almost immediately. Was that the death Mother Earth refused her now because she'd refused the sign when it had come?

She opened her eyes. Sand. Bits of driftwood and a few narrow, yellowed leaves. Beyond them the San Juan slipped wearily by. The sun, dappled by the willows overhead, shone on her face. She stretched out her arm, listlessly picked up a handful of sand, and let it run through her fingers in lieu of the ritual giving of corn meal to Earth. It was dry and lifeless.

Red Moon lay in her bedroll for a long time, not knowing what to do, until the need to pass her water compelled her to get up.

On the pile he had made of her things Rattlesnake had left the two pairs of underpants and all the candy from Ignacio, along with a green branch broken from a tree that stood nearby. Red Moon began to cry again, took the branch and hugged it to her before she went behind the tree.

When she returned, she picked up the branch, stroked its slender leaves and the long twigs that were nearly parallel to the branch. She looked at the tree, touched the narrow webbing of the old bark. It was not a tall tree like the cottonwood of Taos. Its branches forked away from the trunk on a level with her shoulder and branched again and again into long thin fingers, all pointing to the sky, filling the rounded treetop with a delicate maze of leaves. "River Willow," she said. She looked up and down stream and saw the trees that her mother had loved. She sat down on a fallen log, ran her hands over the old loose bark, and watched the trees. There was not much wind, but the branches yielded to it gracefully, swaying like long grasses in waves of green. The motion was so beautiful it seemed to wash over her like the laughter of her mother.

"I am River Willow," she said. "Mother." And her mother's presence was so real that she put her arms around it and hugged it to her, rocking gently on the log. Weeping, she watched the trees ripple as the breezes swept past the Rock with Wings, across the desert and up gentle slope of the San Juan. She saw in the lovely compliance of these trees to the whims of air her mother's graceful acceptance of the man who had drifted in and out with the winds, bringing change and isolation, leaving poverty and a daughter.

I do not even have a daughter, she thought. She tried to project herself into her mother and imagine that River Willow had been left alone. What would she have done? Where would she have gotten the strength to make decisions, to go on living? And then she knew. From Mother Earth.

Red Moon had let herself become too dependent on Rattlesnake and he'd left her. The only thing that would never leave her was Mother Earth. Red Moon ran her hands over the gray wood of the dead tree under her, felt its roots in the sand and in the air, sensed the water flowing through the sand and around roots that could no longer drink it. She accepted the caress of the air as it eddied around her, knew the dance of the Navajo willows as her own obedience to Mother Earth. She would not refuse the sign another time.

CHAPTER 12
RED MOON AND RATTLESNAKE

Red Moon was still at one with the dead roots deep in the sand when a footstep startled her. She froze.

"*Cher?*" Rattlesnake sat down on the other side of the log, reached around her and turned her to him.

"Rattlesnake." Her voice shook with surprise. She pulled away. He would hurt her again.

He held her shoulders. "I'm sorry, Red Moon. I was a fool. Stay with me. Please, stay with me." His voice was different, full of feeling she'd never heard before.

He put his arms around her and held her tighter than he ever had, rocking her like a child. She closed her eyes to all but their oneness and tightened her arms around him, desperate to feel as much of him as possible.

Rattlesnake stroked the back of her head. "I love you, Red Moon. I love you."

Without easing her embrace, Red Moon moved her head until she could see his face. His eyes were full of love and belonging.

"I love you," he said again.

She was crying. He wiped away her tears and pressed her head against his chest.

"I'll never make you cry again." He pulled her head to his. "I rode for a long time, but the farther I got the more you pulled me back. Even *Bontemps* seemed to fight me."

Through the tears, Red Moon smiled up at the panting horse.

"Remember that old sheep pen we saw yesterday afternoon?" he said. "I was almost that far when I just stopped. And I sat there on the horse feeling too much of me was missing. I was stupid not to realize how much I loved you. And then I got scared, yeah. I was afraid you'd be gone and I'd never find you. I made *Bontemps* gallop all the way back."

"I thought I never see you again," she said.

"But you were still here. We're just meant to stay together." He smiled, but then he pulled his lips together and looked away, as if he could see tomorrow. "I don't know what lies ahead, *cher*. It's not easy, a white man and an Indian girl. We just have to keep going till we find a place where we'll be safe. I can't even promise you we'll ever find one." He sighed. "I didn't want to make life so hard for you, but I want you, Red Moon. Please stay with me. I need you."

Red Moon knew they would not stay together, no matter how much he loved her. He wasn't her sign or part of the thing she must do when the sign came. She looked down. "You will leave me again."

He frowned and pulled her face up to make her look at him. "No, I won't. I tried once and couldn't. I promise I won't try again."

She smiled then, sadly, remembering the dream with the broken gray line. "You won't want to, but it will happen. I know it. But we will be together until it does. I love you, Rattlesnake."

They sat holding each other on the old tree for a long time, reluctant to surrender the sensation of each other to the necessities of the day. Red Moon felt a new peace, knowing she could love Rattlesnake without allowing herself to need him so much. The end would come, but she would find a way to go on. Perhaps he would leave her a daughter.

Suddenly, the presence of a child was so strong that she felt the daughter sitting on her lap at a loom. The little back was warm against her breast, and the small fingers curved under hers, awkwardly threading yarn the color of the desert floor through the warp. But she understood now that it was not the blanket that mattered, it was the weaving. The warp was woman, the continuous thread in which a single woman was a length of yarn in the pattern of time, grandmother, mother, daughter, all Red Moon and all River Willow though past and future. For the first time, Red Moon knew she could not break the warp. More than she had ever been conscious of anything, she wanted a daughter to carry her mother through the weaving of life.

The child stirred. She blinked, startled to find Rattlesnake warm against her breast, not the child. She shook her head to clear the image of the daughter.

"What is it, *cher*?" he asked. "You look like you were a million miles away."

"I...," she said. But Rattlesnake wouldn't understand, and besides, he'd already said he didn't want her to have a child. "Still surprised," she said. "You came back. I never thought a white man would come back. I'm glad." She turned to look down her mother's river. "Something happened when you were gone, Rattlesnake. I can't explain it. I feel my mother in this place. Want to know it better. I want to go to the Rock with Wings."

"Why, sure, *cher*, we can stay a day or two."

Rattlesnake looked at her profile and remembered the detached look in her eyes when she said he'd leave her again. There was something different about her, a wholeness he'd never seen before. Her eyes showed him love, just as they always had, but from some strength inside her rather than from need. He was free to love her, not forced to; she was his equal; and she had, in some way beyond his grasp, become a woman.

In the afternoon they moved their camp farther upriver for privacy, and on the following day they rode down to the Rock with Wings. They passed Navajo men and women on the road, and a few scattered hogans. Red Moon sat erect on the mule and stared straight ahead.

Rattlesnake reached over and touched her shoulder. "You think some of these could be..."

"Don't want to know." Red Moon feared her heart would break or she would scream if she saw someone who looked like River Willow. Her mother had feared them, now *she* would ignore them. She focused on the land around them, the place where her mother had walked and woven and sung. The clop of hooves on the dirt road became the beater in the loom; the wind became her mother chanting the weaving song. Red Moon listened, but the voice that was only in her head now hurt too much.

She turned to Rattlesnake. "My mother told me her people believed this rock was the bird that brought them up from a big hole in the ground. They came up from another life through the hole."

Rattlesnake squinted at the rock. "A big hole? You mean the Grand Canyon?"

"Don't know. But when it brought them here it turned to stone so they could honor it."

They rode around the rock, straining their necks to look up at its vertical red-brown spires.

"Even close it doesn't look like Rock with Wings," she said.

Rattlesnake took off his hat and ran his fingers through his hair, looking up. "Well, I guess your people named it that a long time ago. Long before mine named it after a ship. Probably it looked a lot different then. See all those big rocks lying around the bottom?" Long columns of deep red sandstone lay in a jumble at the base. "They must have fallen off and maybe when they were up there it looked more like a bird."

"Maybe."

"I wonder why it's still standing here in the middle of this big desert. Why didn't it just flatten out like the rest?"

They climbed partway up the jumble of rock and sat on a level column, looking southeast. Before them stretched a widely spaced web of dirt roads leading to hogans and sheep pens. Here and there small, scattered herds of sheep foraged on the sparse grass that competed with the sage for water. Toward the east the few buildings of Shiprock lined the river banks, clearly the homes and businesses of white people.

Rattlesnake pointed toward the town and started to say something, but when he glanced at her, he noticed she was gone from him, in some world of her own. He waited.

Sitting with her knees drawn up to her chin on the Rock with Wings, its spires tall and powerful at her back, Red Moon understood. Whether it had ever had wings was not important. It was the way the rock stood, rooted in the earth, like a piece of the earth's spirit there in the desert for The People to touch. She put both hands on the stone at her sides and became one with it. Her warmth radiated back to Father Sky. Her rough surface took the brunt of the sand hurled by the wind. She was its unyielding hardness and its great depth below the desert. She sensed its male nature and understood the oneness of all life, male and female, plant and animal and rock and air. All life flowed through her body, directly from her mother, made urgent by the man she loved.

He stirred next to her, bringing her back to the world of rock and wind and flesh, to feelings she could express in words. "Rattlesnake, I want a baby," she said.

"We will have children, *cher*, someday. But we have to find a place where we can stay first. It might take a long time, but we have all the time in the world." He put his arm around her. "You know,

I don't think you would've been happy here. This is pretty miserable land to live on. I'm glad you're not staying."

"I would not stay here."

"What?" He turned to her and put both hands on her shoulders.

"If you not come back, I leave. Maybe go back where we camped before Farmington, or maybe somewhere else, higher up. I don't know. But not stay here."

"Red Moon, *cher*, do you mean to tell me you would have gone off and tried to survive alone?" He looked into her eyes and knew that she could have done it. Years of loneliness and hiding played out a terrible vision, and he pulled her to him. "I won't let that happen to you. We're together now, and someday, you will have my baby. I promise."

Red Moon knew he meant to keep the promise, but she would try to make the daughter before it was too late.

CHAPTER 13

MAC

The slender bowl of the moon gathered up starlight, grew full, and then scattered it into the night sky again. Its cycle did not relieve the parched summer that lay over the land. The longer nights of waning summer did not grow cool. Plants everywhere were brittle, animals limp.

Red Moon and Rattlesnake traveled north through Colorado, staying in the mountains for the sake of the few streams that were still running; but no gain in altitude diminished the heat. They were on Buckhorn Creek just past Masonville, a clapboard town with a general store, a small church, and an even smaller school. On both ends of the town they passed ranch houses and dusty, yellowed pastures dotted with skinny brown cattle. Fences kept them confined to the road and nervous about the people who stared as they passed.

They had just rounded a bend and were out of sight of ranch houses for the moment.

"Here, *cher*," said Rattlesnake, stopping and handing her his reins. "This looks like pretty good cover if we can get in without cutting the fence." He slid off the horse and pushed through a thicket of willows. He came back and tied *Bontemp's* reins to a bush. "Come on, you can get the mule through, and nobody can see you from the road. No water in the creek, but you can hide here while I ride back and get some matches and find out how far we are from Wyoming."

Red Moon pushed through the branches into a narrow pasture at the bottom of a cliff that blazed red in the late afternoon sun. A few skinny cows standing in the shade of the trees along the streambed stared at her without moving. Salt licks dotted the grass stubble. In front of her, square red stones from the cliff ringed a fireplace. The charred wood in it looked new enough to make her tense, and she hoped Rattlesnake didn't plan to camp here. It was late now, but if they camped this close to the road they couldn't risk a fire to boil the remaining water.

She sat on the stones and waited. It was a long time before Rattlesnake shoved through the willows. He held up a big box of matches, but Red Moon's eyes went to his bulging pockets.

He looked down and pretended surprise. "*Mon dieu*, will you look at this, now. Where do you suppose this stuff came from?" He reached into all his pockets and laid four wrinkled yellow apples and a couple of budding red potatoes on the rocks next to her.

Red Moon wrinkled her brow. She still had the money. How had he gotten the food?

He laughed and stroked her chin and kissed her forehead. "Don't worry, I didn't steal them. They were on the trash bin behind the store." He handed her one of the apples, put other one back in a pocket, and slipped the others with the potatoes into his saddlebag. "Whooeee, I need a drink." He grabbed a water skin, hefted it with a frown, and took a sip. "We sure need more water. Come on, let's eat on the way, *cher*." He started back to the bushes. "You know what? We're closer to Wyoming than I thought. If we just stay on this road here, we'll come to the Cache la Poudre River."

She squinted, trying to understand the name, but he went on without noticing.

"Imagine such a French name way up here. At a place called Rustic, we head north and follow the old stage road right on up to Laramie. Just think of it, when we get that far, we'll be on the old Laramie Trail."

"I don't understand Woming, or that river, or that larmy tail." She took a bite of the apple.

"Well, come on, let's see if we can make it to the river by tonight and I'll tell you about it on the way."

They led the mule onto the road again and started off.

"The river means 'hide the powder' in French. I wonder how it got that name," Rattlesnake was saying as they passed a stone portal topped by weathered posts and a crossbeam, from which hung a board. It was weathered also, but the name MacCauley carved into it was still visible, and next to the name a capital L with a smaller capital M sitting in its lap.

As he stomped up the two steps to his narrow front porch, Lester MacCauley turned and glared at a boy on a huge horse and a dark woman on a mule. His weathered face might have emanated the dignity that often comes to men who work the earth, but there was no peace in it, nor a hint of gentleness in his blue-gray eyes.

His thumbs hooked belligerently into his belt, he watched the two strange riders disappear around a bend. When the sound of hooves on the dirt road died, he leaned his five foot, seven inch frame against the post nearest the steps, its grayed paint roughened and cracked like a sheet of graph paper. In the place where his shoulder always rested, the paint was gone and the wood dark with sweat and dust. He shoved his Stetson back, wiped his forehead on his shirtsleeve, and stood facing east. At the end of his day, he came as close as he ever did to the sensation of peace.

He'd never told even his wife how much he liked looking across the Stove Prairie Road and Buckhorn Creek at the three simple stripes of color at the edge of his world: the narrow green strip of willows on the creek, the intense blue sky above, and between them the deep red of the sandstone bluff. His son had told him it was a fossilized sand dune, one in a string that rose in spectacular formations all along the Front Range. Mac didn't give a damn about the geology. He just liked the three colors, but if anyone asked what he was looking at, he would say he was checking the cattle in the pasture. To admit pleasure in the scene before him would have struck him as womanish.

Mac, known to everyone in the Buckhorn valley as "Mean Mac," never walked; he stomped. He slammed doors, saddled his horses too tightly, threw himself into chairs, frequently broke dishes, and nearly always cut himself shaving. The son of an angry and abusive father, he was perpetually angry himself; and since the death of his wife the anger could only seethe below the surface. He was rarely able to vent it on his only child, Les Jr., who insisted on going to that stupid college down in Greeley and came home only on holidays.

Mac had the good sense to keep his anger in check with his new hired hand, however, a drifter named Brad, who he hoped would stay until winter set in. Not that Brad was any great shakes as a worker, but there were no others in the valley.

When the last rays of sun had slid up the ancient red sand dunes, Mac banged into his house and found Les, Jr., reading in the cowhide chair with his hair slicked back from a bath. "You back already?" he barked. "I thought you wasn't coming till Thanksgiving."

Les plucked at the towel he'd stuck through the lamp stand, a series of old horseshoes stacked and welded end-to-end. "Summer school's over."

Mac looked at the thin face and narrow chin, exactly like his own twenty years ago, only without any stiffening. The blue-gray eyes were staring warily back.

Les shrank a little. "They don't let you stay in the dorm between terms, Pa. I'm starting a new job in town on Monday. I can stay with a friend who lives in Greeley till the dorm opens again."

As usual, Les slouched in the chair, just as he slouched in everything else. Even when he stood, Mac thought, he seemed to slouch, almost cringe. He had his mother's sandy hair and the softness of her eyes, which reflected his gentle nature. It was this very nature that had always irked Mac. Les had never been able to stand up against him. Simply wasn't much of a man. Wasn't ever going to make it as a rancher when he took over.

"Fine." Mac snorted and gave him a sarcastic smile. "You can go hunting with us day after tomorrow. Maybe that'll stiffen you up a little bit."

Les closed his eyes. "You can't go hunting now, Pa. It's out of season."

Mac glared at the closed eyes, just like the mother's when she'd wanted to protest and knew she could never win. "So who's gonna tell? You?" He turned toward the kitchen. "Had to kill another cow last week. Pastures're too dry. Git me three steaks outa the coolin' house." He shoved at the swinging kitchen door. It banged against a cupboard, swung back into the living room, and settled into a diminishing arc.

Les shouted over the noise of the door. "Three?"

Mac shoved at it again as he turned. It slammed into the bottom of the lamp stand and caught on the circle of horseshoes at the base. "Jes git 'em."

The screen door opened and closed quietly, and Brad walked in.

Mac introduced them in his way. "This here's my son Les. Brad."

Les looked confused.

"Hired hand," said Brad when Mac didn't explain.

"I didn't know you hired a new hand," Les said, shaking hands with the worker.

Mac watched the smile that began in Brad's brown eyes and spread over his face. Easy for him to grin like a ninny. He didn't have a whole damn ranch to run and a son who couldn't rope a steer if it fell over in front of him. Les was smiling back at the hired man. Of course. What else? Mac took his time answering and called from the kitchen. "Well, how *would* you know? Gotta have somebody around here, what with you off at that *uneeversitee*." He said the last word in a falsetto drawl.

Les leaned against the worn spot on the porch post, watching Mac march down the road toward the Poudre. He'd said something about looking for a couple of trespassers who might set a camp fire on his property. Les looked up at the stars for a minute, turned back, and sat down in one of the wicker chairs.

In a few minutes Brad joined him. "Dishes is all done." He sat in the other chair and crossed his feet on the porch railing. "Your pa ain't much of a talker, is he?"

"No, there was hardly ever any talking in this house. Came as a big surprise to me in the dining hall at school when everybody sat around talking."

Brad rolled down the sleeves of his red plaid shirt and snapped the cuffs. "Make you realize what you missed, huh?"

Les looked down, embarrassed. "Yeah, I guess. Just before you came in he told me he was going hunting with somebody on Thursday. Would that be you?"

"Probably. He mentioned it. Sure, I'll go if he don't have anything else for me to do."

Brad's calm, handsome profile, lit by the light coming through the living room window and the laughter just below the surface of his voice appealed to Les. He laughed. "Oh, I reckon he wants you to do the cleaning and stuff, if he bags anything. He always made my mother do that part."

Brad made a face and shrugged. "Well, he's paying me."

"I guess I'm expected to go. I'm not much use as a hunter. Pa hates that. Thinks I'm a mama's boy."

Brad raised his eyebrows. "That so? Well, you ain't much like him, that's for sure. What you studying?"

"Education. Pa hates that, too. Thinks teaching's for women." He saw a conspiratorial grin spread over Brad's face and felt a surge of pride. "I'm going to teach science and math. Probably high school. Maybe go for a higher degree, teach in college."

Brad nodded.

"What about you? Where're you from?" asked Les.

Brad waved vaguely with his hand. "Oh, just about everywhere west of the Mississippi. Never stay one place too long, though."

"Well, if I know Pa, you won't be here too long, either. He can get real mean."

Brad let out a puff of derision. "His kind of mean don't scare me. Too solid, if you know what I mean. Don't often flare up, folks that're just mean through and through."

Les was stunned. "You're right. He's so mean all the time he doesn't have to lose his temper. Everybody just does what he wants so they don't have to deal with him. I never thought of it that way." He shook his head. "I'm glad I didn't turn out like him."

"'Course, there's other kinds of mean, too. Now me, I can flash mean. They say I'm a mean drunk. Get real bad. I don't remember anything afterwards, though."

Les looked straight at him and waited a minute. When Brad didn't go on, he repeated the key word, "But you say it's bad?" It was a trick he'd learned in his psychology course to draw a person out.

Brad set his feet on the floor and drew his long legs right up to the edge of the chair. He stared down at his hands clenched in his lap. "Once I beat up a guy pretty bad, I guess. I was working on a ranch down near the New Mexico line. I caught one of the other hands trying to steal my rattlesnake belt. 'Course, I don't own much, but it makes me real mad when anybody messes with my stuff. And this belt...well, it's just important to me. I'd had a few drinks, real strong stuff to boot. They say I messed him up good." He separated his hands and slammed the right fist into the left palm. "Try to stop before I get mean ever since. Scares me what I might do."

Mac came back and the conversation died. Brad went off to his room and father and son stayed on the porch. Mac threw himself into the chair Brad had vacated.

Les waited through the typical silence, conscious of his father's solid meanness. "Not so many mosquitoes this year," he said to drown the quiet hostility.

Mac yanked a twig from the wicker table between them and began to break it into bits. "Too dry. Creek's almost completely dry."

"Yeah," said Les, relieved that the subject had not somehow reverted to himself. "I went down and had a look before supper."

"Tomorrow you go into town and get some beer and ammo for hunting." Mac stood up, banging his chair into the wall behind him.

Les felt the dread rise. This could not go well. "Pa, I don't think..."

Mac slammed the door.

Les sighed. "Good night," he said to the darkness.

CHAPTER 14

In his hurry to get to the river, Rattlesnake set a faster pace, and Red Moon pushed the mule to keep up. She wanted to leave this narrow place with all the fences and white people she had to hide from.

As the road moved closer to the cliffs, they passed from bright heat into deep shadow, and almost immediately the mule stumbled and stopped, breathing hard.

"Rattlesnake," she called, getting down to relieve the mule's load. "Mule is too tired. We have to stop."

Rattlesnake rode back. He took off his hat and blew a breath out from puffed cheeks. "We gotta keep going, *cher*, we need water."

"We passed small stream back there. Maybe has water. I'll walk the mule."

They turned back and found the creek bed. Close to the road, the creek offered only a few tiny pools inhabited by water skaters.

Rattlesnake jumped down. "Well, at least there's a little. It's gotta come from somewhere. Let's follow it up. I'll walk the horse and we'll put the mule's load on her back."

As the gulch closed in, they found a clean trickle over rocks, along with the remnants of a cabin and an old mine. Rattlesnake went into the entrance several feet, holding a match.

Red Moon examined the cabin. It leaned into the rock face behind it, causing the one unbroken glass pane in its window to reflect the tree tops behind her. The smell of coyote rose from inside, but it was better than the bad feeling she'd had on the road.

Rattlesnake came back from the mine, saying, "Not much to see, but that's a good place to hide out from the heat. Downright cold in there." He looked around at the clearing in front of the cabin. "It'd be a nice place to camp a few days, but we need to get to that river tomorrow."

The next morning they rode down to the river, a slip of murky water that trickled through the dark, dry rocks. They watered the animals and started upstream toward Rustic. It was an uneasy ride. The river bed was too rocky for the animals to walk in, and the road was busy with lumber trucks that startled them. Fisherman trying their luck in the shrunken river stared as they passed.

In the afternoon they started up the old stage coach road at Pingree Hill, two steep tracks overgrown with yellowed grasses and brittle sage. The stream bed that followed it for the first quarter mile was dry.

Walking up the steepest parts to spare the mule, they cleared the top of the hill. Below them lay a long valley that stretched from left to right, a mixture of broad meadow, rocky outcroppings, sage, aspen, and fir trees. At the bottom, a road crossed it at right angles. Here and there, mine tailings dotted the slopes like scaly yellow tongues hanging out of black mouths.

Rattlesnake jumped off the horse. "I got to stop for a minute, *cher*, wait here and enjoy the scenery." He disappeared into the trees.

Red Moon got off the mule and walked up to the trees on the other side. When she returned, Rattlesnake was already back, holding a gray board in his hands and laughing.

"Look at this, Red Moon. It's a sign. 'Manhattan, 1/2 mile.' Can you imagine? Look how old it is. Somebody a long time ago was having a good joke, yeah."

He explained about Manhattan and the bargain that somebody had gotten for a few beads, but Red Moon didn't laugh. Dark fear welled in her heart and clamped her breath. From his first days with her came the memory of two gray lines woven together on his map. They became knotted over a place called Manhattan. The knot broke, leaving only one line. There was blood in the memory. Manhattan was not a good place.

As they rode down the hill, the remains of the town came into view. The one street and everything on it slumped toward the stream at the bottom of the valley. On the uphill end of town a few log cabins still stood, but most of the clapboard buildings had already collapsed. Others, at tired angles to their foundations, would succumb to the next heavy snow. The word *Bank* was barely legible on the only building still erect. They dismounted and peered through the broken windows.

It was bare of bank trappings but had been turned into a campsite. All the floor boards had been ripped up, and against its side wall someone had built a stone fire pit and angled sheets of corrugated tin above the broken window to vent it.

"Well, what do you know?" said Rattlesnake, looking around from the front door of the bank. "A real ghost town. I guess there was a Manhattan here after all."

"Don't like it here," said Red Moon, feeling a tingle between her shoulder blades.

Rattlesnake was already headed up the street. "Why not, *cher*?" he called over his shoulder. He wandered from one old house to the next as he continued. "This is a nice spot. We'll stay here a couple of days. We can have a roof over our heads for a change. Look, there's even a little water in the stream down there. No tellin' how far we'll have to go before we find any more."

Red Moon stayed by the bank, watching him with dread, her arms pressed against her chest. "Rattlesnake, come back. I feel death here."

He joined her again, grinning. "Well, that's why they call places like this 'ghost towns.' This used to be a mining town. See all those places on the hill where they dug? Men came here looking for gold or silver, and when there wasn't any more, they left."

"But..."

"There's no death here, *cher*, don't be silly. Come on, we really do need a rest. I don't want to camp in the bank. Too many people been there already, but there's a cabin up there that looks like pretty good shelter for a couple of days."

He led her to a cabin at the end of town. Its windows were intact, but its door screeched when he opened it and the upper hinge let go. A rusty pot-bellied stove stood in the middle of the dirt floor with its chimney still straight. A corner of the roof was missing.

Too tense to speak, Red Moon helped him unload the animals and store their things in a corner. She set a couple of snares along the creek and then they rode up the Red Feather Lakes road to hunt.

After a quarter of a mile they spotted the town's cemetery. The old wagon tracks that led up to it were deeply rutted. Full of enthusiasm, Rattlesnake had to have a closer look.

Red Moon waited, withdrawn and fidgeting with the reins. The sense of death would not leave her. Images of a white blanket in the sand swam before her eyes. "Please, Rattlesnake, can't we leave this place?"

Rattlesnake heard the fear in her voice and took a quick look at the graves inside the single low strand of barbed wire. "Coming," he called and guided *Bontemps* back down. "You should see some of the graves up there, *cher*. They go all the way back to..." He stopped. She was paler than she'd been when the rattler nearly struck her. "Sorry, *cher*, let's go if the graveyard makes you so nervous." For a second, her fear made his heart race, but he laughed at himself. Ghosts. No such thing.

The road made a U around a grassy slope, in the middle of which stood the largest ponderosa pine Rattlesnake had ever seen, more than three feet in diameter. Before he reached the bottom of the U, he came across a sign: "Hangman's Tree." He looked again at the tree. It was so magnificent he wondered why anyone would name it after a hangman. Then he understood. As he rounded the curve, the lowest branch presented its breadth to him. It was easily twelve feet long, sturdy as a mid-sized tree, and exactly the right height for hanging a man.

He turned in his saddle to call Red Moon's attention to it but changed his mind. She was sitting hunched over the mule, and even from around the curve he could see the whites of her knuckles as she clenched the reins. He said simply, "Look at the tree in the clearing, *cher*, did you ever see such a big one?"

Red Moon looked and shook her head.

On the way back from their unsuccessful hunting, they checked the snares and found them empty. "We'd better bag something tomorrow," said Rattlesnake.

Red Moon checked the sticks and thongs of her traps. "Going to be hungry tonight. No more jerky. Just two potatoes and I can pick some of these greens."

They gathered boards from the collapsed buildings and made a fire in the stove to cook the bitter greens. After she'd changed the water three times to make them edible, they sat with their backs to the wall of the cabin and ate together from the pot in the light coming from the stove.

Rattlesnake swallowed the bitter greens and made a face. "They have a big ol' city called Denver down there someplace. I bet they have some good restaurants." He fished another leaf out of the battered pot and dropped it back in. "Yeah, a good restaurant would be nice, that's for sure." He poked the greens aside, speared a chunk of potato, and popped it in his mouth. "Hoooeee, even the potatoes taste bitter now."

Red Moon nodded.

An hour after they'd eaten, Rattlesnake's stomach growled and echoed through the cabin.

Grinning, Red Moon checked her bags again. "I found something for you!" she cried. She held out a single hard candy remaining from Ignacio.

Rattlesnake laughed. "You better save that. We might have to share it tomorrow. But thanks." He kissed her. "I'll settle for this." They made love long and slowly to forget the hunger.

The next morning they left their things in the cabin while they tried again to find fresh meat.

In the late afternoon Mac gunned the motor of his old pick-up, stripped it into first gear, and angled it through the ditch. He gunned it again; and the truck jolted onto the clearing between Manhattan and the road. Les, in the middle, braced himself on the dashboard. Brad grabbed the top of door frame and the back of the seat. In the back, the head of a small buck bounced, and its antlers banged against the truck bed, though its body was lashed down with a rope.

They left a double trail of bent yellow grass and broken sage as they drove up the dead street. Mac parked parallel to the front of the bank and shoved his door open so hard it slammed shut again. He swore and opened it with exaggerated deliberateness.

"You two hang the deer in the shade," he said, getting out. "Cut out the innards except the heart and liver. We'll save 'em for later. I'm going to put the beer in the creek to cool."

Les protested. "Why don't we go on back, Pa? You already got yourself a deer."

Mac turned, shaking his head over his ninny of a son, and counted his reasons out with sarcastic patience, "Number one, buck meat's tough. Number two, I like doe meat better. Number three, it was Brad's shot brought him down. That makes it his deer."

Brad got out and moved to the truck bed. "Yep, this one's mine."

Les stayed in the truck and tried again. "Then why'd you let him shoot the buck? If you get caught with two this time..."

"Jus' hang up the goddamn deer," Mac shouted. He slammed the door again and the sound echoed off the hill behind them.

Les got out and helped Brad haul the deer up the hill. "Someday I'm going to stand up to him," he said through clenched teeth, hardly aware he was speaking aloud.

"One of these days you're gonna have to, son," answered Brad.

They hung the deer from a tree only a few paces from a cabin with its door hanging from the lower hinge. Intent on dressing the deer, they didn't glance inside. Brad slit the throat and let the blood run out on the ground. He made a long slit down the belly; removed the intestines, lungs and spleen; and threw them off into the bushes.

Flies were already buzzing over the offal in the afternoon heat as Brad and Les returned to the bank. They sat in the back, Les and Mac in the corner behind the fire pit, Brad opposite them.

A flash of light hit Rattlesnake just after they passed the cemetery on the way back to Manhattan, empty-handed. The sun reflected off the window of a pick-up parked in front of the bank.

He motioned to Red Moon to be silent. They slid off their animals, took them into the trees, and tied them to a branch. They approached through the woods and hid behind a leaning building. From inside the bank came men's voices.

"We're in the middle of a goddamn depression. No bleeding heart game warden has the right to tell me I can't take a deer." The voice was harsh, aggressive, and blurred with liquor.

"Yep, damn right," said another voice, more pleasant in sound but with the fixed conviction of drunkenness.

"Nobody says you can't hunt, Pa. It's just not the season." The third voice was younger and more sober.

"What do you know, you weak pup? It's time somebody put some backbone in that body of yours. You know what you remind me of? A skinny little grass snake, tryin' to stand on its tail. Got no spine. Jesus. Can't even hold a few beers. Here, drink up like a man."

"Damn right," said the second voice again.

"Is that what you think it takes to prove you're a man? Okay, give me a bottle and I'll match you beer for beer."

Rattlesnake whispered to Red Moon as they crouched behind the weathered boards, "Remember the big tree we saw yesterday? Beyond the cemetery?"

Red Moon nodded, her eyes on the bank.

"Go back and take the horses up to the woods above it. Keep 'em quiet as you can. It sounds like some mean people down there. I'll go get our things and meet you."

Red Moon slipped into the trees.

In the town all was quiet, and Rattlesnake feared the men were preparing to leave. He waited a few minutes, but nothing happened. He tiptoed to the end of the bank and peered around its corner and in the window. The air around the three men seemed to be full of nails and ice picks.

Staying behind the buildings, he ran to the cabin where their bed rolls and saddle bags lay in the corner. He packed the coffee pot, gathered both bundles in his arms and started out the door again.

And there was the deer.

He'd been so intent on watching the bank he hadn't noticed it. Immediately his stomach rumbled beneath the lumpy packs, and he remembered the meager meal of the night before. The deer was meant for him, his for the taking. No, he'd promised Red Moon. No more stealing. But they were starving. He could try to buy a piece of it from the men. No, he'd seen their types before and knew to stay clear of them. His stomach growled again. Red Moon needed this meat, and so did he. He could take it. He'd never gotten caught before. But this was different. He'd never taken anything when the owner was so close by or so clearly dangerous. He went back in the cabin, opened a saddle bag, and took out Red Moon's biggest knife. It wasn't sharp, but maybe he could cut off one foreleg. He checked the bank. It was still quiet, too quiet, but the pull of the meat was strong. He ran to the deer.

Mac lined up six bottles in front of his son, six in front of himself. With exaggerated courtesy, he handed Les the bottle opener.

Les didn't join the show of sarcasm. This was not the way he should stand up to his father. His challenge had sounded brazen enough, but inside he felt defeated, dragged down to the level of his father, and he knew he would be sick. He took the opener without looking up, uncapped the first bottle, and handed it back. He drank the beer as fast as he could but couldn't keep pace with his father.

They went on to the second bottle, then the third. From time to time, Les glanced at Brad, who was matching them without seeming to realize it, his face turning red, his eyes narrowing to hostile slits. "Brad, remember what you said about getting violent when..."

Brad snarled back, "Shut up. That's my business."

After his fifth beer, Les stopped. Mac swilled his and then triumphantly took Les's sixth, lifted it to his son's face as if to make a toast, and drank it. Les's stomach turned. He started to get up, fell forward, and braced himself on his father's knee. Mac shoved his hand aside.

Supporting himself on the wall, Les made it to the front, past the broken window and through the door. He just made it around the side of the building to throw up.

The knife was no use against the tough deer hide, and Rattlesnake wanted to scream in frustration. Against the hide, he saw Red Moon's face drawn with hunger. He pulled out his pocket knife, reached up, and cut the rope just above the knot that held the deer's legs. He brought the bundles from the cabin and laid them on the ground near the deer. Then he hoisted the buck onto his shoulders and reached down to lift the rest.

Les came back around the bank, leaned against the rough gray boards for a moment, more sick with anger and hatred than beer. Someday, he thought, he was going to snap. Someday he was going to kill the old man. Out of the corner of his eye he caught a movement up the hill. It was someone taking the deer. "Hey, that's our deer," he shouted, and regretted it instantly. There was going to be trouble.

Mac and Brad scrambled to their feet, lurched out of the bank, and rushed up the hill, reeling into each other and swearing.

Mac reached Rattlesnake first.

"Hey, mister, could you share...?" Rattlesnake started, sliding the deer off of his shoulders.

Mac shoved him to the ground and dragged the deer toward the tree. "Shut up," he growled.

Brad stepped around him. "That's *my* deer," he snarled and kicked Rattlesnake in the hip.

Rattlesnake tried to scramble away. "Please, you have the deer. I wouldn't have taken it if..."

Mac turned to where Les stood rooted by the bank, "Les, bring me the shotgun," he shouted.

Les ran to the group, his stomach burning with fear. "Pa, you can't shoot him."

Mac grabbed him by the collar. "Oh, yeah? Well, that's the difference 'tween you and me. I'm a man knows how to stand up for what's mine. You know I can..."

Brad kicked Rattlesnake again. "I'm gonna do it. *My* deer."

Mac's face twisted into a smile. "Wait, Les's right. Shootin's too good for a dirty rustler." He grabbed Rattlesnake by the left arm, jerked him violently, and put his face close. "Gonna hang him," he crowed.

Rattlesnake tried to get to his feet. "Please mister, I'll give you anything I got..."

Brad kicked him in the jaw and looked at Mac, confused.

"Got a hangin' tree right up the road."

Les gasped. "Pa!"

"Grab his hands," Mac ordered Brad, loosening the rope from the trunk of the tree.

Brad tied Rattlesnake's hands behind his back.

Les was shaking with horror. "No, Pa."

Mac turned on him, growling. "Shut up, you spineless twit. I'll put you out like a light. Now, git down there and start the truck."

Les swallowed hard and stood straight. "Pa, I'm warn..."

Mac shoved him against the tree, his forearm pressing against his son's throat. "Do it," he growled. He held Les's eyes until he felt his son's will dissolve and then shoved him toward the truck.

"Hey, please, mister..." Rattlesnake pleaded, looking at Les.

Les turned back, looked down at the thief, and saw his own hair color, his own fair skin, his own youth. But it was the helplessness that struck him. His stomach churned. Whose helplessness? His own. He turned back to this father, but Mac's fist hit him in the stomach. He stumbled to the truck.

Brad sat in the bed of the truck with Rattlesnake. Les drove, his face was ashen with fear and hatred and the need to vomit again. Mac sat next to him, facing him, keeping him cowed. When they reached the curve in the road where the hanging tree stood, Les found a place where he could angle across the ditch as his father had done earlier.

Rattlesnake fell to his side as they bounced across the ditch and hit his left shoulder again. His head banged on the bed of the truck. He groaned. The truck came to a jolting stop against a rock about twenty feet from the huge tree.

Mac caught himself on the dashboard and glared at Les. "Get in close there so we can drive the truck out from under him."

"I can't. The truck'll get hung up on those rocks. Pa, give this up."

"Shit. Then we'll just have to string him and pull him up ourselves." Mac got out and pulled Rattlesnake out.

Rattlesnake's knees buckled under his terror. "Mister, you can't do this."

Mac dragged him to the tree and positioned him under the long branch.

"Please, mister!"

Up the hill *Bontemps* nickered at the sound of his voice. Rattlesnake's heart sank. The men fell silent and listened. *Bontemps* nickered again and was cut short.

"I'll go up and see who that is. Keep the rifle on this son of a bitch—and that one, too," Mac said to Brad, nodding at Les. "You sling this rope over the branch and make a noose," he said to Les, shoving the rope into his hands. He ran up the hill, crossed the road and disappeared into the trees on the other side.

"Run, *cher*, run!" screamed Rattlesnake.

Brad shoved the gun in Rattlesnake's ribs and motioned with his head that Les should get the rope ready.

Les threw it and it landed across a side branch. He pulled it down again.

"Do it right this time, goddammit!" Brad commanded.

Rattlesnake watched in the direction Mac had taken. "Please, please, don't let him catch her," he begged any powers that might be listening.

Les prayed the rope would go awry again, but it flew over the branch. Its frayed end dangled before his face.

"You heard your pa. Make a noose," said Brad.

Les's hands were trembling too badly to loop the rope around itself.

Mac came back down the hill, shoving Red Moon from behind with his rifle, leading the animals. Red Moon's rifle was in his left hand. "Lookit here, I got me some kinda squaw," he called down to them.

Red Moon broke into a run as soon as she saw Rattlesnake. She threw her arms around him and they would have fallen together if Brad hadn't shoved Rattlesnake from behind.

Brad looked closely at Red Moon and his head jerked back for a second. He blinked and looked again at the Indian features with the lighter brown hair above the temples. His eyes lit on the snakeskin belt, so much like his own. He shook his head to clear the fuzziness of the alcohol. Jeez, so what if she was some Indian with a snakeskin belt?

"*Cher*, why didn't you run?" asked Rattlesnake.

Red Moon stared wide-eyed at the men. "I scared for you. What they do?"

"We're gonna hang him," sneered Mac. "Gonna hang you too."

Rattlesnake stepped forward until he felt the gun in his ribs again. "Please, mister, she's just a kid. She's got nothing to do with this. Let her go."

"Shut up!" Mac turned to Les. "You get that noose done yet? Jesus Christ, gimme that rope."

Les dropped the rope and leaned against the huge tree trunk, both hands over his face.

"Why?" asked Red Moon, clinging to Rattlesnake's arm.

"They had a deer," he said. "It was hanging right by the cabin."

"Stole it," growled Mac. He tied the noose and threw it over Rattlesnake's head.

"No," cried Red Moon, letting Rattlesnake go and grabbing at the rope. "Please, let him go."

Mac threw her to her knees. "Tie her up, Brad."

"I don't know, Mac. She's just a girl.'

"Do it, dammit."

Les rushed at Mac. "Leave her alone," he yelled. "Leave them both alone!"

Before Mac could answer, Brad rushed Les and propelled him back to the tree. "Goddammit, he stole my deer. If your pa's too goddamn sissypants to do it..."

Mac shoved him aside. "Get back there and guard them two." He shoved the rifle under Les's chin. "I tol' you I'm doing this, and that's that. Now shut up and watch. Put some steel up your back." He hit him in the stomach again.

Red Moon stood and tried to pull the rope off, the rough, knotted end of Rattlesnake's gray line, the vision she couldn't let come true. Not now, not this way. "No, please," she begged. She looked at the two men with the same face, thin, with narrow chins and gray-blue eyes. Only one was full of hate. She turned to the young one. "Please, we just hungry."

Les leaned against the trunk, groaning.

"Shut up girl, if you know what's good for you," said Mac. He yanked her away.

Rattlesnake started toward him. "Leave her alone, for God's..."

Brad slammed the rifle barrel against his nose and blood spurted down his face.

Mac pointed toward the animals. "Get the horse down here," he shouted at Les, kicking at a large rock under the limb.

"Pa, you can't go through with this."

Mac shoved him and he fell over a bush.

Mac climbed on the rock and pulled Rattlesnake up to him. "Bring the goddamned horse," he yelled.

Les led the horse to the rock.

Mac grabbed Rattlesnake's shoulders to steady him. "Git your foot in the stirrup," he ordered.

Rattlesnake winced at the pressure on his shoulder. "No," he cried.

"Do it, or I'll choke you with my bare hands," Mac yelled.

The man's hardened hands at his throat, Rattlesnake searched for the stirrup with his left foot, nearly falling off the uneven rock. When he had his foot in it, Mac shoved him upwards.

"Git on the other side and hold him steady," Mac ordered his son.

Rattlesnake leaned into the horse and began moving his right leg up. Mac shoved, and then he was in the saddle, listing to the other side. Les shoved at his thigh to steady him.

They positioned *Bontemps* under the branch. Mac pulled the rope taut over the branch, looped it over once more, and wrapped it around the trunk several times before knotting it. There was no give in it at all.

Rattlesnake's neck stretched to the pull of the rope. "Please," he begged over and over.

Red Moon tried to run to him. Brad grabbed her arm and held her until she froze in horror.

Mac slapped *Bontemps'* rump hard. She did not bolt away as he expected. She looked up, saw Rattlesnake on her back, and walked forward. Rattlesnake was dragged over the saddle and slid down the back end of his friend. Above him, the rope slipped toward the trunk of the tree and held. Rattlesnake choked. He struggled violently, trying to free his hands, trying to find anything solid under his feet. He found a sage brush and kicked at it, found the rock that he could only brush with his toe. "No," he rasped, "Please. Red..."

The rope cut under his chin. The legs stopped kicking. His face was blue. There was no more sound. And then the body of the man called Rattlesnake was just swinging gently in the back-wash of his struggle to live.

The vertical swaying of the branch came to rest. Silence and afternoon heat stifled the meadow around the tree. A puff of wind turned the body in a full circle.

Red Moon's scream was low and primeval.

The men were stunned, silent, and totally sober.

CHAPTER 15

The creak of the rope swaying with the Rattlesnake's dead weight barely marred the silence around the Hangman's Tree. Red Moon stumbled to the front of the body, looking only at the blue pants and the dusty boots. She could not look at the bloody face. She put her arms around Rattlesnake's legs and struggled to lift him. The dusty denim rubbed against her cheeks and turned wet with her tears as she buried her face between his knees. Her breath came now in gasping moans. Terror and shock removed her from the men like a crack in the air, and she watched them from a different reality.

"Oh, God," Les broke the stunned silence of the men, choking on tears. "Oh, God, what've we done?" He took out a pocket knife and hacked at the rope where it was wrapped around the trunk of the tree.

Mac jerked him away. "Leave him be. Let's get outta here." He started toward the truck.

The anger and the shame boiled up. Les wheeled, ran past his father, and stood directly in his path. He straightened to his full height so that he was half a head taller than Mac, his face full of contempt. He grabbed him under the arm and shoved the point of his knife against his father's throat. "You evil old fool," he screamed. "You've done enough harm in your life. Now you're going to take him down and bury him proper or I'll kill you. You hear me?"

Mac put his hands on his hips, but Les shoved the knife into his throat until it drew blood and propelled him back toward the body. "Get him down. Now."

The girl was still straining to hold the body up, moaning and crying.

Mac stared at his son for a minute, then looked up at the noose, too high for him to reach. Les turned to the hired hand, who stood staring at the bloody blue head dangling in the noose.

"Brad, help Pa with the rope and then take the girl and the horses down to the cemetery back there. It's up the only track the goes off on the left."

Brad shook his head, his face a mask of horror.

"*Brad!*" Les shouted, "Do it. Or I'll kill you, so help me God."

The shouted name jarred Red Moon, and she turned her head toward the tall man without letting go of Rattlesnake's legs. The young man pulled her arms down, and gently led her toward the mule, but she kept her eyes on the one with the name Brad.

Brad shook his head and looked in Red Moon's eyes but lowered his own quickly. "Oh, God, the beer. I shoulda known better." He moved toward Rattlesnake. "I'll do it, Les, don't worry. We done a great wrong here. The least we can do is give him a decent burial."

Les turned to Red Moon. "I'm so sorry, ma'am. I'll see no harm comes to you."

She hardly heard him. That name...Brad. Old visions of her mother and a laughing man whose face she could not see wavered for a minute in the crack that separated her from the men. But there was no laughter in this man's eyes. She watched him strike the shoulder of the old man, who was still standing by the body, looking at the ground.

"Jesus, Mac, all you got to do is untie the rope," he said.

Mac glared at him but undid the knot, worked the rope loose and lowered the body. Brad held Rattlesnake's legs as they laid him in the truck and helped Red Moon onto the mule.

Mac coiled the rope, threw it on top of the body, and drove the truck with Les sitting next to him, knife in sight, both rifles between his knees. He forced the truck up the steep embankment to the old cemetery. As the truck lurched through the ruts, the body in the back jolted against the sides and came to rest crumpled against the back.

Mac stopped at the knee-high strand of rusted barbed wire around the graveyard. Behind the fence a few wooden crosses leaned where the wind had pushed them, their names already weathered into anonymity. A single, plain stone marker stood amid the dozen neglected graves and the dry sage bushes.

"Help me get him out of the truck," ordered Les. They laid the body on the ground next to the wire.

Brad and Red Moon rode up and joined them.

Mac was looking over the fence. "We can't bury him in there. Too many people coming up from the ghost town to look at the cemetery. Somebody'd notice a new grave. We oughta just leave him somewhere in the trees. Shouldn't have a Christian burial anyway, dirty thief. And we gotta do something about that girl. She'll..."

"Shut up!" Les hissed into his face, grabbing him by the front of his shirt. "I watched you kill my mother with your meanness and your temper. You sapped every bit of happiness she ever knew out of her. You couldn't even bother to get her to a doctor when the flu went into pneumonia. You just let her die." Les choked on the old anger and grief. He pushed the knife back into the bead of blood on Mac's neck. "Well, this one time you're gonna listen to me. You're gonna do something decent for a change, if I have to put this knife in you right up to my elbow."

"If he don't, I will," said Brad. He stepped close to Mac and glared down at him. "We all done one murder today. One more ain't gonna matter, and seems to me we'd be doing the world a favor to get you out of it."

Les shoved him toward the trees at the uphill end of the clearing. "Take him up beyond the big ponderosa and start digging."

"I ain't got no shovel."

There was a long silence.

"I have shovel. I bury him," said Red Moon, barely whispering, not wanting to cross into their world.

"Yeah, let her do it," said Mac.

Les thrust a fist at his face and stepped over to her. "No, ma'am. We'll do it. Where's the shovel?"

"Down in cabin in town with ghosts." She was looking at the ground, unable to look at the body, too terrified to look at the men.

Les started to put his hand on her shoulder but dropped it to his side again. "Which cabin, ma'am?"

"One up the hill. Has broken door."

"I'll go get it," said Brad. He jumped into the truck, and the others listened while it bounced down to the road and whined over to Manhattan. The silence of Brad's search seemed to last forever. Les motioned to Mac to help him carry the body to the pine tree.

Red Moon sank to her knees next to *Bontemps'* legs, hugged herself hard, and doubled over with her eyes closed, her mind empty of all but the name Rattlesnake, the feel of his hand on her face, the love in his warm brown eyes. All locked in the body they were carrying away.

The young man came back knelt near her with his head hanging as low as hers.

"I'm so sorry, ma'am," he said.

But Les knew no words of his would ever make this right or ease her pain. He felt his heart shrivel into a tangle of guilt and defeat and shame that would never unravel.

The motor started again and the truck returned. Brad thrust the small shovel into Mac's hand and Les joined the other men at the tree. Mac started digging.

"I brought the rest of your stuff, ma'am," the man called Brad said, coming back to the truck. He laid the packs on the ground and set her rifle on them. He stood for a minute, shifting on his feet.

Red Moon watched the pointed brown boots smash the grass but did not look up at him or at the things he set next to her. From the tree she heard the scratch of the shovel and the thud of earth being thrown aside.

Les prodded Mac. "Hurry up, it's getting dark."

Mac dug faster and finally the three men lifted the body and let it down into the shallow grave, positioning the arms at its sides. They shoved the dirt over it using their boots as well as the shovel. Then Les and Brad stood for a minute with their heads bowed. Les reached up and knocked the hat off his father's head.

While Brad kicked a few rocks toward the grave and Les retrieved the shovel, Mac ran back to Red Moon, who was still on her knees by the horse, and grabbed her arm.

Red Moon shrank from him. The narrow face with the cold blue eyes was not a hand's breadth from hers. The smell of his drunkenness fouled the air between them, and she shoved at his hand, terrified, feeling the rope at her throat, her breath cut off.

"You ain't never gonna say anything about this, you hear, girl?" He rammed a fist into her abdomen so hard she jerked backwards. "Now you just disappear outta this country. If you don't, I'll kill you." He raised his fist to strike her face, but Les grabbed him, shoved him to the truck, and slammed his head into the hood.

Mac slumped to the ground. Brad helped Les dump him in the back of the truck and started the motor.

Les set Red Moon's rifle on top of her pack. "He'll never forget this, ma'am. Don't let him find you again. I'm so sorry."

He got in the truck. It bounced down the embankment and roared off in the direction of Manhattan, leaving a wake of dust.

Red Moon heard it pass the death town and strain up the hill toward the river before the sound faded, leaving her with her belongings and a grave.

CHAPTER 16
BRAD

Silence and dust and gathering darkness settled on Red Moon like death itself. She felt around in the packs until she found her name blanket, spread it on the grave, and lay for a long time with her heart against the earth to embrace Rattlesnake a last time. The smell of the freshly turned dirt rose to her nostrils. Slowly, her hand pushed through it until she felt his hand. She held it, willing the cold of his death to flow into her; but the only cold came from the spirits in the frightening, moonlit air around the cemetery. When she began shaking, she got up, unpacked the two bedrolls, and curled up between them next to Rattlesnake.

She'd hardly gotten warm again when a pain struck and warmth oozed from the secret place where only Rattlesnake had been. She rolled onto the ground and took out the cloth she used for her monthly bleeding. The pain doubled her over, and blood was running down her legs. She stanched the flow and cleaned herself as well as she could in the dark, shaking again with cold. Dropping the cloth into the grass, she barely made it back to the bedroll before she fainted.

The morning sun struck her face with the fierce heat of the drought. Red Moon woke and saw the cemetery to her right, as unconcerned as it was neglected. She didn't look to the left, hoping against memory that the images she'd brought with her into the day were only a dream. But all around her, earth and air stretched away into the silence of being alone.

No tree had died because her love was gone; no thirsty flower had fallen from its stem.

"Please, Mother Earth, please, take me now," she whispered into the silence.

No hole opened up to accept her.

She touched a small sage bush but felt no pull on the water of her body as she had in the San Luis Valley. She'd refused what she'd thought was her sign in order to stay with Rattlesnake, and Mother Earth refused her again now. She was the bleeding gray line that remained at the end of Rattlesnake's time in her life.

She turned on her left side. The mound of fresh earth was there. The name blanket still on it. Trampled grass. Rocks left from the digging. The shovel lying in patches of dirt they hadn't shoved on the grave.

Tears came. She drew her legs up and an echo of the night's pain returned. She picked up a handful of dirt and let it slip through her fingers. The dust blew back in her face. She tried to visualize how she might bury herself with her love, how to cover her arms after she'd buried the rest of her body.

Her stomach growled and the pain returned. She reached for the cloth. Blood. There was so much blood, enough that the wrinkled center was still damp, though the rest was stiff and brown. Then she knew she'd lost more than blood. Her bleeding should have started with the full moon and it was nearly full again. She was late, very late. Because of the hunger, she'd thought. But it wasn't the hunger. There had been a baby. Rattlesnake's baby. Her daughter. She groaned and pulled the cloth toward her. Ants were crawling on it. She shook them off, knelt next to the grave, and dug again into the earth. In the hole she laid the cloth in Rattlesnake's hand, sobbing. "You are Red Moon Dying," she said as she shoved the dirt over the child that was somewhere in all the blood.

"Why?" she asked the grave. "Why did they do this? It's my fault. I didn't help you. I should have shot them. I need to die with you. Mother Earth, why do I not die?"

Mother Earth gave no answer.

She placed both hands on the ground and bent low. "What do I do in this place? Where do I go?" She tried to listen, but the square in Taos flashed across her mind. The cottonwood tree, Mr. Koenig with his bald head, the hogan. The cistern, the glistening rock where the water ran into it. She ached for their comfort and familiarity, but the rock was dark and dry now, the hogan empty, no longer home. She could not go back.

The painful hunger returned to remind her she hadn't eaten anything but a few greens and bits of potato two nights ago. Rattlesnake had been with her. The shock came back. She pressed both fists into her stomach and doubled over, wishing she could ignore the hunger until she died, too.

She raised her head to Father Sky and begged in a ragged voice, "Show me my sign." Father Sky gave her no answer. She bent low over her knees and cried into the grass, "Please, Mother Earth, a sign."

But all she heard was Rattlesnake's voice. "Remember the deer, *cher*," he said into her ear. Her head came up to kiss him, but the dirt lay as before. The deer. The men had not stopped for it last night. She'd heard the truck grind on up the hill behind the town.

She lay down on top of the grave, on the name blanket. "I love you," she sobbed. When she could speak again, she knelt and cupped air from above the dirt, breathed it in, and whispered through clenched teeth, "I am Rattlesnake." Now anger flashed and flared through her whole body and erupted from her heart. She straightened and screamed into the sky, "I am Rattlesnake. I will kill them. I will kill them all!"

She stood up, intending to find something to leave on Rattlesnake's grave before she tried to find them. Her vision went black and she sank to the ground again. When she came to, she knew she could not kill them, she could never do the horror of murder and she was too weak to try.

Moving slowly, she got up and packed the animals, fearing she'd faint again. Under one of the packs she found the gray rope. She stared at it, looked back at the grave, and then tied it onto the pommel. The air was going black again. She rested her head against the horse's withers until her vision cleared. She started to pull herself into the saddle, but the sight of Rattlesnake bouncing out of it and slipping down the horse's rump was too clear. She called the mule and took his reins. She would fall off if she tried to ride him down the steep road from the cemetery. She led both animals down to the road and climbed onto the mule. From his back she turned toward the grave, but all she could see was the tree.

Rattlesnake's voice came again, "Go get the deer, *ma chere* Red Moon."

Crying and swaying on the bony old back of her mule, she rode back to the ghost town, listening for the sound of a truck straining up from the river. At the stream she stopped and filled a skin with water. She rode up the hill to the cabin and found the deer lying by a tree near the cabin, its antlers caught in a currant bush, its hind legs still bound by a rope. The blood on the ground was a swarm of ants and flies.

Next to the blood stain was Rattlesnake's big hat.

She slid off the mule, and the jolt of her feet on the ground brought back the pain. She hugged the hat to her and put it on her head. It fell below her eyes, but she pushed it back and left it on. She stood a minute to see whether she'd start bleeding again before going back into the cabin and making a fire in the stove. She sharpened her knife, cut off a chunk of a hind quarter, washed the insides, and pulled the skin together over the hole to keep flies out. She put the meat and greens in the pot and set it to boil. Then she lay down and fainted again.

When she woke, half the water had boiled out of the pot and the fire was out. She drank part of the broth, fished the meat out with the knife, and bit off the end. It was tough and gamy and mixed with the bitterness of the greens.

She rested again, then drank more of the broth before turning her attention to the problem of the deer. She'd never had so much meat to cure at one time.

It was still in the shade at the edge of the forest, but the sun would be on it soon. There were ants and flies on the eyes and mouth. If she didn't move it to a cold place it would rot before she could cure the meat.

She tied the rope from *Bontemps'* saddle to the legs and dragged the carcass up the hill to the first place where the white men had dug their mines. The hole went far into the mountain and the air in it was cold. She dragged the deer inside by the antlers. She went back down to the death town and moved her things back into the trees near the mine.

She could not stay near Manhattan. The men might come back. She needed another place to keep the carcass cool if she was to use all the meat. And she needed salt and a place where she could build a fire. She remembered the last camping place before the river. It seemed the only place where she might still feel safe.

She ate the remaining piece of meat while she thought about drying such a large animal. After she'd rested, she got up to go back to the grave before she left.

She hadn't taken three steps when a spot of red caught her eye. She crouched behind a rock. The tall man with the name Brad was walking down the road that came from the river, his red shirt glowing in the sun. Carrying a leather bundle over his shoulder, he passed her and cut across to the town.

She watched him, her heart pounding so loudly she feared he could hear it. He walked straight to the tree where she'd found the deer, looked at the black swarm of ants, and went into the cabin. When he came back out, he dropped the pack by the door and circled the spot where the deer had lain. He found the wide track of her dragging the deer. He wanted it back.

Red Moon clamped both hands over her mouth to stifle her scream. How could she have been so stupid not to cover the track? She should have known they would come back.

The man was looking up the hill now, with his hat off. His face had changed. He looked old since yesterday, as if time had scratched his face with bitter sticks. He took a few more steps, coming straight for the mine, so close she could see the horror still burning in his eyes. He stopped, bent left and right, looking through the trees for her.

He stood for a minute, as if torn in two directions. He opened his mouth and closed it again. He took a few steps back toward the town. He turned and looked at the mine again. He put his hat back on and held both hands in front of him, empty. "I know you're there, girl," he shouted.

Panic rush through her. She shrank more into herself. The pine needles beneath her crackled with the shift in her weight, and she held her breath.

"I mean you no harm," he yelled. "I'm very sorry. I did you a great wrong."

Red Moon did not move.

"Girl, I think..." He stopped and the silence lasted a long time.

Red Moon inched to the end of the rock and peered around it.

He was still there, standing with his head down and running his fingers through his brown hair. He made a fist and pulled at it. He looked up. "Child, I think you might be...I don't know. Is your mother a weaver?"

Red Moon jerked back and the breath shot out of her lungs. He *was* Brad. The laughing man. Black swirled about her; all her yearning to know him boiled up from the past. It crashed into the terror of yesterday. And the anger of this minute. He was her father, and he had killed Rattlesnake. The swing of the rifle barrel that had hit her lover in the face swept away any desire she might have had to speak to him. Her father.

"Child, I want to help you. I know I can't make it right, but..."

Red Moon grabbed her rifle and stood up with it aimed at him. "Leave me alone," she screamed.

He stood there staring at her for another minute, his hands still held toward her.

"Oh God, I'm sorry," he said so softly she hardly heard him. He turned and walked back down the hill through the trees. He picked up the leather bundle, looked once more in her direction, and headed for the road at the bottom of the valley. There, he started toward the cemetery, then turned and took the road in the other direction.

Red Moon collapsed onto sharp pine needles. Her breath came in gasps, and tears rolled down her face. All the threads that had tied her to past and future, to life itself, had snapped. All her belief in the man her mother had loved was shattered. She hugged herself for the little Red Moon with her useless hope that her father would come back.

After a long time she remembered she'd wanted to go back to the grave.

When she reached Rattlesnake, buried with a baby too small to see, she cut a large and a small pine branch from the tree and laid them on the new dirt. She placed Rattlesnake's hat over his head and weighted it down with rocks all around the brim. Then she sat at the foot of the tree with her arms around her knees, rocking slightly. When evening fell, she went back for the deer.

With the rope tied around the deer's legs, draped over a branch and tied to *Bontemps'* saddle, she hoisted the animal. She brought the mule under it, guided and pushed until the deer was balanced, and then tied the hind legs to the fore legs under the mule. She would use moonlight to return to the river and make the run downstream to the last camp.

CHAPTER 17

RED MOON RISING

Red Moon reached the campsite in Skin Gulch just after dawn and dragged the deer into the mine. She made a fire, and while another slice of meat cooked, she looked for cow parsnips in place of salt to cure the meat. When she didn't find any, she knew she'd have to go back to the town where Rattlesnake had gotten the potatoes. The thought made her shake. Rattlesnake had been so careful not to let the white people see her.

At mid-morning she set out on *Bontemps*, leaving the rifle under the deer for fear they'd take it from her. She was just past the pasture where she'd waited for Rattlesnake when she heard a familiar motor whining up the road behind her. Terrified, she looked for a place to hide with the horse, but both sides of the road were fenced. The truck drove past her and skidded to a halt.

She jumped from the mare and hid behind her. Dust billowed around her as the man with the narrow, hateful face leaped out and yanked his rifle from the seat.

He fired a shot into the air. "What the hell you doing here, girl?" he shouted. "I oughta shoot you right now. I told you to get outta this country." His words weren't slurred now. His eyes were clear and hard.

Red Moon was speechless, hardly believing he'd found her again. Was he out hunting for her? She did not want to die at his hands, but dying would be better than living. Rattlesnake's bloodied and blue face in the noose swam before her. She stepped out where he could aim at her. "You killed my man and my baby," she said, as he leveled the gun at her. "Kill me, too. I don't care."

The angry face softened slightly and the man lowered the rifle. "I didn't have nothing to do with no baby," he said. Then his face turned to stone again and the rifle pointed at her heart. "And your man was a common thief. Just like you. Nothing but trouble. Now my son's gone for good and my hired hand, too. I got to run this whole goddamn place by myself, and it's your fault." He steadied the gun.

Behind him the sound of another motor rumbled toward them.

His mouth twitched in annoyance and his shoulder dropped, though he didn't lower the rifle. "You get on back down that road and if I find you again, I swear to God I'll shoot you in the back and leave you for the vultures."

A flash of the vultures at her mother's legs hit her. Red Moon drew back in shock, climbed on the horse and started back toward the river, waiting to feel a bullet in her back.

The man slammed the truck's door, gunned the motor several times to turn on the narrow road, and passed her again, spinning his wheels to throw dust in her face. He turned into the great stone gate and got out to watch her pass.

Red Moon's heart was still racing when the second truck passed her. A bend in the road took her out of sight of the man who, she now knew, lived close to where she must cure the deer he'd shot. He would kill her if she let him, and she had no choice but to work where he could find her easily. She was too weak to go on, and the deer would rot.

She began watching the sides of the road for cow parsnips. On her right was the pasture dotted with his salt licks. At the end of the pasture, where it narrowed to a point, a lick lay close to the fence. She slowed and listened. From the house came the sound of a hammer. She turned in the saddle. The road was clear and the fields on both sides empty. She jumped off the horse, feeling the pain jab her belly; ran to the fence; and pulled the block under the barbed wire onto the road. She walked *Bontemps* to the lick and lifted it with difficulty until it was on the saddle. She rode behind the saddle to balance the salt.

Before she got to the creek bed that went up the gulch, she knew she was bleeding again. She returned to the clearing at the head of the gulch and stanched the bleeding. After she'd made sure her rifle was loaded and propped it against a tree, she warmed and ate more soup, chipping a bit of the salt into the broth.

She hoisted the deer into a tree, found a smooth stone in the creek to sharpen her knife and went to work. The smell of flesh just going bad and the intrusion of her hands into the body made her queasy. She reached into the cavity and cut out the liver and the heart.

She stared at the heart in her hand. It was her heart. And the deer was as empty now as she was, all her love places hollow and hurting, her heart ripped out and trying to get into a grave. She walked away. She had to force herself to breathe and each breath was a moan.

When she could continue, she made a spit, speared the heart, and angled it over the fire. She began removing the skin while the heart roasted. The deer was more difficult than rabbit, which separated so cleanly. She cut off the hind quarters and covered them with Rattlesnake's extra shirt, then moved the remainder of the carcass into the mine and laid it on the pants from San Luis. In every pot, pan, and cup she made brine solutions and sliced thin strips from the legs to soak in them. She strung her ropes from tree to tree on the sunny side of the clearing. While the meat soaked, she scraped the remaining sinew and thin layer of fat from the skin and spread a mixture of ashes and water on it.

Then she scraped it again, rubbed it with a paste of brains and liver, and stretched it out on the ground, anchoring the legs with rocks. She wouldn't have time to finish the skin properly; she needed a bigger pot to soak it in, but she'd have to worry about that later.

All through the day's work she made as little noise as possible and kept a wary eye on the stream bed. To do the rest, she had to have smoke, which the man could see from his place.

She built several small fires, using boards from the old cabin and fallen pine branches. She hung some strips in the smoke and others wherever there was sun. She mashed some of the meat with a rock and mixed it with the deer's little fat and a few dried wild currants that grew along the stream. She washed off a rock that would catch the sun for several hours yet and spread the meat mixture over it to dry. From time to time she ate some of the broiled heart with dandelion greens and harebell roots. By the end of the day she had about half of the meat drying and hoped the rest would keep in the mine until the next day.

Shortly before dark she heard a hoof hit a rock far down the gulch. She grabbed her rifle and stationed herself behind a large tree so far downstream from her campsite that he wouldn't see the meat. He was riding up the creek bed on a black horse. He dismounted, tied the horse to a tree and came up the valley with his rifle at his side. He stayed in the trees, trying to find her before she saw him. She stepped out when he was close enough to hear her, the rifle aimed at his head.

"Go back," she ordered.

The man looked as if he thought she was stupid. He started to shift his gun.

"Don't," Red Moon said. "Turn around."

He hesitated.

"Look at cone on tree behind you. Turn around."

He turned, she pulled the trigger, and he jumped. A cone inches from his shoulder had exploded.

She aimed directly at his head again. "I stay here two more days, then I leave. If I see you come up here again, I shoot you between the eyes long before you find me. If you send anyone, I tell them you hanged Rattlesnake and show them the grave."

The man waited a second, his face purple with anger, then walked slowly backwards to his horse, watching her and feeling his way past branches and roots and stones.

Red Moon moved the rifle very slowly to keep his head in her sights. She knew he was watching for a break in her concentration.

He untied the reins and stepped behind the horse as if to mount it. Instead he used it as a shield, laid the rifle across the saddle and tried to aim at her.

She shot him in the right foot and he screamed. "That from Rattlesnake," she shouted, making sure he heard the name. "Drop your rifle. Get on your horse." He threw the rifle into the grass at the side of the stream.

The man kept all the hate of his eyes on her, even as he pulled himself up on the pommel and got his left foot into the stirrup. Grunting and wincing, he swung his right leg over and settled in the saddle. He rode slowly down the rocky stream bed, looking back often. She followed him with the rifle aimed at his head until he crossed the ditch at the bottom of the gulch. Her shoulders ached with the weight of it and with the weight of the anger that was building in her.

He glared down at her after he turned the horse toward his place. The hatred in his eyes stung like scorpions.

"You can't run far enough, girl. You're dead. I'll find you no matter where you go," he growled at her.

"I shoot you first," she yelled at him, wanting to pull the trigger again now, to see a hole in his back and a red circle around it like the full moon in a sandstorm. But deep inside she shook with terror of this man and the others he might bring with him.

She walked out onto the road and waited until he disappeared around a bend. She lowered the rifle and her shoulders slumped.

Deep dusk was settling as she trudged back up the gulch with the rifle stock dragging the ground. He had brought her down. Even though she'd shot him before he could kill her, he'd taken away the last thing that was hers—her ability to love.

Now she understood why she'd felt separated from him and the other men after the hanging. She'd never felt hate before and didn't want to be in the same air with that feeling. But he'd dragged her in, made her feel his hate. If she saw him again, she would kill him, and she would be like him. His air was poison, and she would hide from him, from them all, lest she ever have to breathe it again. If she never loved again, she would never hate, either. Now she understood why her mother would have needed the Enemy Way if she'd gone back to the Rock with Wings and her family.

When she came to the poison-man's rifle, she started to throw it in the water to rust. She caught herself. She would need this rifle. It was exactly like hers, only he had cut a row of little notches in the top of the stock. It had all ten bullets in it, and she could feel each one slam into her body.

At the campsite she doused her fires and took the bed rolls into the old mine shaft. She lay down in front of her deer, where she could see the entrance, both rifles at her side, intending to keep watch all night. She was asleep instantly.

The following day she turned the drying meat and started soaking the rest. By mid-morning the last of it was drying and she worked on the skin. As evening approached, she began to pack her things, leaving only the last strips of meat draped across branches.

The next morning, she was stowing the last of the jerky in the hide when she heard voices coming up the stream bed. She ran for her rifle and was facing downstream with the rifle aimed when two young men with packs on their backs rounded the last bend and spotted her.

"Stop there," she yelled.

The men stopped in their tracks and stared.

"Hey, lady, who're you?" asked the taller one.

Red Moon didn't answer right away. Rattlesnake's laughing voice came back: "I just let the name stick. When you're small like me, it makes you sound mean and tough."

"What're you doing here?" asked the other.

Red Moon answered the first question. "Rattlesnake."

The men jumped and glanced around. The one with the eyeglasses hit the tall one on the arm, looking annoyed with himself. "There's no rattlesnakes around here."

Her breath caught. The dirt mound with Rattlesnake and her baby in it filled her vision and she groaned. Then she regained control and said, "They hanged him on big tree and buried him outside cemetery by Manhattan. Go find body. Tell sheriff."

The boys looked at each other. "She probably escaped from somewhere," said the taller boy. They started toward her. She raised the rifle.

They stopped, but the one with the glasses said, "Come on, lady, let us take..."

Red Moon shot over their heads; they turned and fled almost faster than the shot echoed back and forth across the gulch.

"Tell them about Rattlesnake!" she yelled after them.

She doused her fires, filled her water bags, and made her way out of Skin Gulch. When she reached the road she turned away from the man's ranch, her only choice. She waited near the river until nightfall and started upstream. She rode past the turn-off to Pingree Hill, feeling the pull of her lover buried alone beneath the tree with a pine branch on the dirt to show that someone had loved him. Toward morning she led the animals far enough up a side canyon of the Poudre to be invisible from the road. It was a narrow, dry gulch, strewn with boulders in the buff grass. There was no place for her to lie down, and she padded a rocky place where she could sit. She did not dare build a fire while following the river.

For the next two nights she traveled as fast as the stumbling old mule could go in the moonlight and then rode by day. After a small lake that sparkled through the trees, she left the river and started north through the forest, looking for a place to hide for the winter.

But her passing through the canyon did not go unnoticed. The two students she'd shot at brought others up the gulch to find the crazy Indian who'd shot at them. They found only her blackened fire rings in the trampled grass. The few nighttime drivers on the river road wondered about girl with the long braids and the black skirt with two horses in tow. Early fishermen glimpsed the Indian picking at plants and darting into the gulches where she hid during the day.

The girl who called herself Rattlesnake became a legend along the Poudre River before she reached its headwaters.

CHAPTER 18

L ooking for a safe place to spend the winter, Red Moon wandered north from the Poudre into vast stands of forest dotted by tawny meadows and ancient rock formations. Aspen groves, showing a yellow branch here and there, splashed their late summer green across the dark background of pines. Thin streams tumbled down from peaks to the west in tiny canyons they'd carved in better seasons and curved through the meadows to feed quiet lakes.

On a day cooler than it had been since the snowstorm with Rattlesnake, Red Moon was picking a way through the trees for the mule and *Bontemps*. She was concentrating on the light of a clearing just ahead when she stepped on something sharp under the pine needles and heard a grating sound. She shoved the needles aside. A rusty trap had nearly closed on her foot. Men were here. She jerked her foot back and went still to listen. Only the animals breathing and the wind sighing in the treetops disturbed the silence.

A few more steps brought her out of the forest and to a cabin. With its back to a rock formation, it faced north from the south edge of a meadow. A flat, weathered rock sat in the middle of the clearing.

A stream with a little water in it ran through the north end of the meadow, its route marked by broken beaver dams, aspens, and willow bushes already yellow. There was no sign that man or beaver had lived there for a long time.

On the west side stood a ponderosa that reminded her of the hanging tree. She stopped at the edge of the clearing, trying not to see a body hanging there, her heart pounding with the horror and fear. How long had it been? Already Rattlesnake belonged to a different lifetime, a time of completion and happiness, though the moon had not grown much since he died. If only he hadn't tried to take the deer, he might have stayed with her, at least till the baby came, the baby now at his side in the grave. If only Mother Earth did not have the special thing for her to do... If only... Too many ifs. Useless ifs that belonged to a life she'd never have. She choked on her sob and leaned against another ponderosa to take comfort in the vanilla smell of its flaky brown trunk.

Red Moon led the animals to the stream to graze and sat at the edge of the clearing, watching and listening. Not even a squirrel appeared. She approached the cabin through the woods and tried the door. It screeched on its rusty hinges. Startled, she looked back over her shoulder before stepping inside.

A sooty pot-bellied stove stood in the middle of the floor, a huge enamel kettle on top of it, laced with spider webs. The floor and walls were simple boards, gray and rough, with knotholes open to the air; daylight came in through cracks everywhere. A dirty window on the right wall still had glass in it. The one in the door had its two lower panes broken. The sagging roof didn't let in light, but it wouldn't hold for many more seasons.

She sneezed in the dust she'd disturbed and went out again. The north wind whispered through the trees: "I will bring winter. Stay in this house."

Red Moon camped in the woods for days while she cleaned the cabin and collected plants for the winter, knowing she should have done it while they were young and tender. They would taste bitter but would keep her alive. She hung blanched greens from branches all around the clearing. She took the youngest shoots of mare's tail, violets, and watercress and dug up the roots of cow parsnips and harebells.

On the other side of the stream she came across buffalo berries to use for soap. She stared at the bushes, letting memory have its say. Her mother had picked the berries in the mountains above Taos in place of yucca root. Red Moon hadn't liked them because they made the water orange, though they smelled better than yucca. Now, she picked all the berries she could find.

At last, she moved her things into the cabin and spread them out to take stock of supplies. She had two good knives, a pot, a tin pan, an enamel coffee pot, the spark-maker from Mr. Koenig, and the matches from the last town. There were the two rifles but only a couple of handfuls of bullets. She had a small ax and the shovel; a number of skins for collecting water; woven bags of herbs, teas, and medicines; part of a salt lick; and a large supply of jerky. She didn't have nearly enough greens or roots to get through the winter. She had the few extra clothes she and Rattlesnake had owned, the old sheep skins, two bedrolls, and the spun wool from Taos that Rattlesnake hadn't wanted to bring. She had a small kerosene lantern and a few candles, none of which would last until spring.

For the first time she realized how foolish they'd been not to plan for winter. She sat on her knees, put her arms as far around her body as they would reach and rocked herself as she had when they'd buried Rattlesnake.

In these square, ghostly walls she would have to make a life for herself where there was no sound if she did not make it, no one to take the love she still ached with, no laughing voice to call her "*cher,*" no one to call her anything at all. At the beginning of the third autumn of her womanhood she sat among the few possessions that made up her chances for survival and cried away the tears of her lifetime.

The next morning Red Moon moved the animals closer to the cabin because they'd cropped the grass down to the dirt where they were tethered. She'd have to find other meadows where they could graze. She stroked their faces and whispered to them, still afraid of being heard. The mule ignored her and put his head down to graze again. *Bontemps* nickered and nuzzled her shoulder before doing the same.

Now she collected firewood as well as food. For the present she dragged a few light aspen logs and some pine branches to the cabin. In the evening she made a little flame on the top of the stove, using the spark maker and some dry pine needles. She transferred the flame to the stove. The cabin warmed nicely and she celebrated with extra jerky in the soup of greens and roots. For the first time she felt a little hope. If Rattlesnake were here, he'd be proud of her.

In the middle of a fall night, Red Moon woke with a groan of plea-sure and the last pulses of love. Rattlesnake had been lying with her, making love to get warm. But the warmth faded as fast as the dream into cold reality. His breathing next to her became the wind moaning around the cabin and whistling through cracks and holes.

It was so dark that not the slightest bit of light came through the windows. She forced herself to throw the bedroll off, crawled to the stove, and felt around for the spark maker. Something warm and furry scuttled out from under her hand.

She gasped and jerked her hand away. The animal skittered across the floor and began scratching near the window. Another animal was gnawing at something behind the stove. She found the spark maker and made a flame that she transferred to the stove.

In the meager, comforting light she could see the cabin floor wasn't overrun with mice after all. She pulled her bedroll closer to the stove and stacked some wood where she could add it to the fire without getting up.

The following morning she stayed in the bedroll for a long time, thinking the day would be too cold for hunting. When she went out, the warm, friendly air surprised her. By the stream, a gold light glowed from the aspen trees. Had they been gold yesterday? She hadn't noticed them.

She walked into the trees, listening to the dry rustle of grasses and fallen leaves under her feet. She knelt at the water and ran her hand over gold leaves, curled on their edges and backed up in a dark pool. The sweet smell of earth and of leaves becoming earth rose and mixed with the wind to take her breath away.

Above and around her the air shimmered gold. She stroked the powdery white aspen bark etched with black eyes. She looked up the tree trunks at the fluttering gold against the deep blue sky. The wind stirred the leaves into a whispered song no less beautiful because it told of death in the seasons of life.

Her heart seemed to stop. Rattlesnake would have loved it. Had River Willow ever seen...? She laid her cheek against an aspen trunk. "Mother Earth, why do you not let me join them?" She picked a perfect leaf, held it against the sun, and let its gold light fill her body. She placed it against her heart, trying to take its smooth, beautiful, gold dying into herself.

She went back to the clearing and sat on the flat rock. In its deep weathered cracks grew wild geraniums and grass. She drew her knees up to her chin and put her hands on its rough surface to feel its power as she had on the Rock with Wings. She tried to feel it draw her as the sand had done in the San Luis Valley, but nothing came from it, no pull, no power, and no comfort. She'd asked for a sign so often since Rattlesnake's death, but Mother Earth seemed to have forgotten her.

Bontemps plodded over from the stream and nuzzled her. She reached up and ran her hand down the horse's long neck. In a minute the mule joined them. Her family. She stood up and put her head to the old mule's face. He wasn't friendly the way the horse was, but he'd been with her all her life and reminded her of her mother. He pulled away and reached for a few blades of yellow grass that fringed the bottom of the rock.

She looked back at the cabin, sitting in shadow already, though fall was just starting. No wonder the house had stayed so cold after the sun came up. She pictured the builder as the man with the hate. "Stupid man," she said aloud, then started and looked over her shoulder. "Build a house in shadow like that," she whispered. She thought about the hogan. Why had it not been cold in winter? She remembered her mother repairing the adobe from time to time. The thick walls had kept the hogan cool in summer and warm in winter. She'd have to cover those walls somehow.

She walked down to the stream. The mud between the grass and the water might work. And the boards of the cabin might be rough enough to hold it.

She brought her shovel from the cabin, leaving the door open to let in the warm outside air, and carried mud from the stream. At first the mud she plastered against the boards stuck, but about a hand's breadth off the ground, the rusty nails buckled the boards outwards. The mud refused to stick. For the first time she realized the walls of her mother's hogan had been slightly slanted, allowing the adobe to rest against them.

Discouraged, she put the problem aside while she went in to see about keeping the mice out of her food.

Red Moon stood in the clearing, looking past the bare aspens to the northwest, where a great bank of clouds had swallowed up the trees on higher ground. The wind, bringing the sharp, wet smell of snow, caught her strands of brown hair and blew them in her eyes. She shivered and rubbed her arms.

She led the animals under a shelter she'd built in the trees and rubbed the bony back of the mule, feeling his shaggy winter coat. "I would put Rattlesnake's bedroll over you," she said, running her hands up his neck and over the top of his head. She turned her face to the wind again. "But I need it myself." She threw some grass she'd gathered in other meadows in front of the animals.

She stacked more wood next to the stove. She'd already piled wood against the entire back wall. Just inside the door on the right she'd piled dry leaves and needles for starting fires.

She'd made the cabin her home by the time the first snow fell. Her bedrolls lay on top of a fresh pile of pine needles on the left. In the corner above the bed, the jeans from San Luis hung with the cuffs at the top. Tied off at the waist and cuffs, the pants bulged with dried greens, the food accessible through the buttons. Under the window at the right sat the wool poncho she'd given Rattlesnake, sewn into a bag and filled with roots.

But if she'd made the inside of the house livable, she'd changed the outside completely. From the meadow the cabin had nearly disappeared, only its roof and door still visible. Using the horse and the mule to help lift them, she'd propped pine logs at a slant under the eaves and filled in the gaps with aspens. She'd lost the light from the window but created a triangular space around the outside to insulate the house.

The new, slanted walls were covered with grass. Using *Bontemps* to pull it on the deer skin, she'd hauled sod rather than mud from the stream. It had taken many days. The sod was heavier and harder to dig, but she hoped the matted roots would hold through the winter. To repair the huge black scar her digging had left, she'd scattered grass seeds from other meadows.

She'd piled firewood between the cabin's old boards and her new sod walls and stacked more under the big pine tree. She was as ready for winter as she could be.

Now, as the season sent its first snow, she looked out over the skins that covered the broken panes in the door, and watched the scattered, dry flakes drift into her world. When it got too cold and dark to stand at the window, she started a fire in the stove, leaving its door open. In the dim, orange light she turned her attention to an evening meal.

Already she knew she wouldn't be able to stay in the cabin beyond this winter. The sod wouldn't last more than one season over the loose frame of tree trunks. Her work had given her a poor shelter, too cold and too near collapse. Only the mildness of the drought winter seemed to be in her favor, and perhaps before the spring thaw, Mother Earth would show her where to go.

Each day Red Moon stuck a twig in the meadow, marking the shadow of the rock formation behind the house. The shadow had returned about half way to her starting point, but there was no other sign that winter was waning. She was sitting on the flat rock, leaning back with her legs stretched out to soak up the weak sun, trying to get warm before going to get the animals from another meadow. She let her mind drift back to her time in the mountains above the hogan with Rattlesnake. Summer then, and she saw him making the upside-down rain in the sun.

From the woods to her left came a loud snap, then a crashing sound. Her heart pounding, she darted to the house and grabbed her rifle. The man with the hate in his narrow face. He'd come for her. She stood inside, out of the light, and waited.

An elk with a large dead pine branch caught in his antlers crashed into the meadow, throwing his head about and scattering twigs and tufts of brown needles.

She raised the rifle.

The elk went to the rock she'd been sitting on, froze, and lowered his nose. He bounded for the woods again, but the branch caught on a tree and jerked his head back. He stopped, stalked slowly back to the rock, looking around, and slammed his left antler on the rock. The branch stayed put.

Red Moon watched, amazed. She sighted down the barrel, waited for the second when she could put a bullet directly into his head. Already her mouth was watering. Her finger quivered on the trigger. She steadied the gun on the door frame.

The elk banged his right antler against the rock. It snapped off with a loud crack and fell to his feet. The motion of his head flung the branch to the ground a few steps from him, where it broke into several pieces. The elk jumped. He stepped cautiously to the broken branch, snorted, and used his rear hooves to kick the pieces aside. Then he sniffed the rock and the air and looked directly at the cabin.

Now, Red Moon told herself. She saw herself skinning him, drying the meat. She would have food for a long time. Her finger began its pull on the trigger and stopped. The animal was too big. Too much of the meat would go to waste and the hide wouldn't fit in the pot. Much as she needed his meat and skin, she couldn't use enough of it to justify killing him. And he was too beautiful. She lowered the rifle and watched as he stalked out of the clearing, his head tilting awkwardly to the left.

Red Moon opened her door on a morning late in the winter and stepped up to her ankles in snow. She hadn't felt this storm coming. She checked the animals under in their log shelter between the trees and found *Bontemps* covered with snow and standing over the mule as if to shelter him. The mule was dead.

Her last link with the desert. Taos. The child Red Moon. Her mother. She sank to her knees, brushed the wet snow aside, and stroked the old mule's head. He'd gotten too weak to go up and down the mountain to find grazing, and the grass she'd brought back hadn't been enough. He'd starved to death. "I'm sorry I couldn't take better care of you, mule," she said. "Thank you for your long life. I will keep your skin and you will help me a long time more." Her legs were freezing in the snow. She stood again and hugged *Bontemps'* huge head. "You tried to help him. Thank you." She shoved the snow from the horse's back, ignoring her

freezing hands. She rubbed hard at the winter coat that had gotten thin. The ribs and hip bones were sticking out. The horse was
starving. Red Moon felt her own ribs and knew she was starving,
too. She went into the cabin and looked in the old poncho. More
than two thirds of the roots were gone. She piled a load of them
in her skirt and fed them to *Bontemps*. Somehow, she had to find
more food, or they would both die.

On the afternoon when she finished tanning the mule's skin, Red
Moon went to the stream for water to bathe in. Stooping with her
water bag, she caught her hair in one of the bushes. She pulled
the broken twig out of her hair and saw a fuzzy pussy willow. She
sucked in her breath and looked about.

The stream had more water in it than she'd ever seen. Where
she'd reseeded the bare spot, there were little shoots of green. In
the meadow, tiny green spikes peeked out of the stubs of brown
grass. The cabin was still in shadow, flanked by snow, but the sun
was warm on her face.

Red Moon ran for the horse and led her out of the shelter into
the sun. "*Bontemps*," she shouted, then looked around and changed
to a whisper, "If it's almost spring up here, there must be things for
us to eat farther down the mountain. We'll go look."

She collected what she'd need for a couple of days of camping.
The next morning she packed it on the horse and then stood for
a minute, full of energy and purpose but no direction. "If we go
back to the river, there will be the man with the hate, like before.
We have to go west. We will go out of this Colorado."

She led the weakened horse uphill until she came to stunted,
misshapen trees beyond which lay snowfields too steep and difficult for the horse to climb. They were both breathing too hard
to go on. All she could see to the south was more snow. She went
back down and headed north until she found a gap where she
could continue west. The sun was at the top of its climb when she

began to see daylight through the trees. She looked for a place where she could see what lay ahead but had to go a long way downhill before she found a rocky shelf beyond the trees. She stepped onto it, caught her breath, and fell to her knees.

Before her lay a vast valley, its hilly floor crossed by several rivers trailing willow bushes, a valley so green it took her breath away. It was closed in on three sides by snow-covered mountains; only the north was open. Cows dotted the flatter sections of the valley, and in the middle to her right, far from her ledge, was a town smaller than Taos.

Though no branched scar ran through the valley like the Rio Grande, looking down on it was so much like looking down on the hogan that she felt she'd come home. There would be piñon nuts and yucca and cactus for her to eat, and as she stared the wind brought her the sweet smell of sage in bloom. She put her hands on the rock under her and felt the whole sweep of the valley flow into her, forcing tears to her eyes. It was the most beautiful place she'd ever seen. "Mother Earth," she said.

She looked at the town for a long time, wondering whether it had a square with a big cottonwood tree. The town must be in that Woming Rattlesnake had wanted to reach. Maybe a trader like Mr. Koenig would buy blankets from her. She'd dye the wool, weave some, and take them there. The man with the hate would not follow her to Woming. The thought lifted her heart.

Reluctant to leave the view, she went back and led *Bontemps* down long slopes. They came out behind a ridge that hid her from the town. As soon as they cleared the last trees, *Bontemps* stopped to graze. Red Moon let her have her head and set two traps by holes in the ground. She found piñon pines, but the cones left from last summer had small, unfinished nuts in them. There was no yucca. She found small ground-hugging cacti, already in bloom. Discouraged, she peeled some of the cactus blades and ate the flesh with a little jerky. Then she laid her sleeping roll on the ground and sat down facing south with her back to a rock, reveling in the smell of sage and the intense green of her valley.

She dozed but slept uneasily, dreaming of the man with the hate, and when she woke, the sun hung in the west, hot and angry behind the image of him standing between her and the town, his rifle across his arms. Her own hate rose to her throat, and with it the fear of others like him who could make her hate. She would not go to the town. But there was something here. She'd wait and watch for the sign.

She took a gopher from one of the traps and followed *Bontemps*, who'd left a path of cropped grass as clear as an arrow pointing south. She caught up and pulled the horse's head up, laughing. "Come, horse, you make yourself sick, you eat too much at once," she said, stroking the face that ended in a muzzle gone green. She walked south along the flank of the mountains, keeping the ridge between herself and the town, seeing no one.

Toward evening of the second day she built a fire and stretched out on her bedroll to watch the last rays of sun climb the peaks she'd passed. One of them was separated by a great gap from its southern neighbor, leaving its rocky south cliff in full sun. It must have sun all day, even in winter. Red Moon felt the mountain pull her. From the west the breath of Father Sky whispered past her, swirling through the grass and brushing the pines on its way up the slope.

In the morning she hobbled *Bontemps* and started up. The mid-day sun was shining on her when she felt the earth tug at her feet as if trying to pull down a root. She stood below the towering, layered rock face, just in front of a large overhang. Stunned, she shook her head. Was this where Mother Earth wanted her? There was nothing here. Only a clearing that curved around the cliff like an apron, already pale green in its southern exposure. A thin line of trees hemmed the apron. Maybe past the trees she'd find the task. She went through them and nearly stepped off a cliff.

If she'd fallen, she'd have been badly hurt, and climbing back up would have been impossible.

She turned back. Under that overhang? "I don't understand," she said aloud. "How can I live here?"

Not even a breeze whispered an answer.

"This is my task? To live in this place?" She sat down on a ledge at the back of the overhang. Instantly she felt something close her in. It was not a thing of comfort, but it was a thing of clarity. She was to come here.

If Mother Earth wanted her here, there must be water. She found none on the east side of the cliff but did see that she wasn't far from the cabin and could bring her things here easily once the snow melted. On the west face she found the water slipping over the rocks in two clefts separated by a stack of square boulders. Below her, both streams fell straight down for a long way. She pressed away from the rock wall as far as she dared and tried to see the source of the water, but the slope was too steep.

She returned to the overhang and saw how she could build a shelter the way she'd insulated the cabin. In the trees she saw some of the fallen logs she'd need for walls.

She went back to the west edge of the clearing and found a single large rock where she could sit and see the valley. She stared for a long time at the town, far to the north now, so small the houses looked like matchboxes on a vast green blanket. Surely families lived there, people like those of Taos. But her fear of the white men was great, and her root was here. What would the people down there do if they knew she was here? Someday they would come and tell her she had to leave, she didn't own this land. Maybe they would be kind. Maybe they would give her a little place out in the valley. Or they could tell her where to go. Or perhaps in a few summers the fear would not be so great. She sighed and started back down to *Bontemps,* angry with Mother Earth for demanding such a silly task of her.

CHAPTER 19

Many summers after Red Moon moved to the shelter she'd built under the cliff, she lay asleep on a summer morning dreaming of the square in Taos, smiling at the deep green glow of sunlight in the cottonwood on the square. The leaves waved at her. Chuggies roared in and parked in front of the stores. The people of Taos laughed, going about their business. She blinked. Lonely silence muted the picture; the leaves faded to skin color and became vaguely familiar faces that smiled and hands that beckoned. Throwing off the bedroll, she was half sitting when they disappeared. Confused, she looked around in the meager light coming through the cracks around the door. She flopped back on the bed, trying to find the line between dreaming and waking. In her home under the rocks, the dim gray branches of the tree trunks that made up her walls jabbed in at her like a cactus turned inside-out.

After so many summers, it was the first dream of Taos without Rattlesnake coming back to love her. His face had not been among the leaves. The old cottonwood had been full of the happiness she had known with her mother. The people had smiled and there had been no hate. Was it only a dream? Was it a sign Mother

Earth wanted her to leave now? In the pain of her loneliness she'd begun to think of leaving. Why would Mother Earth give her such a clear sign to stay here but never one to tell her what to do?

She closed her eyes and saw the white people in their bright clothes strolling about the square, and the Indians slipping silently among them. She reached out to them. They all stopped, turned to her and smiled, then walked up the road in the valley, to the town she feared.

"I will go down," she said aloud. "I will not tell them where I stay, and I will come back."

She stepped out to saddle *Bontemps*. Already the sky was dotted with the puffy clouds that would grow into thunderstorms. For days they'd rumbled across the valley in the afternoon and dropped their rain somewhere else. She hesitated, then saddled the horse and rode down.

By the time she approached the ridge that ran between the mountains and the town, the sun had disappeared, and the wind howled toward her from far beyond the valley. Towering darkness stared down at her. She spurred *Bontemps* and they started up the ridge. At the top the wind nearly swept her from the saddle. And still it screamed from the west, lashing the clouds into changing shapes. She looked toward the town and back at her mountain. She was halfway between them, only steps from the road. The first raindrops slapped her face. She untied a deerskin from behind the saddle and wrapped it around her head and shoulders.

She looked again at the sky and gasped. In the screaming turmoil a black face bore down on her, eyes and mouth shifting angrily. To the left of the face a finger was forming, a twisting, furious finger that pointed her back the way she'd come. It dropped briefly toward the ground and then pointed again at her mountain. Lightning flashed out of the eyes and struck a fence post on the other side of the road. The post flashed into fire, and light bolted along the wires to the next posts, setting them on fire as well. *Bontemps* reared, terrified. The rain fell in huge drops mixed with hailstones. Red Moon turned *Bontemps* and they fled back across the valley.

Many more summers passed. On a rocky slope not far from her shelter under the cliff, Red Moon stood looking down at the little flat pea pods in her hand. She had picked ripe ones and new ones to compare the flavor. She bit off half of a small one and chewed it slowly. It was not bad and the little bean inside tasted nutty. She waited a few minutes to see whether her stomach reacted to it. Then she bit off part of the riper pod. "Bitter, too old," she said. She tried the peas in it. They were peppery, very tasty. She put the rest of the peas in a bag. "Wish not so small," she said. "Have to pick so many, take so much time." She wondered whether the plants reseeded themselves or came back from the roots. She dug a few up and wrapped a skin around the roots to try planting them nearer her shelter. She sighed. River Willow would have known.

After planting some of the peas in her sod walls and some in the clearing that flanked the cliff, she went over to the rock where she always sat, taking the elk antler she'd brought with her from the cabin. She needed tools. One of her big knives had broken when she used it to take apart the old stove in the cabin. She tried not to use the other except for cutting. The antler might provide her with a drill as well as buttons.

Her black skirt was hanging in rags and she had only squirrel, rabbit, and chipmunk skins to make into clothing. She had no sharp instruments for making holes to lace the pieces together.

She glanced down at the valley, at the people who never came to tell her to leave. They had everything down there. If only she could trade with them as her mother had done in Taos, but they didn't seem to know she lived on their mountain. She'd guessed that the wind blowing from the west kept them from seeing her smoke and even hearing the noise she made.

"You not see I take your corn?" she asked the town. Last summer they'd planted a small field of corn not far from her mountain. The growing season had been too short. They'd let the stunted ears dry on the stalks and then not picked them. With *Bontemps* gone, her leg broken three summers ago when she'd shied at a bear, Red Moon had taken several trips to bring most of it up. She would have dry corn for a long time.

Loneliness overcame her again. She sighed and went back to the antler. She tried to break off a piece of it with her hands, tapped it against the rock, hit it harder. She slammed it with all her might against the rock and finally a piece broke off. "Didn't know so strong," she muttered, picking up the broken prong. If she could break the antler into small enough pieces, rub them flat on the rock, and bore holes in them, she could use them for buttons.

She slammed the tine against the rock again to break off a smaller piece. It broke into several pieces, none small enough to be worn down for buttons. She picked up the longest piece, held it against the edge of a sharp rock and hammered at it with another. Nothing happened. Her brown temple hair was blowing in her eyes and she shoved it back into her band, her brow knitted with frustration. There would be no buttons.

She took up a tapered piece and rubbed it against the rock to make a drill. A small chip flew out of the point. The chipped point chewed into the rabbit skin and went through. She went back to the shelter and brought out a pile of soft skins and her broken knife to cut them into patches and thongs.

As the sun set she got up and draped her new patchwork skirt around her, tied it with a thong, and went in to eat her peas. She did not glance down to see how it looked.

Since the time with Rattlesnake when she was a girl, Red Moon hadn't known such a hot, dry season. Even though it was still early morning, she'd unlaced the lower skins from her skirt and was sitting on her rock, rubbing the chaff from wild grass seeds. She'd waited for days for the wind to die down and allow her to thresh the seeds. They were so small they blew away with the chaff in a strong wind. She'd picked the seeds half a day to fill the rabbit skin bag. If she threshed all of them, she might have two handfuls of seed to grind and use for thickening soups. She looked down at the spot where she'd started grinding many summers ago. It had worn into the rock and the stone she used to grind with was smooth on both sides.

Something caught her eye as she looked back at the seeds in her hands. Across the valley a column of smoke was rising from the forest. She forgot the seeds and watched as the fire spread in all directions. The smoke was already high in the sky. Now chuggies made dust trails toward the fire, and the wind came up, blowing the dust and the smoke toward the east. She covered the seeds.

A little later she heard a loud droning noise behind her. A huge machine flew right past her mountain, trailing a kind of bucket. Red Moon leaped off her rock and took shelter behind it, scattering her seeds over the ground. The machine did not fall out of the sky. It roared on across the valley and disappeared into the smoke. Another came, and others flew into the valley from the north. Then another one roared over her. They all went into and out of the smoke and flew back the way they'd come. All day the valley droned with the machines. By sunset the smoke column had grown smaller, but as the stars came out she could see many small red fires on the mountain.

In the morning the smoke was up again, the wind strong, and for the rest of the day and the next the machines with the big buckets worked the fire. Ashes rained on her. Red Moon hiked past her streams, both just trickles, and climbed as high as she could, looking for fire on this side of the valley. The smoke was strong in her nostrils.

On the fourth day there were only a few wisps of smoke rising from the mountain and a big scar covered most of its slope, like a black face glaring at her across the valley. She shuddered and looked away.

Red Moon glanced at the town. She didn't expect them to come any more, and she was used to being alone. She was not waiting for them, she would not go to them, even though she no longer feared the man with the hate. It had been so long. He must be dead by now. She wondered whether she was still waiting for a sign from Mother Earth. She hadn't thought of the sign for a long time.

Red Moon went looking for another patch of grass. It was good she did not have to care for anyone else. There would not be much this winter.

CHAPTER 20

GINNY

Ginny MacCauley moved around her surveyor's tripod to put her back to the wind. God, up this close to timberline the wind could drive you crazy some days. As she moved, something flashed in her peripheral vision through the stunted trees. She glanced toward it but saw nothing. She must have imagined it.

Her Colorado Forest Service hat blew off and she chased it. She hadn't set the transit yet, but Alan Wooten at the other end of the quadrant would just have to wait. "Geez, blow all the way to Kansas why don't you?" she yelled after the hat tumbling through the trees. At last it banged into a fallen log and settled ten feet from a cliff. She picked it up, slapped dust off the brim, held her light brown hair so it would stay under the hat, and jammed it back on. She glanced at the terrain she would've had to cover if it hadn't stopped.

The cliff in front of her was the beginning of the great dip that gave West Baldy on the other side its huge southern exposure. Light flashed again from across the pass, as if someone were holding a small mirror in the sun. Worried about fire, Ginny stared down at the spot, saw nothing. It had come from above a stand of spruce that made a kind of necklace below the rock face. She waited, wondering what could flash out of a grassy slope. Just as she was about to give up, the flash came again. She frowned, looked toward Alan, who was a quarter of a mile away on top of a rock, and back at the spot on the mountain. She looked at her watch. It was ten of twelve. She'd adjust the transit, get the binoculars and have a closer look. If Alan complained, she'd just have to apologize.

With the binocular case slung over her shoulder, she took her lunch sack and went back. She trained the binoculars on the spot where she thought she'd seen the flash. Nothing. She moved the glasses over the entire grassy clearing below the cliff and then back to the middle. No, wait. There *was* something. Right in the grassy slope there was a faint gray rectangle. Then the flash came again, the rectangle became black, and went back to gray. There was someone standing there. No. There was no way that could be a door. There were no walls, only the grass. The figure moved around to the west side of the cliff. Ginny strained her eyes, tried to adjust the binoculars. The figure was so far away it danced on the light waves. Still, it was unmistakably human. Strange, whoever it was certainly blended into the scenery. Anyone not looking closely would have mistaken him for a deer. He disappeared.

She put the binoculars on her lap and reached absently for her lunch. A flood of memories came back, her years at Colorado State University in Fort Collins, the stories that had passed through generations of students about the wild Indian woman who lived up the Poudre somewhere. Years ago two students had sworn they'd seen her, talked to her, and she'd shot at them. Everyone always said she must be dead by now, but every year the fraternities hazed the pledges by making them hike up Skin Gulch on the Stove Prairie Road looking for Rattlesnake. They always set off a few fire crackers for effect.

Other, more unsettling memories returned—her mother's reluctance to talk about the father Ginny had never known, that awful visit to her grandfather's ranch. She shoved the old feelings aside, finished her sandwich and returned to her observation. Now there was nothing. The figure was gone, she could barely make out the gray rectangle because a cloud shaded the mountain. She searched the area again at the end of her work and found nothing.

Ginny sat across the fire from Alan at the campsite they'd set up for the surveying work. The logs crackled in the silence that had fallen between them after the division of supper chores. Firelight turned the trees around them into ghost branches and the tents into flat canvas.

Alan spooned a second helping of stew onto his tin plate and cleared his throat. "You lived in Fort Collins all your life?"

Ginny wrapped her fingers around her coffee cup to warm them. He was a nice enough guy, this Fed, with his short red beard and mustache and his blue eyes. "No, I lived in Denver for four years after my mother died. Lived with an aunt, went to high school there and then came back to Fort Collins for college. What about you?" It was a habit, turning the focus back to the other person, though she was getting over the fear of being close that had made her short marriage so difficult. She tried to find a comfortable position. Her small frame did nothing to cushion the rock she was sitting on. She should have gotten her camp stool out like Alan.

Alan took his U.S. Forestry Service hat off, ran his hand through his thinning red hair. "I guess I'm what you people call a 'flatlander.' Ohio. Came out here and worked one summer in the national park as part of my training." He gave her a sheepish smile. "Fell in love with the mountains. Like all flatlanders, I guess." He poured hot water into a mug and added a spoonful of instant coffee. "When I got out of college there weren't any openings in Colorado, so I came on out and did construction work in Winter Park for a couple of years. Pestered the Service until something came up." He waited for a minute. "Your family was from Fort Collins?"

Ginny shifted nervously, put her coffee cup on the ground. She rested her elbows on her knees and put her small chin in her hands, looking at him across the flames. "Well, around Fort Collins. My grandfather had a ranch up near Masonville. I inherited it, as a matter of fact."

Alan just smiled, waiting. It made her uncomfortable.

She stared into the flames. "You remind me of the shrink I went to right after my divorce."

"Why?"

"He always just looked at me and waited. Made me real nervous. If I told him anything about my past, he just said, 'How did you feel about that?'"

Alan laughed. "And how did you feel about *that*?"

"Like he was pulling teeth."

He lowered the coffee cup and stretched his back. "Listen, I don't mean to pry. Anything you might want to talk about is fine. How about the mapping? Want to get started tonight?"

"No, I like to do that on a good surface with better light than lanterns."

"Me, too."

Awkward moments passed.

Ginny squirmed. "I know I'm not good company, Alan. I'm just a little reserved. It's a bad habit I'm working on."

"I like your company just fine," he said.

"Tell me about your family if you don't mind my asking."

"The usual. Except for one brother. He got on drugs, ran away to California, and ended up in jail for dealing." He waited for her reaction.

Ginny looked into his eyes. He was deliberately giving her an opening, asking for a level of trust she wasn't sure she could give. He was nearly a stranger. She'd only known him since somebody'd made the decision to put one Colorado and one Federal surveyor on each team because the proposed Rawah National Wilderness Area was right on the border of the state forest. After a minute she took a deep breath and asked, "Do you ever think that whatever made him addicted to drugs might be in you, too. Ever fear you'll end up the same way?"

"Yeah, I do. Or used to. The older I get, the more I trust myself, though." For a minute the crackling of the fire dominated the silence of the mountainside. The logs shifted. Sparks flew up and died. He poked at the logs with a stick. "The question comes from way inside, doesn't it?"

"Yeah." She looked up. There was something about the way he was holding his head, the warm directness of his eyes looking into hers. He wasn't smiling, but there was an open gentleness to his face that she'd never seen in a man.

She picked up the coffee cup and shifted it from hand to hand. "I guess I have some fear of family traits, too. My grandfather was a man of pure evil." She shuddered. "My mother never had any contact with him, but she told me where he lived not long before she died. She told me a lot of stuff before she died."

Alan moved his camp stool closer.

Ginny glanced at him and then stared back into the orange flames. "It was easy enough to find him. I went there one day while I was in college. He came limping to the door. I didn't want him to know who I was, so I told him I was doing a survey for a class. He was a little man, no taller than I am, had my eyes and probably my thin face, although you couldn't see much under his beard. When he saw me he looked shocked. I guess I look a lot like my father." For a second the picture she'd found among her mother's things flashed before her. She closed her eyes to it. "Anyway, I asked him if he would answer a few questions for a college project. Instead, he practically spat at me. '*Uneeversitee* again,' he said, whatever that meant. 'Can't you read? I got a sign on the gate says "no trespassing." You got no right comin' in here.' I thought he'd slam the door in my face, but he just stood there staring at me. The air coming out of the house was awful. Stale beer and sheets that hadn't been washed in ages. But it was his eyes that were the worst. Cold eyes full of hate and anger. And they were my eyes."

Alan put his hand on her forearm. "Your eyes are not cold, Ginny. Take that from one who's only known you for a short time. If they were we wouldn't be having this conversation. And they're certainly not full of hate and anger."

Ginny glanced at the hand and into his eyes before looking back into the fire. "Thanks."

Alan withdrew the hand. "What happened then?"

"I finally stammered, 'Sorry I bothered you' and left. From the gate I looked back. He was still standing in the door. The house was all run down, the barns, too. I didn't see more than a couple of cows."

"Did you say you inherited this place?"

"Yeah. About two years ago. A lawyer for the county got in touch with me in 1962. My grandfather died without a will and it took them a year to find me. The lawyer had known him from a fight he had with his neighbor over a fence line. Said he was probably just too mean to leave his property to anyone. I guess I was his only heir."

"What did you do with the place?"

"Nothing. Except pay property taxes. I thought about selling it. I go back to look at it from time to time, but it gives me the creeps. Maybe someday I'll tear down the old house and build something I can live in or spend vacations in. It's actually a pretty spot."

"Show it to me sometime?"

She looked up, surprised. "Yeah, sure."

"Ever marry again after your divorce?"

"No, I guess I hid my head in the mountains, so to speak. They don't hurt you. What about you?"

He grinned. "Never tried it."

The following weekend Ginny drove her Jeep back up to the place they'd been surveying. She camped down the hill from her observation post so a fire wouldn't be visible at night and scare the man off. She brought the strongest binoculars she could find and settled in to watch West Baldy.

She'd been watching for hours before the figure on the mountain appeared. She gasped. It was a woman. Tiny as she still was in the stronger binoculars, the two braids were clearly visible hanging down the skin colored clothing. Everything about her movements suggested a woman. Ginny lowered the glasses to relieve her aching shoulders and stared into space. There must actually be a Rattlesnake woman. But that was years ago, decades. She couldn't possibly still be alive.

She looked again. Rattlesnake disappeared into her door in the grass, then reappeared and walked down into the trees that lined the clearing. It took a minute to pick her out, standing behind the first trees, staring down into the North Park valley. Ginny moved the binoculars in that direction. Several trails of dust lined the valley floor, the wakes of earth movers. They were grading highway 14 below Walden. Why on earth didn't they just go ahead and pave it? She let her eyes wander over the ranges that surrounded the huge horseshoe-shaped valley, all still covered with snow, the Park Range, the Rabbit Ears and the Never Summer Ranges, and what she could see of the Medicine Bow Range. It was so beautiful it almost made her cry. She wondered whether Rattlesnake found it beautiful. She trained the glasses on the trees, but couldn't spot the woman again.

Ginny watched all afternoon. She thought back to where the transit had been when her hat blew off, to the lines they'd sighted, and realized that Rattlesnake must be camped on federal land, almost on the border between the wilderness area and the state forest.

Rattlesnake reappeared just before dusk and went inside. After she'd watched for another half hour, Ginny walked slowly back to her camp through the gathering dark and made a fire. "How could she stand to be alone like that?" she asked aloud. She sucked in her breath. "*Alone*, my God, I never knew what the word meant till now. It must be how long? At least thirty years. It can't be. No one can survive in this wilderness for that long alone. And even if you could, you'd go crazy."

Ginny tried to picture herself living alone in the mountains for even a year. She'd been alone on camping trips several times, especially after her divorce. It was an eerie feeling. She always found herself looking over her shoulder in the silence, as if there must be a deer or at least a coyote around. Such complete solitude wasn't quite believable. Your own footsteps were an affront to the silence. At night in her tent it had rung in her ears. Of course, she'd enjoyed it, had been less depressed in the mountains than in town; but she'd always known she'd be back with civilization soon. Noisy thing, civilization. Getting more depressing all the time.

But to live like Rattlesnake, without the return to the world. You'd be little more than an animal in a few years, scratching for food, trying to keep warm in winter.

"God, I'd like to get to know her, find out how she made it all these years," she said aloud as she was washing her supper dishes. She looked over her shoulder and laughed at herself. "I wonder if *she* talks to herself."

After she settled in her tent, memories she'd shoved aside when she'd first seen Rattlesnake forced their way into consciousness. Her mother had said her father and grandfather had victimized Rattlesnake in some terrible way. The legend always mentioned a hanging, but no one knew who'd been hanged, or why. A distant guilt prickled her thoughts, but she shook her head in the dark tent. "I didn't have anything to do with it," she told herself, "whatever it was."

Early Sunday morning she packed her things back down to the Jeep and set out for West Baldy to find this Rattlesnake woman.

The next week Ginny and Alan worked farther south along the ridge that separated Colorado forest and Federal land. Her happiness at seeing him again had surprised her. His presence felt good, but so had Ron's in the beginning.

"How was your weekend in Denver?" she asked over supper on Monday night.

"Fine. My friend didn't have as much time as he thought, so I spent some time just driving around the city. It's nice as cities go, but I guess I'm just a small town boy. What did you do?"

"I went camping back at the place we were surveying last Thursday." Should she tell him about Rattlesnake, about almost making contact with her?

"How about showing me your ranch on Saturday? I'd really like to see it."

"Well, sure, okay."

"Do you like to go square dancing?"

"I've tried it a few times. I'm afraid I'm not a very good dancer, and I don't know the names of the steps. Do you dance?"

Alan stood up and bowed with his hat in front of his chest. "Ma'am, you happen to be talking to the most avid square dancer in Larimer County, who asks you for the favor of your company at the Hoedown in Fort Collins on Saturday evening."

Ginny grinned at him. "Wear your most protective boots."

They picnicked at the ranch before the hoedown, and as the sun set, they stood together on the dilapidated porch. Across the road the narrow pasture was lush green in the June growth, the rocks behind it bright orange in the last sun. Alan was leaning against the post and had his arm around her shoulder.

"Don't you like those three stripes of color?" she asked. "The grass, the rocks, the sky?"

He nodded. "You told me this was your grandfather's place. What about your father? Why didn't he inherit it?"

"He was already dead."

"I'm sorry to hear that. When did he die?"

She'd known this was coming. Well, if he was as eager to get a relationship going as he seemed to be, he might as well know now. She moved to the post at the other side of the steps. "Couple of months before I was born." She hesitated. "He committed suicide. Hanged himself."

Alan put his hands on her shoulders and turned her to him. "Was that what sent you to the therapist?"

His voice was full of concern, not condemnation. The warmth of his hands traveled up her neck and she felt her face flush. "Well, that plus being brought up by a mother who never got over it, living with an aunt who didn't give a damn, a frightening encounter with an evil grandfather, and a messy divorce. Those were the Roman numerals on my shrink's list, but by far the worst was my grandfather."

He put his arms around her and held her head against his chest. "So you think you somehow inherited his evil nature?"

Ginny let go of her reserve and leaned into him. "Not really. I worried about it for a long time. But I've never done anything awful, never hurt anyone, at least not if I could avoid it. I've never contemplated suicide, even after the divorce."

He smiled down at her, stroked her small chin. "I think you're great."

In his Jeep going back to Fort Collins he asked, "Did your mother know why he committed suicide?"

"She said it had something to do with my grandfather. My father should have saved someone from him. Some man who was about his age at the time. There was a girl involved, too." She couldn't quite bring herself to mention the woman on the mountain.

The next morning, Alan woke her by stroking her chin down to its point. His eyes were grinning into hers when she opened them. "Thanks for doing such drastic injury to my toes. This was a much better idea than dancing anyway."

She smiled back, at ease with him after an evening of laughter and warmth that had turned to passion. She couldn't remember ever being so comfortable with anyone. "It's a service I can provide anytime. Bodily injury, that is." She sat up and looked around his efficiency apartment. She pulled the spread off the bed for a wrap and went to the book-shelves. "Good library," she said. "I take it you like to read."

"Do you?"

"Love to. No animals? Not even a goldfish?"

"Nope. I used to have dogs at home, but here it would be too cruel. Other pets don't interest me much. And basically I love wild animals. What's wild should be wild. Maybe that's really why I'm in this business."

She turned to look at him.

"What's the matter?"

"You really believe that?"

"What?"

"That what's wild should stay wild?"

"Really."

"Alan, will you go camping with me next weekend? There's something I want to show you."

The following Saturday they returned to their first campsite and hiked up to the edge of the cliff. They'd both brought binoculars.

"Can you see the sort of gray rectangle in the grass?"

"No...yeah, I do see it."

"It's a door."

"Can't be. It's gotta be a rock."

"I saw it open, and somebody came out."

He lowered the binoculars and stared at her.

"I think it's a plain old wooden door with a pane of glass in it. I saw it because when it opens there's a flash of light if the sun is right. And then I saw the woman."

"Are you telling me there are people living over there in some kind of cave?"

"Not people. A woman. Alone."

"You can't be serious."

"Have you ever heard anyone around here mention Rattlesnake?"

"A rattlesnake?"

"No, Rattlesnake. She's supposed to be an old Indian woman who lives somewhere up the Poudre, shoots at people if they get too close."

"Come on!"

"The story's been around for ages. But, Alan, the thing is, I think she was the one I told you about with my father and grand-father. There was supposed to be a young Indian girl involved in whatever it was."

"So you think that woman has been living there since before you were born?!"

"Wait till you see her."

Alan raised the binoculars again. "I see something," he cried. "Just the tail end of something going around the side of the mountain."

Ginny brought her binoculars up so quickly she hurt her nose. The door in the mountain was propped open, making a black hole in the grass. "She must be coming back soon." She let the binoculars dangle around her neck and faced him. "You remember I told you I'd gone camping two weekends ago? Well, this was why."

Alan turned to face her.

"I watched her all day Saturday. On Sunday I tried to get closer. I thought I'd give her something, so I took a whole box of matches. I drove up that old logging road..."

Alan looked puzzled.

"...you know the one behind Chambers Lake?"

"Ah, right."

"...and then started hiking. I was wearing my running shoes, so I wasn't making much noise. I had scrambled up a rock face to a meadow that was still way down the east slope. Just as I cleared the top I saw her." Ginny shook her head at the image. "She was sitting by the side of a stream about two hundred feet ahead of me and seemed to be completely engrossed in something. I started toward her, but the last rock I stepped on gave way and I grabbed for support on a dead aspen tree. It snapped right off and I lost my footing. By the time I was standing again, all I could see was her braids disappearing around the rocks on the other side of the stream."

"Did you follow her?"

"Uh-uh. I thought about it for a minute and then just left my matches where she'd been sitting. She was scared of me, Alan. That's why I brought you here instead of going closer."

Alan trained his binoculars on the slope again and they waited. It was almost an hour before Rattlesnake returned with an arm-load of wood and went inside. She seemed to be wearing clothing made of skins, but not of one color. She came back out, stopped a minute to do something with her hair, and retraced her steps. The sun was setting before she reappeared with more wood. In the last rays of the sun shining directly on her face two streaks of gray above her temples were clearly visible. Before the door closed they saw the faint yellow glow of a fire, and as twilight settled over them smoke rose from somewhere above the door and drifted off to the east.

They watched her the next day. She brought things back to the clearing and seemed to be hanging them on branches. She carried something around to the left side of the mountain and brought it back much heavier and rounder than it had been when she left. She did not walk easily.

"I can't believe what I saw up there," Alan said as they drove down the Poudre to Fort Collins. "She certainly is old enough to have been a girl when your father was around. I'd give anything to get to know her. And why not? We don't mean her any harm."

"I thought about that a lot, Alan. I've wanted to go up and knock on that strange door ever since I saw her. But whatever my grandfather and my father did to her years ago is what made her a hermit, so I feel guilty about it."

"Oh, now, wait..."

"Well, not really guilty, but very bad. I decided I didn't want to make her drag it up again after all these years. I'm afraid even my appearance would traumatize her, since I look so much like my father. And if I could avoid reminding her of the past, what good would I do her? There's no way I could ever make it up to her. Finally, I realized that the kindest thing I can do for her is leave her alone. I even wonder whether leaving the matches was the right thing. Can you imagine what she must be like by now?"

"Stir crazy. Lonely."

"I doubt she can even communicate any more. She's like a wild animal." Ginny waited a minute to let that sink in. "The thing is, Alan, I think she's probably just inside the wilderness. So we have to decide what's to become of her."

"My God, you're right."

"You know you said 'wild things should be wild'?"

"Yeah."

"Well Rattlesnake certainly qualifies. If we tell anyone about her, they'll have her in some kind of home before you can say *wild woman*. Imagine what that world would be like for her."

Alan didn't answer quickly. He stopped the car in a pull-out next to the river. "It'd be a nightmare," he said, staring absently at the steering wheel.

"Even if the Forest Service allowed her to stay in the wilderness area, you know what happens as soon as a wilderness is established. Thousands of hikers who want to 'pack it in, pack it out' and experience 'nature as it should be.' She'd never have another moment's peace."

He turned to look at her. "What are you suggesting, Ginny?"

"That she's probably in poor health and can't live much longer. You saw how she was limping. Let's leave her alone."

"How can we do that? If she's on federal land like you said..."

Ginny didn't answer. The decision had to come from him.

"Let me think about it. And the matches were a good idea," he said, reaching over to caress her cheek.

The surveying was done and the maps were in the files of the United States and the Colorado Forestry Services. Ginny's Colorado survey showed the border of the wilderness an eighth of a mile north of the peak of West Baldy. Alan's map for the US Forest service showed it an eighth of a mile south.

"Let's go up and check on her from time to time," said Alan. They were putting steaks on her grill, celebrating the final reports.

"Maybe if we ever see she needs help we can do something." Ginny handed him the barbecue sauce.

"We could leave things, more matches, some dried food."

"Well, maybe. Salt would be good."

"You know," said Alan, running his fingers down her nose, "someday somebody's going to find out those lines are wrong."

"We were young, we made a mistake."

They grinned at each other.

"Got everything ready to start tearing down your grandfather's house tomorrow?" he asked. "The guys are coming with the bulldozer at nine."

"I just have to pack the lunch in the morning."

"Dancing tonight?"

She tugged at the ends of his mustache to pull his head down. "Wear your loafers. I'll have you home in no time," she whispered into his lips.

CHAPTER 21

RED MOON

Red Moon bent to pick up the large rabbit she'd trapped. The gray hair above her temples blew into her eyes in the cool wind that spoke of winter coming down. She straightened under the gold, fluttering aspens and flung the rabbit to break its neck. After she'd thanked it for its life, she looked down at the meadow where the woman came. It was the woman who'd almost found her when she was sitting near a small stream, watching a hummingbird take a bath, hovering just above the water and splashing it up, like Rattlesnake making upside-down rain in the sun. She'd completely forgotten to listen for danger, and the woman had climbed up from below, slipped, and made a lot of noise.

Now the woman came every year with her man and child, although they hadn't come this summer. Sometimes Red Moon watched them play about the meadow, but mostly that was too painful in her loneliness. Silly people, they always forgot things when they left—matches, salt, once a thick shirt that she'd left there because it might still be good when they came again.

When she'd taken a few steps toward home, she heard a noise and turned back. She gasped. There they were. They hadn't been there when she'd checked her trap just minutes ago. Now they tramped noisily into the clearing, carrying bundles and a green box.

She crouched behind a rock and watched. They wore reds and blues and yellows, and the man and woman wore hats with wide brims all around. The little boy wore a hat that looked like a duck bill.

They put up their green cloth building and unfolded a table. The woman put the big green box on the table and opened the top while the man and boy went away. In a few minutes they returned, carrying between them a big red box with a white top. The little boy struggled with his side, but when the man tried to take both sides, he put both hands in a handle, and they finally set the box next to the table.

For a while, all three of them threw something back and forth to each other. It looked like a squashed brown melon. They laughed and called to each other.

Red Moon began to cry. She hadn't cried since the first night in that old winter cabin, longing for Rattlesnake and the family he'd promised her. Now here was this family again, loving each other. Such good people loving the boy the way her mother had loved her.

With a heavy sigh, she picked up the rabbit and started back to her home. Her chest tightened as she climbed up the mountain. She hugged the rabbit, but it wasn't her child. She thanked it again. At least she wouldn't have to hunt again for several days.

The next morning, tears came again. The family in the meadow played in front of her eyes, no matter where she looked. They were good people, like ones she'd have wanted for her family. Not people who would hang Rattlesnake or want to kill her.

Would they be kind if she went down to them? Immediately her chest tightened again and her heart raced. But they were so loving with each other. They would not want to harm her.

She ran her fingers through her hair and rebraided it, tucking the grey strands into a headband made of a chipmunk skin. She pulled at her skin skirt. She put some rabbit jerky in a skin bag and started toward the meadow, almost hoping the people would be gone.

When she reached the first aspens before the clearing, she stopped, her heart pounding hotly. Mother Earth had not given her any sign that she should go to these people. Still, she hadn't sent a storm with a forbidding black face in it to stop her, either.

Red Moon stepped slowly through the aspens, hearing the crunch of dry vegetation beneath her skin shoes like the steps of a big, noisy bear.

The woman was alone now with her bare head down, standing at the table, washing something in a metal pan. Facing Red Moon.

Red Moon took another step, leaving the shelter of the last tree.

The woman looked up. She dropped whatever she was holding and smiled.

It was the face. The narrow chin, the blue eyes. The face of the man with the hate and the foul breath. Red Moon turned and ran.

CHAPTER 22

CARVER

In the silence of Red Moon's ledge on the mountain, time drifted by with only the seasons to color the sameness of the days. Far away, in Denver, time strutted by to the clank and roar of bulldozers leveling earth and trees. It marched forward on the city's concrete arms stretching onto the plains and into the foothills, sprouting houses like rampant warts.

And in the middle of the hubbub, as the moon was setting behind the construction area next to the city's hospital, Momma Powers gave birth to her second son in May of 1963. When the nurse brought the baby to her in the maternity ward, she was watching the day's work rumble to life. She tried to smile at him, but she was tired from all the labor and worried about another mouth to feed with Manny paying no support. Her welfare worker wasn't going to be happy.

"Come to Momma, child," she said with a sigh, resigning herself to his fate as well as her own. "I ain't going nowhere and you ain't neither." She glanced at the dirty, noisy construction site. "Well, maybe *you* can carve a life for yourself in this shitty city. Gonna name you Carver." She took the small bottle the nurse provided and shoved it against his lips.

And Carver grew in the way of ghetto children.

He lived with his mother and two brothers north of downtown in a project that stretched from Barristan to Granite and from 32nd to 38th, as grim as abandoned army barracks. Rusted Cadillacs and Pontiacs lined the streets, most of them with four flat tires, all of them sprayed with blue gang turf markers. The trees in the packed-dirt grounds of the project barely clung to life through annual infestations of elm beetles and perennial assaults of switch-blades, battered baseball bats, and the scores of things ghetto children use to vent their anger. The screens on most of the windows were torn, the panes cracked; and from every apartment the beat of joyless music competed with the screams of children fighting over use of the swings on the playground.

Momma Powers, a rolling fat woman with huge hanging breasts, had ruled her household for four years, ever since her last boy-friend, the father of her youngest, had left under a barrage of beer cans and frying pans and taken up with a woman of more man-ageable size. She had had four sons, but now she had only three. The two smaller boys were LaRon and Odelle, whom she sent off to school on days when she could get out of bed early enough to make it worthwhile.

At fourteen, Carver was still small for his age, but his father had been nearly six feet. There was no childhood innocence left in his face, though his natural sweetness, which had been steamrolled by urban strife, occasionally surfaced at home. His hair was carved into a perfect boxtop, and at the back of his shaved head a small amount of hair grew in the shape of a pistol. He was very proud of it.

At home Carver was a tractable teenager, intimidated as he was by the sheer size of his Momma. With his gang on the streets he was tough and ruthless, and it was not a show. They wouldn't have voted him in if he'd shied from the sound of gunfire or could not handle a little coke. After the shooting of his older brother

Keeno, who'd had the same father, he'd seen the necessity of gang protection. Someday he'd probably end up just like Keeno, but if he was lucky, the gang could be a leg up to the sweet life, like those big basketball players had. He never felt quite right about lying to Momma about being in the gang, but "there's just things a man's gotta do," he told himself.

On a fall afternoon, Carver stood in his room, totally concentrated on the revolver he was handling, shifting it from hand to hand. It was a beautiful thing, glinting bluish in the light from the window, and it made him feel ten feet tall. He jerked into the cop stance he'd seen on TV and pointed at himself in the mirror. He fired off an imaginary round and fell backwards onto the yellowed sheets of his unmade bed. Then he rolled off the bed and aimed across it at the door just as his mother's bulk filled it. He smiled and pulled off another round. "Gotcha!"

Her face scrunched into lumps like the knuckles of two fists, and her hands went to her hips. "Where'd you find that gun?" she asked in her rich, deep voice.

Carver put it behind him.

"You gimme that gun, boy. It ain't no toy, and you got no business with it. You gonna get hurt." She clumped forward, creaking the floorboards.

"Aw, Momma, lemme keep it. It ain't loaded." Man, he wanted to crow about being the best shot in the gang, but Momma'd be mad as a Blood after a Crips raid.

She stood there like a tank with her hand out, bobbing it up and down.

"Come on, Momma. It was my daddy's gun. It belongs to me now."

She put one knee on the bed, bowing the mattress, and yanked him up by the collar. She snatched the gun away.

Carver followed her and peeked through the crack in her bedroom door to watch where she put it. He shook his head. She put it right back where he'd gotten it, behind the shoe box full of coupons and food stamps on her closet shelf.

Three days later, on an afternoon when even the project basked peacefully in the October sunlight, Momma Powers called up the stairs, "Carver, come down here. I got a job for you."

There was no answer. Momma Powers listened. From above she heard a thud and then a burst of laughter. She heaved herself up the stairs. The steps bent and protested under her feet in the men's slippers with bunion holes cut out of the toes.

Carver crouched behind a Kenmore washing machine box at the end of the hall. He yelled, "Now!"

LaRon dashed across the hall from one bedroom to the other.

Carver pulled the trigger on a toy gun with suction-tipped arrows. He hit LaRon in the hip without even taking time to aim. LaRon stopped, keeled over, and died dramatically. It was Odelle's turn.

"Now!" yelled Carver once more at the same time Momma yelled, "Carver, you cut that out. Where you get that gun, boy?"

"You should see Carver, Momma," piped up Odelle, coming out of the bedroom. "He hit us every time."

She lumbered down the hall like a locomotive and grabbed the toy.

Carver slammed his fist into the box. "My frien' give it to me. You give it back."

"You tell your frien's don' be givin' you no guns. All you gonna do is get in trouble. Get up, boy." She put a huge, heavy hand under his right shoulder and hauled him up. "Come on." She shoved him from behind. "You gotta go downtown and pay the 'lectric bill."

"Aw, Momma, that's a kid's job. I'm a man now. Send LaRon."

She let go and bent forward till her face bumped his. "You don' learn how to do stuff like this regular, you ain't never gonna be no man."

"Okay, okay." Carver stepped toward her bedroom. "Can I wear my daddy's Bronco jacket?"

"Yeah, it'll be cool by the time you get back. Here forty dollars. The bill's thirty-six twenty."

Carver wheedled, "Can I have the money that's left?"

"If you hurry up and get there before they close. But don' be spendin' it on no blood'n'guts comic books."

"I know, Momma. That's kid stuff. I'm a man now."

"You a man? You a piece o' chicken shit." But she was smiling as she turned toward the stairs.

While she plodded down, Carver went to her closet and took out his father's worn blue and orange jacket with the right pocket flap torn open. He reached for his father's gun behind the shoe box. He loaded it with the last four bullets from the box next to it, shoved it into his belt, and closed the bottom snaps of the jacket. It was time he brought his own gun instead of practicing with somebody else's. Besides, they were doing Otis's initiation tonight, and you never knew what might happen. On his way out he picked up his boom box and his blue baseball cap, which he tucked into the jacket till he was out of sight.

Momma watched him down the street, approving the self-confidence of his almost limp-like gait, his free left hand swinging in time to the beat, palm backwards. She could still hear the boom box long after he'd rounded the corner.

LaRon and Odelle were standing at the bottom of the stairs.

"Go watch TV till dinner," she said. She went to the laundry room in the next building and did a load of wash. Then she put on water to boil for the hot dogs. When Carver didn't come home for supper they ate and went back to the television set.

"Ain't Carver coming home?" asked Odelle during a commercial.

"He probably just met up with some of his frien's and ate at MacDonald's."

"Is Carver a man now?"

"He think so."

Carver sat next to the window in the back seat of the Honda Civic Otis had stolen. It was a shit-car, all rusted around the tire wells and ragged on the inside like some tiger had sharpened its claws on the seats. Sheeit, the window next to him wouldn't even close. They'd been driving around with it for hours, trying to use up the gas before they took it to the chop shop, but the fuckin' thing seemed to make gas instead of burning it.

He was trying to ignore a squishy feeling in his stomach. Hot Papa and the other leaders had ragged him earlier about not doing a single thing for the gang after the car he'd stolen for his own initiation. Carver's reminder that he was the best shot hadn't cut a sliver of ice. They wanted him to be more "valuable," but he didn't want to do the drug stuff. Too many got caught pushing dope. Maybe he'd do a drive-by in Blood turf.

He stole a glance at Hot Papa, who'd been arguing with the other leader for the last half hour about whether the Civic oughta count for the initiation since it was so beat-up. He turned in the driver's seat and grinned at Carver. "Hey, Pistolhead, what you think? This little crate good enough?"

Carver stroked his chin thinking about it and felt the gun under his arm. He rubbed his elbow across the butt, feeling the power of the gun stiffen the squishes in his gut. By shit, he'd do something soon to make the gang proud. Maybe knock over a liquor store and score big time. "I dunno. It's pretty shitty. I got fuzz all over me and wires stickin' in my ass. I ain't any older than Otis, and I stole a new Acura."

"True. True," said Hot Papa as he turned into the street where the chop shop was. "Okay, it's decided. You gotta steal something else, Otis. Maybe a cop car."

Everybody howled at that one. Otis, jammed into the middle of the back seat, rammed his elbow into Carver's ribs.

Before Carver could hit him back, Hot Papa let out a "ssshhee-it." He pointed ahead. Half a block away a red Cadillac de Ville as long as a semi stood at the gate of the warped plywood fence around the chop shop. Several Bloods in their red caps leaned against it while one negotiated with the owner of the shop.

A Blood shoved himself away from the Caddy and pointed at the Civic. "Sheeit, man, look what the Crips dragged in."

That set off a round of knee-slapping laughter.

"Best they could do," yelled another.

"Hey, ain't that Carver Powers?" shouted another. "Man, they lettin' fuckin' babies in the Crips these days."

"Crips creeps, mother fuckin' losers!" crowed the leader.

Hot Papa gunned the motor and the Civic shot forward. He screeched to a stop and jumped out with his gun drawn.

Carver's insides froze.

The Bloods began to step toward them, still laughing.

Behind them the Caddy's back door flew open and a woman jumped out, her jogging suit ripped, her blond hair torn out of its pony tail. "Help me," she screamed, running toward the Civic.

Carver's hand came up automatically with the pistol in it and went through the window before he knew what he was doing. The gun went off by itself. The bang deafened him. The kick brought his hand back inside the car. He stared at the gun in it, smoking and smelling like firecrackers.

When he looked out again, the woman lay still on the street and the Bloods were leaping back into the Cadillac.

"Oh, momma, oh shit," he cried.

Hot Papa jumped back in the car and they screeched away.

"You fuckin' dumb-ass fool, Pistolhead. Why'd you do that?"

"She was moving. I didn't mean to do it. The fuckin' thing just went off."

Hot Papa squealed onto Sheridan Street. "You shithead, you're gonna have the fuzz *and* the Bloods all over us. You dead meat if them Bloods get you. An' if they don't, I might."

Shadows of the Rockies followed the ghostly light of the setting moon up the sides of the skyscrapers. In the dead hours of the

early morning the city seemed abandoned, a well-preserved ruin in steel and glass and concrete. No breeze, no street sweeper disturbed the sleep of the MacDonald's cups and cigarette butts in the gutters. In the project, silence lay over the buildings like a sheet of gritty, yellowed newspaper waiting for the next wind.

The Civic whined around the corner and screeched to a stop in front of the Powers' entrance. Its door opened and banged shut and then it screeched away, leaving the smell of burning rubber rising from tire marks. Carver ran up the three chipped concrete steps to his door. He turned on the hall light.

"That you, boy?" Momma called down from her room, her voice muffled by sleep.

"Yeah." He ran upstairs.

"You pay that bill?"

"Yeah."

"Well, go to bed and don' wake your brothers. In the morning you can tell me where you been so long."

His voice was shaky but determined. "I gotta leave, Momma."

She turned on the light by her bed and squinted at him. "Say wha'? Come here, boy. What you done?"

Carver was changed. He stood at the foot of her bed, hunched forward, his arms hanging straight at his sides. The last sweetness was gone from his face. His lips were tight and a muscle clenched constantly in his jaw. His gaze shifted about like a nervous flea, but when his eyes paused on her face they were scared and begged for help.

The story came reluctantly. He told her about the gang and the name-calling and the shooting. He didn't tell her the woman had just been asking for help. Or that she was white.

As he talked, Momma's face sagged and grew hopeless.

"I'm a man now, Momma. He called me a baby. A man can't take that kinda shit off nobody."

She threw the covers off her great hulk and grabbed him by the shoulders. "He? He ain't the one you shot. Yeah, you some kinda man. The kind tha's gonna end up jus' like your brother. Gang," she spat out, shaking him hard. "Didn' I tell you stay outta that business? I swear, if I didn' have to save your life, I'd whup you to death." She shoved him toward the door. "You gotta go fast. Get the gray jacket outta the hall closet."

She went to her own closet and took out the fifty dollar bill she'd kept hidden in the old winter coat that was eight sizes too small.

"You hear any cars comin' when you come in?" she asked, lumbering down the steps.

"No, I think they hadda ditch the Caddie first."

Carver meekly followed his mother's frantic activity. She ran to the kitchen and threw whatever food she could grab quickly into a Safeway sack. She stripped the Bronco jacket off of him and threw it into a corner. When the gun in it banged against the radiator, she retrieved it with a tsk and a shake of her head. She helped him into the old suit coat, pressed the fifty dollars into the left pocket and the gun into the right.

"Gimme that hat," she demanded.

"Naw, momma. How the Crips gonna know me?"

"It ain't the Crips you gotta worry about." She snatched the cap and threw it on top of the jacket. "How many bullets you got left in that gun?"

"Three."

"Get some more outta the box."

"They ain't no more."

Momma sighed and her shoulders sagged a little more. "Well, git, then. And look out for the cops. They prob'ly after you by now, too. Here, don' forget the sack."

She gave Carver a hug, shoved him out the back door, and watched him run away.

When she turned back, LaRon was leaning sleepily against the kitchen door. "Where's Carver going?"

"He doin' his 'man' thing." Her voice was heavy with sarcasm and despair.

Momma climbed once more up the creaky stairs. In another minute the bed springs groaned rhythmically to her sobbing.

Carver slung the Safeway sack over his shoulder. He headed left through the playground, away from the direction in which the Bloods would come. There were no lights in the buildings yet, and the dim pre-dawn light had an eerie, hostile quality that made him run crouched along the walls. Daylight would be even more dangerous. He had to find a place to hide where neither the cops nor the Bloods would think to look.

At the last building before 37th Street, he peered around the corner. There. On the left. Something moving. He drew his head back and waited, his hand on the gun. He peered again. A wino was trying to get into one of the garbage cans, his shopping cart waiting on the sidewalk, loaded with the lumpy belongings of the homeless. The wino dropped the lid and it crashed onto the sidewalk like a cymbal. Carver cowered to the ground, but no window flew open, no lights came on. The wino had his back to Carver, poking in the trash.

Carver dashed across the street, ran through the last block of the tenement with no clear goal in mind and stopped at the last building, as he'd done before. Across 38th was a park. Beyond that was the old newspaper building, scheduled for demolition. There was a chain link fence around it with a huge sign advertising Mile Hi Demolition. If he could get in, he might be safe until night fell again.

The park was empty. He looked up the street. There were headlights a couple of blocks to the right. They were moving slowly, but he didn't risk it. He ran back to a carousel in the playground and lay down behind it. The car took a long time, and it was a squad car. Carver tried to hug the ground closer, his heart banging like his boom box. The revolver pressed into his hip but he dared not move. The searchlight flashed through the playground and the park; the car slowed to a crawl but didn't stop.

When the sound of its motor and its crackling radio died out, Carver checked 38th again and dashed across to the park. From several blocks away came the screeching of tires forced too fast around a corner. He knew it was the Bloods. There were only a few bushes in the park, all already bare, and the few trees were too far away for him to reach. The car would pass the park in seconds. He raced to the nearest bush, thanking his mother that he was no longer wearing the bright Bronco jacket. He lay flat behind the bush and watched as a wood-paneled station wagon thundered by on 38th full of boys, all wearing red caps.

He lay still for a few more minutes. Over in the project the first lights went on. The sun would be up in a few minutes. He sat up and brushed the dust from his coat. Now he remembered the food sack. He must have left it behind the carousel. "Sheeeit," he swore, picking himself up.

Half way to the end of the park he heard the Bloods coming back on 39th. He made it to a tree whose trunk was barely as wide as his shoulders and stood sideways behind it, the gun hanging in his right hand. The car slowed almost to a halt. Carver used the sound to guide him as he slowly moved around the tree. He didn't know what they were doing but didn't dare move his head to see.

The car stopped, a door opened, and seconds later he heard one of the Bloods running toward the chain link fence. He peered around just enough to see the glint of a gun. Carver's gun trembled in his hand, but he didn't shoot. When the Blood had checked out the abandoned building with a flashlight, the car screeched off.

He ran for the fence, his half-laced high tops silent on the pavement. It was an eight foot fence, and the toes of his shoes were too wide to hook into the wire. He had to haul most of his weight up on his hands. They were scratched and bleeding by the time he vaulted over the top.

He landed in rubble left from the gutting of the building, twisted his ankle and involuntarily cried out. He got up from the old studs and scraps of dry wall, tearing holes in his jeans and catching the left pocket of the gray coat on nails. The pocket came apart, the fifty dollar bill fluttered to the ground and settled under a toilet resting on its side.

Carver picked his way to a cleared area between the rubble and the building. He was limping toward the entrance when the search beam from a squad car caught him.

"Freeze. Police," he heard behind him.

CHAPTER 23

Carver sat in the conference room of the Byers Juvenile Home on 13th and Claymore waiting for some case worker they'd assigned to him. He glanced around. The walls were full of those stupid posters he'd seen in school, like that cute little kitten advising him to hang in there. Stupid cat had no business on the clothesline, anyway. Deserved to get hung. The furniture must have come from the schools, too, after it'd gotten all beat-up.

He was using his key to gouge the word *bullshit* deeper into the table when he heard the doorknob rattle behind him. He stashed the key and assumed the position he'd used all the way through the questioning and the trial: crossed arms, relaxed slump into the chair, right ankle on left knee, his face a mask of indifference.

The door opened and closed. The case worker stayed behind him, his clothes rustling as he took off his jacket and hung it on the coat rack in the corner. Sheeit, the dude was taking his time. Carver waited. He heard a briefcase open and papers being slipped out. More rustling and he could hear breathing, but nothing happened. He felt his face soften with curiosity and hardened it up again. Come on, dude, get around here and check out my cool. Another rustle and paper being shuffled. Carver turned to look. Sheeit, another honky.

He looked at Carver and waited.

Carver turned back and still the dude said nothing. Carver waited. Papers shuffled again and the case worker moved but didn't come into sight. Carver couldn't stand it anymore. "You come in here to read or what?"

"Hmmm."

"Well, I got better things to do with my time." Carver got up and turned toward the door.

The honky was standing in front of it, a file folder open in his hands. "Sit down. And let's get things straight from the outset. This is *my* time," he said calmly. "We will be here one hour three times a week whether either of us says a word or not." He came around to the other side of the table. A dude not much taller than Carver but built like a wrestler. He was wearing a loose brown sweater with a blue plaid shirt under it, old jeans and hiking boots. He had shoulder length brown hair, a mustache, a short beard, and round steel-rimmed glasses over a straight thin nose. He could be twenty-two or forty-two. He had about as much style as some ol' honky preacher.

"I'm Mister Lathrop."

Carver resumed his position in the chair and screened his face with contempt.

The honky sat down and leaned back with both hands behind his head. "Tell me why you're here."

"You ain't my Momma. I don' gotta talk to you."

Mr. Lathrop glanced through the file in his lap. "Reckless endangerment, firearm without permit, accessory to auto theft, attempted manslaughter. Quite a list. Lucky you just grazed her hip and the woman had the breath knocked out of her." He ran the thumb and index finger of his left hand along the bottom of his moustache and continued. "Apparently the arresting officer wasn't your 'Momma,' either, or the D.A., or the judge."

Carver shifted his weight and looked disgustedly at the floor to his left. "Buncha honkies."

"I see. Well, you can make up your mind about talking to this honky later. For now you just listen. These are the conditions of your staying here rather than in jail. One: you will keep your area clean and neat and will help with the general work. A duty sheet is posted every week in the common room. You do your share without complaining, and do it right the first time. Two: you will go to school every day and meet all your classes. Tomorrow you and I go to East High and get you registered."

Out of the corner of his eyes Carver watched him take out a pile of forms and slide them over the table till they rested on top of *bullshit*.

"Every Friday," he droned on, "you will bring home a progress report with each teacher's signature in ink. It will show the number of absences and tardies, your attitude, and a grade for the week. I check regularly that all the signatures and comments are genuine."

He sat back and looked calmly at his hands. "Three: you will be in the home at the prescribed times. That means thirty minutes after your last class until the next morning. There's a basketball court behind the building and a ping-pong table and some weight equipment in the basement. Any questions before I go on?"

Carver gave him a sniff for an answer.

"Four: Tuesdays, Thursdays, and Fridays you meet me here at 7:30. We use that time to try to get you on a track that doesn't lead to prison. We go over any problems that come up in school and I check homework. It's going to be hard in the beginning. Believe me, I won't like it any better than you, but within a couple of months you'll realize I'm the one person who's on your side. And that about covers it."

Carver glanced at him, snorted slightly, and tossed his head.

"No questions? Okay, let's get started filling out the forms." He shoved registration forms, emergency cards, and class offerings along the table.

Carver shifted slowly around. He took the first self-duplicating form with his thumb and forefinger as if it smelled of chicken bones when his Momma forgot to take out the trash.

Mr. Lathrop shoved a Bic pen across the table.

Carver took it and started filling in the blanks automatically. He'd get outta this shit soon. He'd find a way. He'd go...where?

CHAPTER 24

Two months later, Carver sat wedged in the middle of the back seat of the home's van. On his left sat Luke Tobler, the honky he'd been paired with for the weekend. On his right was "High" Dodd, a mulatto and a cool enough dude if he hadn't been a fuckin' Blood. Mr. Lathrop was driving and Mr. Johnson, the black counselor of the home, had the other front seat. The Tom actually seemed to be enjoying his little chat with Dipstick Lathrop.

It was the Memorial Day Weekend and the two shitheads had arranged for a "survival experience" somewhere in the mountains. They were headed up some fuckin' river with a French name that sounded like Pooder. Mr. Johnson had explained about it as they'd turned off of the interstate and driven through Fort Collins. Johnson and Lathrop had been classmates at the college there. No sheeit. Carver made a cool display of inattention. But once in the canyon he couldn't help sneaking a look past Luke or High, depending on whose side the river was on.

"Hey look, there's a road named Stove Prairie," Luke practically yelled in his ear. Everybody thought that was real funny.

"There's a story about that road," said Lathrop. "They say there used to be an old Indian woman who lived somewhere up there.

They called her Rattlesnake. Lived all alone for years and years. She supposedly shot at people who tried to get too close to her."

Yeah, right.

"Why don't you go up and see if you can find her, Mr. Lathrop?" asked High. "Maybe she'd shoot you and put us out of our misery."

"Yeah, go look her up,"

"Go check her out," yelled the others.

What was this, a fuckin' chorus?

Lathrop turned and grinned. "No such luck, High. Then the cops'd get her and they'd have to put her away somewhere. You know how overcrowded the prisons are. They'd probably have to put her in with you."

They all howled and shoved at High. Carver allowed himself a small snort of amusement.

The river shifted to the other side of the road just before they entered The Narrows. Carver looked out at the huge mass of churning water that was almost up to the pavement, but he had to look past Luke-the-spook and it made him queasy. Better not think I'm looking at *him*. Sheeit, don't make me puke.

The sun went in and the air turned so cool it felt like winter again. After lunch in a restaurant full of stuffed heads and animal skins, the trip up to the Cameron Pass campground was quiet. Just like him, most of the dudes had never been out of the city before. Nobody liked the "sleeping arrangements" the counselors had announced, a black and a white boy to each tent, sleeping bags on rubber mats.

The more Carver thought of it, the angrier he became. They had no right to force him to do anything this stupid. A three day weekend with no running water or TV or even radio. "Activities" in which he and Luke had to work together. Fuckin' Luke, Mr. Johnson's little pet, always talking about how stupid he'd been to end up in the home, how he was going to go to college when he got out. Ass-licker. Carver snorted and shook his head. Everyone else was looking at Poudre Falls on the right.

By the time they reached the campground the sun was out again. The counselors assigned them to camp sites and showed them how to pitch their tents. Luke picked up their tent, and Carver followed him to a site, dragging the sleeping bags across the damp dirt road, breathing like he was running from the cops. He stopped. The air was different up here, not like in Denver at all.

Carver tried to look at his watch, but the tent was too dark. And it was cold. The air felt like so much fuckin' ice biting at his nose and ears and all around his head where it was shaved. Even the pistol left unshaven on the back felt cold. He tried to pull the sleeping bag up over his head. Stupid Luke was sleeping like the baby that he was. There wasn't a sound in the whole camp ground except for the wind flapping at the side of the tent. Too fuckin' quiet. What time was it anyway?

He reached out of the sleeping bag and pulled the flap open. Outside, the campground was almost as bright as day in the full moon, but a new thought made him forget to look at his watch. He could get away if he left now. Yeah, just run. It was the chance he'd been waiting for. When they found out he'd left, they'd think he'd headed back to Denver. What he'd do was, he'd go in the other direction, through the woods. He was tough. How far could it be to the next town? He'd take out a filling station or an all-night Safeway or something and head for...where? Someplace where it didn't get this fuckin' cold. L.A. maybe.

He eased out of the sleeping bag without unzipping it and crawled out of the tent. Luke never moved a muscle. Sheeit, that wind was cold. He reached in and grabbed the down jacket the home had provided and slipped into it. He drew the sleeping bag out and carried it to the picnic table to roll it up. Dipstick Lathrop had said it was a good down bag. Ought to be worth something.

He checked his watch. It wasn't even eleven thirty. He listened. The wind had stopped for a minute and it was so damn quiet his ears were ringing. He shook his head and listened again. Not a single sound. He looked at the moon. Jeez, it was bright. He'd never seen it so white. Clear air up here. He shivered. "Well, sheeit," he whispered, "if I'm gonna leave, what the hell am I doing standing around staring at the stupid moon?"

He rummaged in the ice chest on the next table, took out a package of hot dogs and a six-pack of Cokes. He was about to stuff everything into his jacket when he spotted Dipstick's back pack lying on the bench. There were some things in the bottom of it, and when he'd stuffed the sleeping bag into it there was no more room for the Cokes. He jammed the hot dogs into a front pocket, slung the pack over his left shoulder, and grabbed the six-pack.

As he set out, the wind kicked the back of his head, cold and stronger than before, pushing him forward. He'd gone halfway through the moonlit campground before he realized he was headed back toward the road when he wanted to go the other way. A big cloud bank was hanging over the mountains in that direction, too. Angrily retracing his steps, he tiptoed past the sleeping counselors.

The moon was directly above him, lighting his way; the wind was at his back, biting through his jeans. Other than that, this was a piece of cake. That shithead honky Lathrop. Couldn't even figure out someone would just take off like this.

Where the trail entered the forest, Carver turned around for one more look, gave a little snort of contempt that turned into silent laughter, and strode off through the trees.

Two hundred yards later he shifted the Cokes to his left hand and put the right in his pocket. Sheeit, why hadn't they given them any gloves? Probably wanted them to get frost bit. It took about two minutes for his left hand to be too cold to carry the six-pack. He unzipped the jacket and stuffed the cokes inside. Before he even tried to zip it up again, the cold wet cans sent a shudder through his whole body and he took them out. He stopped and set the back pack down on a rock. He took out the sleeping bag to see what was in the bottom of the pack.

The clouds caught up with the moon and suddenly there was no light.

"Holy mother fuckin' sheeit," he swore aloud.

He started at the sound of his own voice and peered around in the dark. Even when his eyes had adjusted, he still couldn't make out what he was carrying under the sleeping bag. He stuffed the bag back in, shouldered the pack, and set out again, leaving the six-pack behind the rock. He stopped to think. The campground was behind him, right? So if he just kept his back to the wind...

It was much harder now. Uphill all the time, and he was breathing like an elephant. Ahead of him through the trees he could see a few stars. Here it was so dark he couldn't even tell whether he was still on a trail. Sheeit, why hadn't he thought to look for a flashlight? He put his hands behind him and poked at the bottom of the pack. A branch with a thousand needles hit him in the face, in the eye. He stopped, waited for his eye to stop watering, and from then on kept his hands at eye level in front of him.

He was making so much noise. With every movement the down jacket gave a squeaky swish. If anything came at him, he probably wouldn't even hear it. He stopped to listen. Nothing. Except this ringing in his ears. Would that block the sound of somebody behind him? He turned around. "Chicken," he whispered and started out again. To his left something snorted and bounded away through the trees. Carver stopped, pumping adrenaline, his heart pounding. The dark was squeezing everything out of him, making him very small.

"Hadda be some kinda animal, a deer," he forced himself to say aloud. "Couldn't be a bear; that woulda made a lot more noise.

Wouldn't it? Just so fuckin' sudden." His hand found a tree and he leaned against it for support.

He started out again. He was going downhill now and had to watch his footing. "Watch." He snorted at his own choice of words. "As if I could fuckin' *see*." He knelt and tied his high-tops all the way to the top, fumbling with the laces and the holes in the dark. "Whadda they wear 'em with the tongues hanging out like that for anyway?" he said as he started again. His hands brushed a branch in front of his face and it snapped from the tree, banging like a rifle.

"Sheeit, I can't see where I'm going. I could end up back in the campground. That's all I need. Dipstick and the Tom organizing the others into a posse to look for me. Laugh theyselfs silly if I showed up there again with Dipstick's pack." He pushed on and crashed head-on into a tree.

He knew he'd been walking for hours through the forest, most of the time downhill. Now it was all uphill. His heart was prob'ly getting' blisters banging against his ribs that way. And always the fuckin' wind blowing down his collar. Finally, he reached a clearing and the going was easier. He stumbled over a big rock and then sat down on it to rest. He was breathing hard. Holy sheeit, the rock was cold under him. In fact, the air felt colder than when he'd left the camp, even though he'd been on the move and should be warmed up. A few flakes hit him in the face. Behind him came a hoo-hoo sound. He whipped around. For a few seconds there was silence again; then a rhythmic whushing came right at him. Something huge and darker than the night brushed his head. Carver stumbled toward the trees without thinking of the direction.

A few feet into the trees again, he dropped the back pack and sat down with his back to a tree. He couldn't seem to catch his breath, his legs were exhausted, his feet hurt, and he was thirsty.

Jeez, he needed something hot to drink. How far could it be to the next town? "Wish I'd'a took High with me," he thought. "Be a fuckin' sight better with two."

It was no good sitting. He was freezing. And if the cold didn't kill him, he'd die of thirst. Goddamn fuckin' Lathrop. He got up, shouldered the pack, and set out again. This time he wouldn't stop until he reached a town. In his determination, he set a pace that he could keep.

It was almost dawn, and he knew he was about a million miles from the campground. It was gonna to be a lousy day, already spitting snow. He was trudging uphill through rock formations that were small mountains, a few open meadows, and trees. He was so fuckin' sick of the trees.

Ahead of him he heard water running. He came to a stream that was about six feet down an embankment. On the other side a trail led around the rocks that towered over the stream. He was directly at the head of a narrow path down to the water. Must be an animal trail. With a cry of relief he threw off the pack and started down. Something caught at his left foot and he lurched forward, tried to catch his balance, turned his foot as he came down wrong on a rock, and pitched headlong down the embankment. He heard a loud crack and thought he'd been shot. One end of the aspen log he'd broken rolled into the water. The other bounced up, came back down and banged his head into a rock. His last thought was that he'd die here. Fuckin' Lathrop.

CHAPTER 25

Red Moon limped around the last outcropping of the rock above the stream where she'd set her snare, hoping for an animal large enough to last for several days. It was snowing already, and the pain in her hip told her the snow would be deep and very wet.

She stopped and stared. On the other side, a man was lying with both legs stretched up the bank and his head almost in the water, hidden by a broken aspen log. She backed behind the rock, her heart beating, making a hot pain across her chest. She listened a minute, but he was not making any noise. She peeped around the rock. He hadn't moved. She inched closer to the stream, looked again, and gasped. His face was black. She slapped her hand over her mouth with her hand to prevent another sound.

She stepped behind a tree and watched. His eyes were closed, but a blue jacket bloated up like dead deer moved a little with his breathing. He was alive. Pictures swirled in her mind. She shook her head in quick jerks. A blurred, smiling face with a thin beard appeared. He'd told her there were black people. What did he say? They came from far away.

At the top of the other bank, a coyote approached, went down on her belly, and sniffed warily at a green bag with a lot of belts on it. Her two pups romped down the bank and sniffed at the man. She yipped to call them back, the man twitched, and they raced to their mother. All three coyotes disappeared without another sound.

The black man groaned. Through the flat lower branches of the fir tree she saw him reach up and rub the back of his head. Then he tried to sit up, moaned, and lay down again slowly. In a minute he turned onto his side and drew his feet down. He let out a scream loud enough for them to hear all the way down in the town.

Red Moon flinched and looked around.

Slowly, he shoved himself to his knees and faced up the bank away from her. He tried to stand, let out another cry and went back down. He sat with his back to her and rubbed his right ankle, whimpering like a wounded coyote.

She should leave him alone. She looked at the top of the embankment where he'd torn out her snare. She checked beyond the green bag for other people. There were always more than one and they wore such bright clothes that she could spot them long before they saw her. This time there was no one. She should leave him alone. The man was hurt. She did not want them to come. But this one was black. Perhaps the black ones were different. If she helped him would he bring others to find her? Would they hang her from a tree? But it was all so long ago. Maybe the time of hate was over. The man was hurt.

The black faces had come so often over the winters on the mountain, the ones in the threatening clouds, the one left by the fire, which had glared across the valley at her for many seasons. She remembered waiting for a sign, but it could not have been the black faces. They were just something she'd heard from her mother and Rattlesnake, she was sure. Almost. He was hurt. Could she run from him?

Had she been waiting all this time for this black man? It wasn't possible. Mother Earth would not make her wait until she was too old and then send the special thing. She turned to slip away before he knew she was there. But he was hurt.

Red Moon stepped from behind the tree and inched down the bank without making a sound or taking her eyes off the man. It hurt her left hip, climbing so slowly in the damp, cold air. She stepped across the water on rocks and came up behind him. He was still whimpering. She stared at his head. It was all square on the top and on the back the hair grew in the shape of a gun. It made the pain shoot across her chest again. Above the gun was a big bump that had bled a little.

He still didn't know she was there. She could get back to the rocks without giving herself away.

He was talking to himself. "Sheeit, mother fuckin' ankle's broke."

She looked at the smooth black skin at the back of his neck. He must be young, calling for his mother like that.

She put her hand out and touched his shoulder. The boy jumped, screamed in pain, and turned around. He looked at her and screamed again. Red Moon gasped and backed into the stream. He scrambled backwards up the bank, shoving himself with his left foot, and stopped out of her reach. He grabbed his right foot, screaming "aaaaah," and stared at her. His eyes were about to pop out and his face had turned the color of ashes.

"Hey, man!" he yelled.

Red Moon panicked and jumped behind a rock to hide. She looked out. There was no man. The boy was still yelling. He did not look at all like Rattlesnake with black skin. Mother Earth could not have sent him.

"Jesus," he said, "You scare the shit outa me sneakin' up like that. Who you, anyway?"

Red Moon did not understand any of it. All the words punched through the air at her like fists. She looked around again to be sure there was no one else and edged closer. She kept her eyes on his but reached for his foot. He pushed away with the left foot. She grabbed the bottom of the left leg and put her other hand up with the palm toward him. She relaxed her grip on his leg and he stopped. She picked his right leg up by the calf and pulled up the bottom of the jeans. He had on a strange cloth boot tied right up around his ankle, but the dark skin puffed out around the top of it. She looked back at his face. He was still staring at her.

She sat back on her knees. Binding it would not do much good now. She could poultice it.

"You think it's broke?"

She motioned to him to get up.

"Hey, man, you think it's broke?"

She glanced around again. He thought...? "Not man, woman." She stepped up to where she could get her hands under his right shoulder and pulled. He struggled up, and she put his arm around her shoulders and reached around his waist. Her arm sank right into his strange coat till it found something solid. She looked up at the box of wiry hair and shook her head.

"What you looking at, man? Ain't you never seen a boxtop before?"

"Not man, woman."

She headed him down toward the stream.

"This the way to L.A.?"

Red Moon frowned, trying to understand. He stopped and turned back. She let go. He teetered for a minute and then hopped back toward the slope where he'd fallen. He tried to put his weight on his right foot.

"Aaaaah, sheeit," he said. "Come on, man—woman, I gotta go this way. Help me up the bank."

"Help you here," said Red Moon, pointing up the other side of the stream.

"What, you from some town around here? I gotta find a place to take care of this ankle, then I'm splitting, hear?"

She supported him again and they made their way slowly up toward the rocks.

At the top of the bank he growled some more ugly words, turned around again, and pointed at the green bag. "Gotta get the backpack," he said when she pulled at him.

"I come back."

He banged into tree limbs, smashed crackling pine cones under his foot, and yelled at her about the cold and snow all the way through the woods and around the face of the cliff. When she let him stand alone for a minute while she opened the door he stopped talking. She looked back, expecting him to hop in after her. He was just standing there with all his weight on his left foot, his mouth open and his eyes about to jump out again.

She helped him in and pointed to the old bear skin, but he was looking everywhere else. She led him to it and pointed at it across the log that was holding up the weak spot in her wall. He just stood there. What was wrong with him? The pine needles under it were fresh; she'd changed them as soon as the ground was dry after the last snow.

She forced him slowly under the log and then down until he was sitting. She shoved a few pieces of firewood under the bear skin where his swollen foot would rest. Then she made him lie down. She dropped some herbs into the warm water left from breakfast and soaked a woven strap that she used to bundle firewood. She untied the lace of his shoe and pulled it out before taking the shoe off. There was a dirty white sock under it, bunched around his heel. It smelled like the mule after a trip to the Rio Grande. She pulled it off, too, and this time he yelled. She wrapped the poultice around the foot and ankle and tied it with a strip of squirrel skin. Now he was staring at that.

"I come back," she said, and started back to get the bag he wanted.

CHAPTER 26

"Hey, man!" yelled Carver Powers as the last of her shadow disappeared from the doorway. He leaned back on his elbows, shifted his foot on the skin, and stared around him.

"Jesus H. Christ, I don' believe this," he muttered. The old woman had brought him to some kinda Hallowe'en cave and then just left. He lay on the skin hardly conscious of his throbbing ankle or the ache in his head. This was some woman from the stone ages. The place smelled like smoke and leather. There was only dim light coming in through the door she'd left open, dumb woman, and snow flakes were piling in. The door was tied to a tree trunk by leather thongs through the old hinges. In fact, the whole wall was made out of trunks with branches still on them. His skin began to crawl. There were furry things hanging from all the branches, and some kind of burlap sacks. A lot of them had pictures of plants on them.

Past the shafted light, in the dark reaches of her cave, hung an old mat or towel, kind of gray-green with a crazy reddish circle in the middle. Or was it a diamond? Why'd anybody keep an old rag like that? Man, even when it was new, the thing must have come from the Good Will.

The tops of all the tree trunks that made up the wall rested against a rock ledge; the sloping ceiling of the room looked like rock, too, only it was all black. A chimney went out from the top of an old stove through a crack in the rock. Two little stone walls supported the stove, with openings to the sides of the room. A pile of ashes and a couple of half-burned pieces of wood lay under the stove. Man, the guys were never going to believe this.

Close to the thing he was lying on was a thinner trunk jammed between the floor near the back of the room and one of the tree trunks that made up the wall. He peered up at the point where the two trunks joined. Looked like a crack in the wall, but it was hard to tell in the dim light. On the other side of the stove there was something made of upright logs.

"Man, this is unreal. What kinda person live like this?" Her face came back to him, all leathery like Momma's brown slippers before she finally threw 'em away. Two gray braids so long he didn't even see the end of 'em. Sorta bald above the temples. What the hell kinda clothes was she wearing, anyway? Looked like a buncha squirrel skins sewed together. Hands like old claws, dried and cracked. Skinny as a line of coke.

The light changed for a second and the backpack thumped to the floor. He jumped. "Hey, man! Don' go sneakin' up on people like that. Somebody gonna off you one day you keep doin' that." Jesus, she hadn't made a sound coming back.

CHAPTER 27

R ed Moon looked down at the figure on her bed. She pointed
at the green bag.

"Yeah, thanks," he said. His stomach growled loudly. "You got
anything to eat around here?" he asked. His words still felt like a
fist punching the air.

She understood "eat." She moved to the ledge behind the stove
and took a piece of jerky out of the old poncho bag.

"Wa's this?" he said, taking it between his thumb and first finger. He held it to his nose and made his face very ugly. "Hey, man,
I got some hot dogs!" he said, throwing the jerky on the floor. He
pulled his bag toward him and opened a pocket, making a terrible
ripping noise. He took out a shiny package with pink fingers in it.
"Gimme a knife," he said without looking at her.

Red Moon took the strange package and turned it around in
her hands.

"Hey." He grabbed the package and glared up at her. "You get
your own food. You can eat that tree bark if you wanna. Not me,
man, no way."

She looked in his black eyes. A pair of gray-blue eyes took their
place, full of hatred. She backed away. Then he put out his hand,
waiting for something.

"Gimme a knife, man."

"I am woman, boy."

He put his hands on the skin and shoved himself forward with his chin out. "Look, man, don' you go be callin' me 'boy'!"

Red Moon looked again hard. The chest was still covered by the coat, but there was some hair growing out of the chin. She'd thought the voice was a boy's. "You girl?!"

He clicked with his tongue and looked pained. "No, I ain't no girl. Look, didn't nobody never tell you you don't go around calling black boys 'boy'?"

Red Moon understood some of the words but not the question. She was trying to figure out an answer when he said, "Okay, maybe nobody ever did. You call me Carver, see. My name's Carver."

"Carver."

"So wha's your name?"

Red Moon looked in the eyes again, the eyes that had no happiness. "Rattlesnake."

"Say wha'?"

"Rattle..."

"Yeah, I hear ya. Man, Old Dipstick was telling us about a old Indian woman name o' Rattlesnake. That you?"

"I am Rattlesnake."

"You ever shoot people come too close?" He looked around and spotted the two old rifles behind the loom. His eyes widened.

"Shoot at people try to hurt me. Not kill them. Before long time." She would not tell him she hadn't had any bullets since she shot the bear.

"Listen, man—Rattlesnake, I ain't come here to hurt you. I didn't even know you was here."

Red Moon waited. His stomach growled into the silence. She looked at the package in his hands.

"Yeah, the hot dogs. You got a knife, Rattlesnake? I can open 'em with my teeth, but it's better with a knife."

Red Moon took her knife from the board that was stretched across two of the tree branches. It had once been a big knife but she'd sharpened it on the rocks so many times it had worn through in the middle and then broken. All that was left was a point of sharp metal sticking out of a big handle. She picked up one of the rifles before returning to the bed and handing Carver the knife.

He backed as far from her as he could on the bed. "Look, lady, I told you, I ain't trying to hurt you. Here, you can open 'em yourself." He handed her the package and the knife.

Red Moon leaned the rifle against a log, took the knife in one hand, the package in the other, and made a slit across the middle, slicing through all of the fingers.

"Naw!" yelled Carver.

She dropped the package and jumped back, holding the knife in front of her.

"That ain't how you do it. Ain't you never seen a hot dog before?"

Red Moon looked at him.

"Give 'em to me. Maybe they be one in there you ain't ruint."

She shoved them across the dirt floor with her foot.

He slapped his forehead and groaned. "You don't know nothing, do you, woman?" He picked up the package. It was still holding together on one side. He took out a piece of a finger and brushed it off with his other hand. Then he put it in his mouth. He made the ugly face again. "You got some boiling water?"

Red Moon poured a cup of water from the old coffee pot.

"Naw, man, I mean *hot* water."

She shook her head.

"You got a coat hanger?"

Red Moon didn't understand the question, but it made him laugh. He looked around her house.

"A coat hanger!" he said again, still laughing. It was not a nice laugh. "Okay, you got a thin stick?"

She went to the pile of kindling wood and came back with a stick as long as her hand. That set him off again.

"I need a *long* stick to roast this weenie on, see?"

Red Moon took out a stick as long as her forearm and as big around as her little finger.

"Can you make me a fire?"

Red Moon clicked the spark maker under a few dry leaves. Nothing happened. She tried several more times before the leaves caught. The spark maker would be useless soon.

When the fire was going Carver stuck his "hot dog" on the end of the stick. "Pretty neat you can reach the fire from the bed," he said. He held the food over the fire. The smell was fatty but it made Red Moon's mouth water. He took it out again after a while. It was all black, and he blew on it for a minute before putting it in his mouth and pulling it off the stick.

He burned almost all of them the same way. When there were only a couple of the fingers left, he glanced up at her. She looked away and stopped working her mouth. "Hey, Rattlesnake," he said, "you want one? I ain't got nothing else to eat, but they ain't enough left for another meal, anyway. You can try one."

Red Moon inched forward and he put another one on the stick and burned it for her. He handed it to her; she blew on it and then pulled it off the stick. It was the fattiest thing she'd ever eaten, but it tasted good. She nodded. He almost smiled.

"Well, it ain't a Big Mac. Man, what I wouldn't give for a Big Mac," he said. "You want another one?" Red Moon ate another, and he gave her the last one. Then he lay down. "Holy, sheeit, I'm tired," he said. He closed his eyes. Within a minute he was asleep.

She covered him, put more wood on the fire, and then left, closing the door behind her. The wind was howling down from the north and the snow was coming down harder than before. Already it was drifting onto the ledge above her wall. She'd better find a rabbit or a squirrel in a trap to feed this mean boy.

The taste of the hot dog rumbled up from her stomach all afternoon. It tasted awful the second time around. She should have left him alone.

CHAPTER 27

Carver woke to the sound of someone mumbling and looked around, confused. Oh, yeah, that cave place. At the stove the old Indian woman was muttering away and doing a weird little bow toward the pot on the stove. The room would have been totally dark except for the fire. He started to sit up and dragged his ankle over the logs she'd put under his legs. It hurt like hell. No way he was gonna walk on it now. He was stuck with the old bat till he could.

As he pulled himself up, he noticed the cover she'd laid over him. Some kind of woven thing that looked like strips of fur with a lot of feathers stuck in it. Smelled like leather, only not so strong. Where'd she get all this junk, anyway? And what the hell was she doing? "Hey, man, who you talking to?"

The woman jumped and turned toward him.

"Rabbit," she said, and pointed at the pot.

He grated up a sound from his throat to show how stupid *that* was. "You call your pot 'rabbit'?"

"Rabbit *in* pot. Thank him for life. Have to kill him to eat."

"Man, you mean to tell me you thank the rabbit 'cause you hadda off him?"

She drew her old leather forehead into a million cracks like she did when she couldn't understand plain English.

"You...had...to...*kill*...him?"

"Yes. Thank all things of Mother Earth for help."

"Holy mother fuckin' sheeit, she feel bad about offin' a dumb rabbit. Wait'll the guys hear about this!"

She gave him that look again.

"I gotta tell my friends about you."

"No."

"Come on, man, you like some cave woman I met gettin' off a time machine. Why not?"

"No."

Carver shrugged. How was the old bag of bones gonna know if he told, anyway? "How long you been living in this spook-cave, Rattlesnake?" He pointed at the creepy branch-thorns of her wall.

"Long. Many winter."

"Why?"

She lowered her head and stirred the pot without even looking at him.

"Well, it don't matter to me. What time is it?" He tried to see his watch but the room was too dim. The door was closed now. There was a small window in it, two glass panes. Below them a board was tied through its knotholes to the panels of the door. There was no light coming through the glass, but the wind was whining through the cracks. "Is it still snowing?"

The old woman nodded.

The fire had warmed the small room. He unzipped his jacket and took it off. The woman stared and then picked the jacket up off the floor. She looked at the zipper for a long time and listened to the nylon whistle under her ragged nails.

The smell of the food was getting to him.

"Guess it's supper time, huh? Man, I could eat a horse."

"No more horse. Eat before long time."

Carver rolled his eyes. "Jeez."

She took a hollowed out piece of wood, spooned some stuff out of the pot into it, and handed it to him. It smelled funny. Carver held it low to the light. It looked sorta like spinach, all greeny and slimy. "Jesus H. Christ, man, you got dandelion flowers swimmin' in there. You gotta be crazy if you think I'm gonna eat flowers." He picked the flowers out as if as if they might shock him and dropped them one by one onto the dirt floor. He peered into the bowl again. There was some lumpy white stuff with bones sticking out of it in the bottom of a broth, some things that looked like French fries they forgot to cook, and fingery leaves with thorns all around them. He gingerly picked a leaf out of the soup and wrinkled his nose.

"This stuff gonna tear my mouth apart! Ain't you got nothing else?" He stared at the hugely serrated leaf. "What is this stuff?"

"Thistle."

"Jeez, man, I could eat thistle every day of my life if I wanted to. Grows all around the playground. Who ever heard of eating thistles? How you know this stuff ain't poisonous?"

"Eat all my life. Taste good. This young plant."

"Who cares how old it is? You sure no dogs pissed on it?"

"Piss?"

He let his shoulders droop with impatience. "Peed. Jeez. Wee-weed. Went...to...the...bathroom?"

"No dog."

Carver shook his head. "Soon's my foot's better, I gotta get outa here and get some real food."

She handed him a wooden spoon. She started eating out of the pot with another wooden spoon. Her very first mouthful was one with flowers, and she looked him straight in the eye while she chewed it.

Carver took another whiff, listened to the rumble of his stomach, and put the spoon to his lips. It tasted greeny, all right, but it wasn't as slimy as he'd expected. He put a spoonful in his mouth. The thorns on the leaves sort of prickled. The stew wasn't too bad, a little like bland soup.

"You got any salt?"

The woman got up from whatever she was sittin' on—Jesus, it looked like an old saddle—and went behind the stove. She made a chipping noise and came back, holding out her hand with some teeny white lumps in the palm.

"I don't know why I expected a salt shaker. Where you buy stuff like this?"

"Not buy. Find on ground down in big...don't know word." She pointed past him. "Down there."

"What, a valley? Okay, well, where I come from we just run in the 24-hour Safeway and get it off a shelf."

"Where you come from?"

"Denver, of course. Where'd you think?"

"Across big water."

"Naw, ain't no big water between here and Denver, 'less you mean that river down there with the French name. Ain't you never been nowhere, Rattlesnake?"

"Taos."

"Where's that at?"

"South."

"You mean like Florida?"

She didn't answer. Man, the woman was dumb.

"You never even been down to Denver?"

She didn't answer again.

"It's the big ol' city at the foot of the mountains."

"We stayed in mountain. Too hot. Dry."

"Who's 'we'?"

"Me and Rattlesnake."

"I thought *you* was Rattlesnake," he said around a lump with a bone in it.

"My man was Rattlesnake."

"I don' get it."

"You have mother in Denver?"

"Yeah, sure, my Momma an' my two brothers LaRon and Odelle. I used to have another brother, Keeno, but they shot him."

She jerked back from him. "Who?"

"The Bloods."

She was giving him that look again.

"That's the other big gang. See, they wear red and they have their turf where they control the drugs and all. And the Crips, we wear blue and we mark our turf with blue spray paint. Keeno, he didn't wanna be in no gang, and my Momma woulda beat the living shit outta him, anyway. One night me and Keeno was throwing a football out in the park on Thirty-eighth. The Bloods drove by and sprayed the park with bullets instead of paint, and Keeno caught it."

"What mean, 'caught it'?"

Carver hardly heard the question. Before his eyes, the yellow police tape rolled off the reel from tree to tree; the sirens screamed and the red and blue lights flashed. Keeno's body lay in the bare dirt, face down with his right arm up, still trying to catch that football, the blood flowing slowly out from under his chest and leg. And ten-year-old Carver was kneeling in the blood, poking his brother in the shoulder, trying to make him not be dead. And Carver was mad. So damn mad at the Bloods. And not crying because he knew crying wasn't tough.

"What mean 'caught it'?"

He turned from her. "Keeno be dead, man."

"I am sorry," said Rattlesnake.

Carver swallowed the lump in his throat and glared at her to keep her sympathy away. "Yeah, well, it happens all the time. No big deal. Anyway, I joined the Crips when I got old enough, and we got back at 'em." He shrugged. "That's the way it goes, man, back and forth. If I hadn'a' got caught, I mighta..."

She was just staring again.

"The cops got me on a whole buncha charges, see? So I ended up in the home and the counselors decided to do this dumb survival weekend." He sat straighter and puffed out a scornful snort. "As if I didn' know how to survive. I'm already older than Keeno ever got."

Rattlesnake didn't look impressed. In fact, she looked like she hadn't heard a word. "They hanged Rattlesnake."

"Who, the pigs?...the cops?...Jesus, the sheriff?"

"Men who had deer. Rattlesnake tried to take because we hungry. Three men with hate. Only one was kind to me after they hanged Rattlesnake, but not help before."

"They hung his ass just 'cause he tried to steal a deer? Man, they don't hang nobody no more. How long ago you talking about?"

"Don't know. Many winter."

"How old was you then?"

"I was not long woman."

"Say wha'? If you mean what I think you mean, you been living like this maybe forty, fifty years. You ever have a radio, Rattlesnake? You know men have been to the moon and back? I wasn't born yet but it was all on TV. Course you ain't got no TV. Man, I couldn' live without TV. You oughta get you one. What you do at night around here?"

"Sleep."

"Come on, man, the nights get awful long in winter. You telling me you go to bed whenever it gets dark?"

She moved her head toward the posts on the other side of the stove. "Sometime weave."

Carver ran his hand over the cover of feathers and skins. 'Yeah, right." He looked at the bowl with the few bones in the bottom of it. "Man, I forgot to pay any attention to what that tasted like. First time I ever ate rabbit. Old Dipstick Lathrop gonna be bumping his gums over this for-*ever.*"

She took the bowl and spoon away and put them in an ancient tin pan with water from the coffee pot. After she'd scattered some berries in the water and washed the dishes, she threw the water outside. She made some adjustment to the board tied to the door, and lay down on the floor on the other side of the stove, her head toward the door.

"You gonna sleep like that?"

"Yes."

"You ain't even got no cover."

"Keep fire going."

"Naw, look, I got a sleeping bag." He opened the fastening at the top of the backpack and Rattlesnake's head jerked up. "Velcro," he laughed, ripping it a couple more times. She was on her knees watching. He started pulling the sleeping bag out. She knelt there and stared as it just kept coming and coming. "You can have your cover," he said, starting to move it toward her.

She put her hands on the sleeping bag and let the fabric slip under her bony fingers. He showed her how to work the zipper. The old leathery face was just like Odelle's the time Carver had shoplifted the bubble-blowing stuff from K-Mart and showed him how to make the bubbles.

He grinned at her. "You wanna try this one?"

She nodded. She laid the bag on the floor, crawled into it, and got the zipper caught trying to pull it up. Carver dragged himself gingerly under the log supporting her wall, loosened it, and zipped it up. She put her head on the saddle and looked up at him. There was half a smile hiding in the old wrinkles.

Carver crawled back to the skin and covered himself with the furs and feathers. Silence settled over the room. Even the fire wasn't crackling any more, just glowing a little. He could feel her feeling him in the room. She'd given him her bed and her only cover without even thinking about it. She really was somethin' else.

"Goodnight, man."

"Goodnight, boy."

CHAPTER 28

R ed Moon did not go to sleep. She listened to the boy's breathing, a sound she'd completely forgotten. The deepening but fitful rhythm filled her home with his thorny presence. Then the peaceful sound of her mother's breath came back, and the straining forward of Rattlesnake's light snoring, as if he were eager to put the sleep behind him and get on with his journey. She wondered whether her own breath sounded as if it were trying to stop.

The sleeping bag warmed and warmed until she was too hot, and she knew the opener would get caught again if she tried to push it back down. She lay with her head on the saddle, seeing this boy's black eyes again, so full of hate. They faded to a cold blue and the hate made her feel tired. Then the warm brown ones took their place. The brown ones used to come often, with the light hair above them and the thin beard below. In the beginning the memory of them made her feel hot, and if they came in the night she'd wake to the rhythm of love-making. Then they made her feel bitter because he'd tried to take the deer and gotten caught. He'd left her. Now the eyes didn't come often. They made her feel sad but soft.

There was another pair, too, so faded only the feel of them remained. Nothing of the face was left, but the hands came, the fingers that flew into the strings, opened them with a flat stick, weaving. She heard the voice chanting but couldn't make out the words. Then they were all there, pulling her in too many directions: Rattlesnake in her memories, his cold hand pulling her to a grave under a pine tree; the couple in the winter meadow, who came every summer and had drawn her to them until she'd seen the woman's face; her mother under the white blanket in the sand, calling her to come and sing a death song at the loom; Carver on her bear skin with his slapping words, his face blended with the blue-black face of Rattlesnake's death and all the black faces that had been her sign.

The pull was strong in all directions; then she came apart with loud snap. Something fell across her and made an angry pain in her left leg. Something else flew down and crashed into her right shoulder. The room filled with howling, flying snow.

"Oh Momma, oh Momma," the boy screamed. "I been shot. I'm blind. Oh God, I'm blind. I'm freezin' to death. Aw, man, it's cold as the morgue. Oh Momma, I been shot." He started kicking at his cover. "Aaaaahh, sheeit, my foot," he yelled.

Red Moon shoved at her cover, but she was trapped in the boy's noisy sleeping roll. She tried to slip out of it, but her left thigh was nailed to the floor. She groaned softly.

"Boy, you not shot. Wall fall down. Wait, I make light."

"Oh, sheeit, I'm still in that fuckin' cave."

She couldn't sit up with the thing crushing her leg and her shoulder in pain. She clenched her teeth, groped for the spark maker, and remembered it was on the other side of the fireplace.

He was yelling "Aaah, aaah," and shoving the snow at her from his face and chest. If he didn't stop moving he might make another log fall.

"Boy!" she said. What was his name? "Carver! Stop now. You make more wall fall."

He was quieter but still breathing hard.

"You have to help. My arm hurt. I can't move. Need the fire maker to make light. On rock by stove. You give me."

"Okay, man, hold on. Gotta get out from under stuff." One of the aspen logs hit the floor, she heard him strain toward the fireplace. He hit something and it crashed against the wall at the back. "Aw, shit." He was feeling around. "Here, this it?" he said, finally.

Red Moon groped in the dark with her left hand till she found his with the spark maker in it. She couldn't reach the kindling or the dry leaves. "Give me feathers from your blanket. Break off piece of the wood that fell on you and give to me."

"Here."

She put the little pile of feathers on the floor next to her and clicked the spark maker. Nothing happened. She tried again... and again...and again.

"Wha's happenin', man?"

"No spark." Fear stung at her like the snowflakes slapping her face. No fire. Her home was broken and freezing. The image of a dead spring flashed back and a frightened girl leaning over a dry cistern, knowing she had to leave her home.

"Holy mother fuckin' shit. This is a helluva time for you to find that out. Why didn't you get a new one?"

"No fire now. I can't..."

"Hey, wait, maybe I got something."

She heard him feeling around and then ripping that bag open.

"Aw-*right*," he yelled, and in a minute he pointed light as bright as the sun in her face. "Old Dipstick had a flashlight in there after all."

She put her hand over her eyes and he moved the light away and pointed it down in the bag. "Hey, yeah, this is where he kept his 'five ways to build a fire.' Looky here." Hunched against the cold, he started pulling things out and showing them to her in the light. Snow whirled into the beam and out again. "A candle.

A magnifying glass. A big old box of matches. A waterproof match holder. *And* a cigarette lighter. Well, thank *you*, Boy Scout. Whaddaya think of that, Rattlesnake?" She could see him grinning at her in the indirect light from the beam.

Red Moon smiled back. "I know matches, I make fire." She started to light it on the floor next to her and then thought better of it. "Can you make fire under stove? I can't move."

Carver pointed the light toward her legs. The pine log had missed the fireplace and fallen across the room so that it blocked the space between him and her. One of the branches pinned her thigh to the floor.

"Your leg broke?"

"Don't know."

"Man, that must hurt."

"Yes."

"You sure don't say nothing an' I'm over here yelling my head off. Lemme get over there and see if I can get you out." He threw off the cover and started to get off the bed. "Damn, it's cold," he said, and reached for the fat coat.

He crawled behind the stove with the light jumping around the room as he moved. He hit his ankle on the rock at the end of the fireplace. A short "Ah" came out, but he looked at her and bit his lip. He set the light on the end of the fireplace with the beam pointed toward the log.

"They ain't much room here. I ain't got a good angle to lift with. You be ready to pull yourself out when I got it up a little."

He strained and Red Moon tried to pull. She felt the hip begin to pull out of the joint again, the way it had the day she backed away from the bear. She groaned. Carver let the log down again slowly. He looked at her and fear crossed his face. Then he said, "Listen, I'm gonna get you outta here, they gotta be another way." He looked behind him at the logs of the loom. "Lemme see if I can use one of them as a lever."

He stepped across her on his knees and untied the side beam. Then he returned and straddled her feet. He put the lever under the end of the log and tried to lift. Red Moon groaned. The lever turned the log and shoved the branch deeper into her thigh. She bit her bottom lip. He let the log down again slowly. He'd made it worse.

He looked at her and then knelt down as far as he could without sitting on her legs. He propped the lever against his right leg, lifted, and pulled back on the log at the same time so that it moved straight up from her leg. His face was drawn with pain but he looked in her eyes. "Now try."

She eased her body back toward the door. She was free.

"Pull the bag out," he said. She jerked it; it snagged on the branch but slid out. He let the lever go and the log fell to the floor, breaking the branch that had pinned her down.

He was grinning. "Can you get up?"

Red Moon tried to support herself on the saddle and the fireplace, but they were too low. Carver crawled over the log and helped, and she was able to stand but couldn't walk.

"You think it's broke?" he asked.

She tried her weight on her left leg. "No, but hurt much."

Carver shook his head. "Man, if I hurt like that, I'd be hollering for a doctor."

They started the fire and when it was going she looked up at snow whirling in through the gap and the pile of it on the floor next to the bed. The mule skin had rotted and now it had torn through most of its length, letting snow in through a long slit that was wider at the top.

Carver was poking around in the bag again and brought out another package.

"Lemme see what this is," he said. He unfolded a cloth made of silver. "Thermal, waterproof blanket," he said, looking at the package. "Let's see if we can use it to keep out the snow."

She fingered the cloth and shook her head before she hopped slowly to the hole and tore a piece of the skin off. She stroked it, remembering. "This mule came with me from hogan," she said. "Died when I stayed in house in shadow. Before came here."

Carver looked up from the bag, where he was still pulling things out. "You mean to tell me when the mule died you cut off his skin and..."

"Tan it. Have many skins between logs and grass. Keep water out better."

"Where you get all them skins?"

"Shoot deer."

"And all them rabbits for the blanket, too?"

"No, trap rabbits and squirrels." Red Moon stopped for a moment. But he had saved her life. He could not want to hurt her now. "No more bullets after shoot bear."

He stopped pulling a thin yellow rope out of the bag and put his hands on his hips. "You mean didn't even have no bullets for the gun you scared me with yesterday?"

"No. You scare me, too."

He frowned at her and then nodded. "I guess we scared the shit outta each other."

"What mean 'shit'?"

"A whole lot." He shrugged with one shoulder. "Well, sort of."

"I guess we scare the shit outta each other," she repeated under her breath.

He reached up with the silver blanket and the rope. "Here, tie the blanket across the hole."

Red Moon looked up. It was too high.

"You ain't got no ladder or nothing to stand on, huh?"

"No."

"Okay, wait a minute." Carver struggled to his feet and hopped to her. It was too high for him, too. "I'm gonna pick you up. Let's just hope I don't fall over and we pull the whole wall down. Where's your leg hurt?"

When she showed him, he bent down and grabbed her around the knees. She balanced herself by holding on to his shoulder and some of the branches as he raised her. The snow lashed her face. He was struggling to stand steady for her, with his weight on his left leg. Ignoring the cold and the pain in her shoulder, she tied the upper corners of the blanket to the tops of the logs on either side of the hole and shoved the edges under the old skin. Carver let her down and she tied off the lower corners. The shiny surface picked up the yellow firelight and glowed into the room.

"How long you think that'll hold?" he asked.

"Not long. Snow heavy. Pull it out again. I make us tea," she said. "Warm us." She poked at the patched wall. "Maybe fire melt snow, make it run down."

Carver took the light beam and pointed it to the other logs of her wall. "I don't see no more weak spots," he said. "Hey, Rattlesnake, who built this thing for you, anyway? Or'd you find it like this?"

"No, build myself. Had horse then. Big horse. And rope from the...men." She scooped some snow from the pile on the floor into the battered coffee pot that had once been blue. "Pulled logs up to top of rock. Worked two summer to get grass up to make warm and hard to see, but winters then dry, not cold like now."

"Where'd you get this stove?"

"From house in shadow."

"Is that the whole stove? Sure is funny looking."

"No, whole stove make too dark. Leave bottom because need light from fire."

He stopped talking. She glanced at him as she took down a rabbit skin with rose hips drawn on it. He was watching her, his eyes pressed together, but he seemed to be somewhere else.

"And Old Lathrop think he know all about survival," he said.

CHAPTER 29

While Rattlesnake made the tea, Carver sat down on the bed, propping his foot on the bear skin. Once he was settled, he looked down at the skin and then put his fingers into the fur where it was still thick around the edges. "This the bear you killed?"

"Yes."

"Musta been one big mother fucker. You musta held a whole pow-wow thanking it. Listen, I think you better sleep here now. You ain't too good with that sleeping bag."

He drank the tea she gave him and it felt good going down, even if it did taste like some kind of flower. They traded beds. Carver slipped into the sleeping bag and lay down parallel to the fallen log. Silence surrounded him again like a mass of black cotton.

"Hey, Rattlesnake, I feel like I'm in a grave. Is it always this quiet here?"

"Yes."

"Man, the silence rings in my ear like I was hearin' a siren from way down in Denver. I ain't never heard such quiet. At home there's always some kinda noise going on."

"That why you talk so loud?"

"I don't talk loud."

"Sound loud to me."

"Well, I guess it would if there's nobody to talk to you."

Rattlesnake didn't say anything, but he heard her swallow hard. He looked over at her in the dim light from the coals. She was lying flat on her back, staring up, and he knew he'd hurt her. Man, a old woman like that. Who'd'a thought she'd have any feelings? Several minutes went by. He couldn't think of anything to say that wouldn't hurt her again.

She sighed and after a long time said, "Thank you."

"What for?" he asked, wondering whether she was being sarcastic.

"You pulled tree off me. Hurt your foot."

"Hey, no sweat."

The silence took over again and Carver strained to hear the sounds that must be just beyond the ringing in his ears. He tried to think of the Bloods, of Momma, even of Dipstick. They were in another world, might as well be on the other side of the sun. He looked up at the shadowy room above him with the tree branches holding the old woman's tea and no telling what else. He put his arm out of the sleeping bag and touched the log he'd lifted for her. I bet I saved her life, he thought. Yeah, for sure. She'd'a been pinned under there till she froze. An' he'd'a probly tried to walk someplace and broke his ankle and froze, too. Then he knew he'd saved her because he was scared he'd die up here without her. He needed her. She'd saved his life, too.

"Hey, Rattlesnake, you still awake?" he asked softly enough not to wake her if she was already asleep.

"Yes."

"Thank you, too."

"What for?"

"You saved my life."

There was a smile in her voice when she said, "I guess we saved the shit outta each other."

When Carver woke the door was standing open and there was a pile of snow in front of it. The sun was streaming in. Even though it wasn't shining right on him, he could feel the difference it made. He glanced up at the sagging thermal blanket. Water dripped from the bottom of it. She must have knocked most of the snow off it before she went out. He pulled himself up and struggled into his shoes, doing the right one gingerly. Without thinking, he tied the laces halfway, as he'd always done in Denver.

"Jesus, my teeth are swimming," he muttered. "The old woman gotta have some kind of bathroom around here." He got up and tested his foot on the way to the door. It still hurt. He grabbed one of the aspen logs that had supported the weak spot in the wall and braced himself on it.

The sun on the snow hit him like a flashbulb that kept on shining. It took him a minute to spot her in her fur clothes. She was standing on a big rock over by the trees on the right. She'd brushed the snow off and steam was rising from the rock in the warm sun.

"Hey, Rattlesnake, you got a bathroom 'round here anyplace?" he yelled, shielding his eyes.

She turned around and her face scrunched up with pain. She motioned him to the right side of the mountain.

Carver stepped away from her door, using the log and placing his feet in the footprints she'd already made. The loose high-tops scooped snow. The light blinded him. He turned away from the sun and gasped. Almost straight up from the top of the shelter was a rock wall taller than the United Bank Building, for Chrissakes, dripping and steaming. But the pressure on his bladder was too great for him to stand around looking at some mountain. He followed her footprints around the west side of the cliff, past a tiny, babbling waterfall to a second stream that slipped silently down a vertical wall between layers of boulders.

"This is the bathroom? Holy shit," he said. Then he giggled at his own pun. On the rock ledges of the mountain's face she had built what could only be a kind of toilet. A couple of sturdy pine logs made up the floor, stretched across the gap and held in place by trees on either side of the slip. On the next higher ledge she'd laid two thick aspen logs, left a space and laid two more. They were all wet with little snow piles on the ends, and the very sight of them sent an icy track down his spine. Far down the sheer slip, the water disappeared into the woods and there was small evidence that this was indeed a toilet.

Cautiously Carver turned around, sat down and gasped. "Man, the woman sure got some weird ways to get her jollies," he muttered as the west wind blew across his bare parts. He used an old Kleenex to clean himself and dropped it down the gap. There were no others. "Gross!"

"Hey, Rattlesnake, ain't you never heard of water pollution?" he yelled, making his way back along the snow covered path. She didn't turn around. She was sitting now on the dry top of the rock. As he approached she moved to make room for him. He repeated the question.

"No."

"Naw, I guess you ain't." He settled next to her. The sun on his back felt great. "Hey, look there. They got a town down there in the middle of nowhere. Must be some sorry town. I bet they don't got a single building over two stories, do they? In Denver we got buildings a hunnerd stories high." He waited to see what impression that made on her. She just glanced at him, barely turning her head.

"You know what town that is?"

"No."

"You mean to tell me you ain't never been down there?"

"No."

He stared at her.

She picked at a spot on her skin skirt. "Tried to go once, but Mother Earth tell me go back. Thought they come, tell me where I go. No one come."

Carver's breath left him as if he'd gotten a fist to the chest. "You been here since you was a teenager? You mean you ain't seen *no one* in what...fifty years?"

She turned her head away. "Sometime see someone."

"Well, what happened? Why didn't you make friends with 'em or something?"

It was a long time before the old woman answered. "Afraid," she said.

Carver looked at her. He started to say something but he saw himself cowering behind a playground carousel, then trying to flatten himself into the dirt behind a bare bush. Sheeit, he'd been scared too, but who'd'a scared an old woman like this?

"Yeah, I hear ya. Well, listen, Rattlesnake, you gotta leave here. You gettin' old now and your house is all broke. They got homes where they take care of ol' people. You gotta sign up for the welfare, but they'd let you live someplace nicer than this. An' you don't gotta be scared no more. Nobody's gonna hurt you now."

She looked at him a long time, almost as if she wasn't really seeing him, and smiled a little. Then she looked back out over the valley. Carver followed her gaze. The whole damn thing was green with just a few patches of snow. To the south and west were mountain ranges, blue at the bottom, the peaks all covered with new snow. The sky was bluer than he had ever seen it. For a minute he could hardly breathe. Jeez, it was so...clean. He couldn't hear a thing. But yeah, there was something, a dripping sound. "What's that?" he asked.

She looked at him with that big question mark all over her face.

"That dripping sound."

She listened for a second. "Snow melt."

Sheeit, it was so fucking quiet you could hear the snow melt. "Man, you don't get that kinda quiet down in Denver. You got your radios goin' all the time, police cars and ambulances and fire trucks with their sirens, traffic noise, people shooting at each other. Always somethin' going on." He listened to the snow again and rubbed his ankle.

Below him a pick-up pulling a camper drove out of the mountains somewhere to the left and headed toward the town, but it was so far away that the melting snow was louder. He swallowed hard. And then the sound intruded after all. It became louder, droning his way from above, and he realized it wasn't the pick-up.

"Damn, a plane!" he yelled and jumped from the rock. "Aw, shit, my foot. They gotta be looking for me. I gotta make 'em see me."

"No," said Rattlesnake, slowly pushing off the rock. "They come here, they see me, too."

"So what, don't you wanna get outa here? Shit, where the hell is that plane?" He started running down the clearing to the trees lining the south edge, limping badly.

"No," yelled the old woman. "Not that way, you fall."

"You stupid old bitch, you just don't want me to get rescued," he yelled without looking back. He pushed through the deep snow in the trees and then there was nothing under his feet. He was flying. He screamed. Not flying. He was falling down a cliff, banging his head, his shoulders, his foot. He was going to die. The full length of his body hit a narrow ledge. In his momentum he nearly rolled off it but threw his downhill shoulder back uphill and came to a stop. His left leg was hanging over the side. Slowly he pulled it back and leaned both knees into the cliff. He lay still for a minute to see if he would die, but all he did was hurt. Overhead the plane droned past. It was way too high to be looking for anybody.

"Carver," Rattlesnake called from above.

"Yeah."

Her head appeared at the top. She was miles above him.

"Can you move?"

He tried. "Yeah, I don't think I broke nothing. I don't know why. Shit, I practic'ly fell all the way to sea level." He stood up and nearly fell the rest of the way down the mountain. The ledge was barely wide enough to allow him to turn around. Every inch of his body hurt.

He peered below and felt a wave of terror swirl through his gut. About another hundred feet almost straight down he'd have hit a field of jagged rocks. Slowly he turned to face the cliff. Steep as a ladder propped against a wall, only no steps. Most of the snow had already melted, leaving the little dirt spongy and wet. He could smell the water in the air. Grasses and sage bushes covered most of the slope and would rip out of the wet ground if he tried to pull himself up on them. It was too steep for him to climb. The few rocks sticking out were far apart.

"Wait," called Rattlesnake.

Carver snorted. As if he could do anything else. "Naw, I think I'll go on home now," he yelled up, but she'd disappeared. In a few minutes she returned and threw a kind of rope over the side. Its end landed about fifteen feet above his head. "Gimme some more rope. I can't reach it."

"No more rope. You come up."

"Yeah, sure, I'll go right off the side," he said, but he began to check for hand holds. He looked down at his feet. "I gotta tie my shoes all the way," he yelled up at her. "Lotsa luck," he muttered to himself, trying to keep his balance on the narrow ledge. His feet were freezing in the wet shoes and socks. Finally, the laces were done and he turned again to the mountainside. Above him Rattlesnake was inching her way out of the trees.

"Wait there, man, lemme try to get up some. You got a bad arm and a bad leg. You gonna hurt yourself again."

"Try rock before you step. Maybe loose."

"Okay, thanks for the warning." He glanced down again and went faint and dizzy. All that open air for him to fall through. He tried to swallow the panic, but he knew that below the air the rocks were waiting for one false move.

To his right was a rock below a sage bush. He leaned far into the slope and slowly moved his right foot up to it. His hip hurt and the sprained foot was throbbing, shooting pain up his leg. He found the rock and started inching his weight onto it. It held but was so rounded that his foot started slipping. He strained his ankle, the pain rocketed up his leg, and he winced. He had no choice but to keep going.

Feeling the air behind him, he looked up at Rattlesnake. She was watching, and she actually looked worried. He was glad he'd said he didn't want her to hurt herself again instead of saying she might come crashing down behind him and then they'd both fall off the mountain. Suddenly he realized why he had said it. He'd meant it. He didn't want her hurt any more.

Through the pain and panic and the effort to keep his balance, the image of the woman at the chop shop came back, flat on her face and not moving. He hadn't felt anything then, even when he'd thought he'd killed her. This was a helluva time to start feeling bad about her. He shoved the image aside and looked for another foothold.

He held his weight on his right foot and inched his left foot onto another rock, smaller but with a good surface. He started looking for another hold and found none above him. Fuck it anyway, why hadn't he checked out the whole slope before he started? He looked to the left of the ledge he'd been standing on and saw several rocks much closer together where he could probably climb, but they would put him to the left of the rope.

"Hey, Rattlesnake, can you let the rope out about ten feet to your right?"

"You find place to come up. I put rope down there."

Carver was balanced on two small rocks, neither of which had room for both his feet. He started to inch back down to his ledge, found himself losing control, sliding toward the rock field. Very slowly drew himself back to the position on both rocks. He had to move across to the spot where he wanted to climb but could only do it by putting both feet on the rock under his left foot. He lay as flat as he could against the slope, the smells of the grass, the wet earth, and the little sage bushes very strong in his nose. Three inches from his eyes were the smallest flowers he'd ever seen, white blossoms the size of a pinhead on skinny red stems.

He inched his left foot to the side of the rock until all his weight was on his heel. Slowly, keeping all his attention on his heel, he shoved himself up and dragged his right foot over until both heels were resting on the rock.

To his left were two stones, the farther one about four feet away. If he could reach it with his left foot he could put his right on the other, but he needed his left foot free with his whole right foot on the rock. Lying against the slope with both feet slewed, his right ankle screaming in pain, he frog-legged his knees down and gave a shove. While his weight was suspended, he freed his left foot and moved the right onto the rock. He was breathing as if he'd been slam-dunking for hours.

He moved his body as far as he could to the left and started stretching for the second rock. He hit the nearer one and felt it loosen. Finally he had the second rock, but it was so high that he couldn't shift his balance to it. He looked up for something to pull himself up on. There was a sage bush, but to reach it he would have to jump his weight to it with his right foot. If the sage let go, he would have no hold at all.

He looked up. Rattlesnake was directly above him, watching anxiously.

"Don't worry, man, I almost got it."

He looked at the bush for a hold. He would only have one chance, and the ledge was no longer below him. There was room for his hand near the root. He shoved with his right foot, grabbed the sage brush, and tried to find the rock. His right foot found it; it fell out and crashed down the mountain. Frantic, he rammed his foot into the hole and his toe caught, sending his ankle into screeching pain. He'd yanked the bush out completely. He let it go and it slid into his face.

He could not see and hardly dared move. He inched his torso to the left as far as he could and then pushed with his right toe to move his hips. His hands searched for anything to hang onto. He found a clump of grass and tried to do no more than maintain his balance with it. Very slowly he inched his body over his left foot.

His hands continued to search and he found the end of the rope. He looked up. Rattlesnake was looking down, smiling and nodding.

"Hey, Rat, I love you, man!" he yelled up at her. She was lying down, her left arm around a tree, the other stretched down, holding the rope. Carver knew she couldn't hold all his weight even with two good arms. He checked ahead and planned his holds for the next several feet, then inched up, using the rope only for security. At last, he called up, "Hey, Rattlesnake, you got enough rope now to wrap it around the tree?"

She got up and wrapped it twice around the trunk. He tested its strength and then scrambled up to her. He was wet and filthy, every part of his body ached, and he felt dizzy. But there was solid ground under his feet. He looked at Rattlesnake and grinned. He took a step forward and started to hug her.

"You hurt your foot?" she asked.

He stopped. "Yeah, some."

"Have to bind it again."

"I dunno. Maybe it's not that bad." He looked back down the cliff and grabbed a branch as the swoon started again. "Funny, it don't look so steep from up here. Man, I nearly killed myself on it though."

She started curling the rope around her hand and elbow, and her face wrinkled with pain.

"Thanks, Rattlesnake."

"Next time, listen."

He looked at the ground and remembered calling her a stupid old bitch, using street talk like that when he really kind of liked the old scarecrow. Well, she probably didn't know what it meant anyway. "Yeah, right. I will." He took the rope from her and finished coiling it.

They started back to the shelter. Carver looked up at the rock face above it. White clouds bottoming to gray were crowding in behind it. The smell of the wet earth filled his nostrils again, a light breeze brought a sweet, warm smell up from the valley. "This some place you got here, man."

She was a little ahead of him. She was limping a lot worse than he was. "That log really hurt your leg, huh, Rattlesnake?"

"Hurt some, but hip hurt more. Old hurt."

"Yeah, when'd that happen?"

"When I shoot bear."

"How'd you shoot it?"

She turned to him, moving her hand from the bald spot above her temple toward her ear, like she had hair there or something. "That bear scare me..."

CHAPTER 30

R ed Moon had returned to her shelter, leading *Bontemps* up the steep trail. They were both carrying loads of grass. Up here it was nearly winter.

She looked critically at her wall, at the sod she'd transferred from several meadows down on the east slope of the mountain. It was taking well, but settling, and the skins were showing through at the top. She would have to fill it in under the overhang again.

She stopped short. Her door was hanging from the leather thongs in the top hinge. The others had been ripped open. She dropped *Bontemps'* reins and the load she was carrying at the edge of the clearing and stepped closer, her heart pounding. They must have come for her. Still, they didn't have to break her door.

A shuffing noise and a growl came from inside. Something fell over and the growl became a roar. She froze, realizing it was an animal, a very large animal to have broken the door from its hinge. Her rifle was in the shelter.

A large brown head appeared in the door and a bear stepped out dragging a lot of the wool she'd brought from Taos. He seemed to smell her long before he could see her in the sudden light. He cocked his head, bared his teeth, and growled.

Bontemps, who hadn't quite cleared the trees, bolted back down the mountain. Something cracked; there was a crash. The horse screamed.

The bear reared on his hind legs and clawed the air. Paralyzed with fear, Red Moon couldn't turn to her horse. The bear was blocking the door to the shelter where her only weapon lay, and her last bullet. She had to get him away from the door.

Down the cliff *Bontemps* was still screaming. Red Moon ran at the bear and veered away as he came down an all four legs. He took a couple of steps toward her. *Bontemps* screamed again and the bear looked in her direction. Red Moon charged him again, waving her arms and shouting. He followed her for a few steps and stopped to listen to the horse. Red Moon dashed around him and into her house. Inside was a jumble. The stove was askew, the chimney dangling over it. The overturned loom lay on top of the rifle.

Outside the bear roared and started toward the door. Her hands shaking, Red Moon shoved the loom beams aside, grabbed the rifle, and cocked it to be sure the bullet was in it. The bear appeared in the door. *Bontemps* screamed again. The bear hesitated then backed away. Red Moon stepped cautiously to the door, the rifle in position to shoot.

The bear turned from the house and shuffled toward the horse. Red Moon stepped out, raced around to the left and stepped in front of him. She yelled. She had to have him standing so she could shoot through the neck into the spine. If she only injured the bear with the single bullet, he would kill her. She stood her ground and yelled again.

The bear reared up, she aimed quickly and pulled the trigger. He staggered and fell to his right into her wall. Red Moon heard a log crack. The bear rolled to his feet and started toward her. Backing away, she reached the trees above the trail. Below her *Bontemps* was groaning now. The bear was on her, his rancid breath in her nostrils. He reached out with his paw and clawed across her left hip. She fell backwards through the trees, down the mountain. Her left foot caught in a cleft stump and she jolted to a stop. She felt her left hip joint pull out of the socket.

The bear watched her, started after her. He lurched forward and fell toward her. His huge body caught between two trees and he stopped. His feet twitched, pawing the air, and then he was still. Red Moon heard her own breathing, *Bontemps'* moaning, and the wind whispering through the trees.

She lay still for a minute, then pushed her weight back up the slope, using a tree for support. Her joint slipped back into place, and she groaned with the pain. She pulled her foot out of the stump with her hands. Slowly she rolled over and let herself slide down to where *Bontemps* was lying among the trees.

At her touch the horse stopped moaning but rolled her great brown eyes, breathing with difficulty. There was a gash in her neck and a large dead pine branch hung from her load.

Relieved that it was an injury she could cure, she let herself lean against the horse to ease the pain in her hip. *Bontemps* screamed again and Red Moon sat up. She looked more closely. *Bontemps'* right rear hoof was sticking out from under her in a way that could only mean her leg was broken.

Red Moon moaned, wanted to throw her arms around the horse's neck, but did not want to hurt her again. Unwillingly, through the blur of tears, she pulled at the pack with the big knife in it. *Bontemps* moved a little to help and then settled on it again, moaning. Red Moon worked the knife out and sharpened it on a rock, her heart aching for her last friend.

She slit the horse's throat.

CHAPTER 31

Red Moon wiped away a tear that tracked down her cheek with the memory of the friendly horse and the man who'd ridden it into and out of her life. She felt the hands of the man named Brad on her arms, holding her still as *Bontemps* walked forward and Rattlesnake bumped over the back of the saddle and slid down her rump. She saw the legs kicking and the sway of the branch and the tight rope. And then she heard the silence of his death. She pressed her hand against her heart to stop the ache that spread heat across her chest.

"Man, you hadda kill your horse? Why didn't you fix its leg?"

Startled, she opened her eyes, and stared around her. She was sitting on the saddle in her home on the mountain, and the boy who yelled all the time was still sprawled on her bed, waiting for an answer.

"Why didn't you fix it, like you fixed my ankle?"

She took a breath to make room in her chest for the answer. "Leg broke. Horse can't walk, it die. Hurt too much. Have to kill her. Eat her meat."

Carver jerked himself upright. "Man, you ate your pet? How could you? That's horrible." He glared at her with his ugly face, like at the beginning.

Red Moon sighed. He made her tired with all the chattering and the meanness. "I work hard so that horse life stay with me. I thank her every time I eat."

He turned his lips down. "I don't care. You gotta eat animals, I know that. But that one was your friend."

"Yes, my friend. Her life part of me. All life part of all life, boy. I think you don't understand that. I honor that horse when take her life into me. Honor every rabbit and every thistle."

Carver opened his mouth and closed it again. He squinted at her; a look of denial passed over his face. "I never heard o' such a thing. All life connected like that." He shook his head. "You can believe that if you wanna. Not me. Still, it's a bummer having to kill your friend. I hate it when something happens to animals. 'Cause they can't fight back, you know?" He rubbed his hand across his stomach. "All that talk of eatin' makes me hungry. We got anything to eat, Rattlesnake? We ain't got no more hot dogs."

She struggled up and brought him a piece of jerky. "This. This what you can eat."

He turned it over, sniffed it, and tapped it like a piece of wood. He stuck a corner of it into the side of his mouth and broke off a bit so small that the piece in his hand looked unchanged. He worked his mouth over it, looking up at the chimney. She had not seen that look since Rattlesnake had eaten a cactus fruit. She frowned softly at the memory. She had seen so many memories since Carver came.

Carver looked at her and grinned.

"Not Big Mac," she said, answering his grin, and now the pain in her chest eased.

"Hey, it ain't bad, man, really." He gnawed off a big bite and chewed mightily. He put his hand down on the bear skin. "This the one you shot, huh? The one that broke your house."

"Yes."

Carver laughed. "Bet you didn't thank this one, did ya?"

"Yes."

"Say wha'? Come on, man, he woulda killed ya."

"He maybe think my home was good place for winter sleep. He did what bear had to do. I had meat long time, still have skin."

Carver's mouth flew open, showing the half chewed jerky. "You shittin' me! You ate that bear?"

"Yes, some. Too much meat to work, smell bad, and had horse same time. Much waste."

Carver looked at her sideways a minute. "Would you of killed him if he hadn'a tried to kill you?"

"No. Too big, and only one bullet."

Carver was quiet for a long time. He lay back and put his foot on the wood piled under the skin. He pushed his fingers into the fur that was still thick on the sides of the bear's skin. Red Moon couldn't tell what he was thinking.

She shoved herself up and checked the patch in her wall.

Carver turned his head and looked, too. "Good thing I came when I did," he said. "I don't think your house gonna hold up much longer."

She glanced down at him. "Don't need much longer. But have to fix before more snow."

"Aw, man, it ain't gonna snow again, is it? We gotta get outta here."

"Sometime snow in summer, sometime not. Maybe snow to-night. Don't know."

"Okay, listen, I'll help you fix it this afternoon. Just need a little time off my foot. And you need to get off your hip. Then we leave as soon as we can get out through the snow. You know where the campground is?"

"Where people put up blue and green house near river?"

"Yeah, that's gotta be it. Can you get us there?"

Red Moon nodded. Her heart began to pound and hurt again. There would be people there. How would it be after all this time?

The old, old loneliness pushed in at her from every direction, making it hard to breathe. Could she have now what she'd wanted so long ago? Did she even still want it? She ran her finger over the ragged edge of the mule skin.

Carver seemed to read her thoughts. "Listen, Rat, I been thinking about it. I ain't gonna make it to L.A. nohow with this bum foot and all. Ain't no way around it. I'm gonna have to go back to Denver. But I'm gonna take you back with me an' find a home for you." His face lit and he hit himself on the forehead. "Wow, you know what? They probly gonna put you on TV. An' me, too. Man, I'll be famous, and rich. And you too. But never mind that. You just don' gotta be afraid no more. When we get down there, I ain't gonna let nobody hurt you. Man, you gonna love it in Denver. There's so many people, more'n a million. We got big ol' streets and buildings made outa glass as high as your mountain here. And lots of cars. You ever been in a car, Rat?"

"Car. Don't know car."

He closed his eyes and shook his head. "That's a machine on wheels that goes real fast. You know, like those things down there on that road. You been in one?"

"No. See many. In Taos. My mother call 'chuggies.'"

"Oh, wow, you got a lotta surprises waiting for you. You know how fast you go in a car?"

She waited.

"Sixty, seventy, a hunnerd miles an hour."

Red Moon heard the awe in his voice and another, gentler voice from the past. "We must be in Colorado now, *cher*. Just think, we're in another state." It was something to be respected. She nodded.

"You don't really understand, do you?"

"No."

"Okay, you know how long it takes you to go from here to… where you found me?"

"Yes."

"Well, in a car you'd go from here to the other side of the big valley in that much time."

Red Moon held onto one of the logs, trying to sense the speed.

"It's great, man. I'm gonna show you everything."

He put his hands behind his head and gazed up at the rock that was her roof. After a few minutes he went to sleep.

Red Moon went back out and sat looking over the valley. She tried to see the buildings as high as mountains, chuggies moving so fast around the square they made her dizzy. She tried to imagine the noises Carver had talked about, and all the people. He'd said they would help her and not hurt her. Would they all be like Carver? He made her feel like a small cactus in a windstorm, struggling to keep its roots against the howling sand.

Why was Carver here? If the black faces had been the sign after all, what could Mother Earth want her to do with him? She could not keep him here. She could barely find enough food for herself. He could not help her. He knew nothing about plants or animals. Perhaps that was it. She was to teach him how to survive in the mountains. It was all she could give him. Maybe Mother Earth had a special thing for him here, too.

She went back into her shelter for a bag, planning to go check her snares. Looking down at him, she thought better of it. "I think you must get hungry before learn to hunt," she said. She lay down on the floor with his noisy sleeping bag thrown over her and went to sleep.

When she woke, Carver was shoving at the silver blanket in her wall.

"We need a better light here," he said. "The light coming in from the door blinds you."

Red Moon got up and limped to the ledge behind the stove. She took out a sun-bleached cloth of skins and laid it in the shaft of sunlight coming through the door. A soft white light filled the room.

Carver looked at her with his mouth open. He shook his head. "I was just gonna grab the flashlight. Okay, let's get the old log outta here first."

"Need old log for stand on."

"Right."

They stood looking at the patch for a minute.

"You think we're going to be able to drag a log that's long enough all the way in here and set it up in the hole?" Carver asked.

Red Moon looked at the height of the roof and the depth of her room. "No."

"Okay, we gotta do a better job with the water-proof blanket and back it with something." His eyes lit on her shelf, one of the boards from the old cabin. "You got any more of those?"

"Some, very old." She rummaged behind the loom and brought out a couple of boards. Carver had taken down the silver sheet and was running his hands between the logs and the skins.

"Man, all this stuff's pretty soggy. Heavy, too. Gonna be hard to jam anything in there."

She set the boards down.

"Those're way too long," he said. "You got a saw to cut 'em up?"

"Have ax."

"Okay, let's try that. Where'd you get this stuff anyway? It's gotta be a million years old."

"House where lived first winter. Very cold house."

"Yeah, I can imagine."

He brought the old hatchet down on the side of one board. It splintered lengthwise into several pieces.

"Well, this stuff ain't no good. Gotta use something else."

"Have to use aspen. Cut easy."

"Okay, let's see what we can do. First we gotta double the sheet and jam it in better on both sides. I'll start loosening the stuff up there and you hand the sheet up to me."

He hoisted himself onto the log. She handed the waterproof sheet up to him and he began to stuff it under both edges of the gap.

By the time the sun went down, they had a row of aspen logs backing the blanket and new sod on the outside. They had cut the smaller end off the old log, angled it up and maneuvered it out the door. Carver looked at the job they'd done and grinned. "Gimme high five!" He held her right hand up at the level of her face and hit it with his. "Awww-right!" he said.

"Awww, thank you," said Red Moon, and hit his hand again.

CHAPTER 32

C arver woke needing to use the bathroom immediately. "Chipmunk, for Chrissakes!" he muttered. She'd fed him chipmunk soup for supper, all full o' teeny pieces of meat and a little bitty rib here and there.

He stopped in the door. She was standing in the middle of the clearing facing the rising sun. She bowed a few times, muttering something. Jeez, she was probably thanking the sun for shining. Like it had a choice or something. Then she went over to the rock, sat down and stared off to the west.

He joined her after he'd used her toilet. "Morning, man," he said.

"Morning, boy."

He sat down next to her. The peace of her valley struck him suddenly, so green, so clean, so...earth before people trashed it. His eyes buzzed hotly. Sheeit, that wasn't no tears, was it? No way he was gonna cry over some dumb scenery. He rubbed fiercely at his eyes to hide the tears, hoping the old woman hadn't noticed them. He watched her out of the corner of his eye. She was staring straight ahead, way far away in her mind. He tried to focus on going home. But there was something here. Something about time.

Or the way she believed it was all connected. He couldn't put his finger on it. Jeez, she'd even thanked the chipmunk. The thought of it made his stomach rumble into the silence. To his surprise, Rattlesnake nodded and looked satisfied.

Still, even hungry, it was funny how good he felt. He'd expected to hurt all over after the fall and then all that work yesterday. He looked back at the section they'd sodded yesterday. I did a good job, he thought. Man, I made a place for somebody to be safe in. Well, fixed it up, anyway. Well, helped. He felt Rattlesnake next to him on the rock, scrawny little cave woman. Sheeit, she done the whole fuckin' thing alone. He looked down at the beautiful valley and felt tears start again. He stifled the impulse to put his arm around her shoulder. She'd been alone all that time and no one had helped her. He didn't want her to be alone any more.

He tried to see her in Denver. The projects would never do. He couldn't stick her someplace like that. The din came back, the blaring music, the TV's after all the silence. He looked at her out of the corner of his eyes. She looked troubled, torn. Well, he'd just have to find a good place for her.

"Hey, man, you know what?"

She looked at him.

"I think I'm gonna get a job building houses when we get back. Gotta get my diploma, of course, and then I'm gonna build houses. You think I can do that?"

"Yes, you strong. You can do anything. Just have to learn to listen."

Old Dipstick's face popped up right in front of his eyes. "Yeah, I guess I do," he said. Wouldn't be easy. Hard to change, especially around people he'd dissed for so long, 'specially Dipstick. He could ask for another counselor. And then Carver knew. The easy way out didn't work if you wanted to build places to make people safe. He sighed. "Gotta start doing the hard stuff."

He reached down and picked a dandelion that had opened to the morning sun. "You just eat these things like this, no cooking or nothing?" She nodded. He closed his eyes and bit off half of it. The petals felt funny, like confetti, but the inside tasted nutty, almost sweet. He ate the rest. "How you learn what stuff you could eat up here, Rattlesnake?"

"Learn some from my mother. In mountains by Taos. Not everything from there is here, like yucca and cactus. Some plants here new. Don't know names. Watch bird and other animal, but sometime plant they eat make me sick. Have to eat little piece first."

Carver shook his head. "Man," he said, looking around for another flower.

"I show you to find things to eat, to hunt," she said.

"You show me how to hunt? Yeah, aw-right!" He jammed an imaginary rifle against his shoulder and fired off a round, bringing down a lion or maybe an elephant.

"Go behind mountain," she said, pointing with her thumb past the shelter to the east side. "You find willow by stream where you hurt your leg. Bring long stem to make trap." She motioned with her hands that they should bend easily.

"Naw, man, I'm gonna get lost in the woods again."

"Go."

Carver hesitated. She looked at him and her eyes looked just like Momma's. "Okay, okay, I'm goin'. If I get lost, I'm gonna yell till those people down there come on up and smoke you out." He grinned and shoved himself off the rock.

He was tired, slogging through all the mud and snow with the ax in the backpack poking him in the shoulder blade and his feet frozen solid. "Hey, I thought we was going hunting. Are we gonna walk clear to hell and back first or what?" He'd no sooner said it than Rattlesnake stopped in front of a pile of rocks and motioned him to be quiet.

"Still some rabbit here," she said, looking around.

"Where?"

"Look at ground."

He looked. "I don't see no rabbits."

She pointed down at some little brown pellets. "Not too old. Put your hand on them."

"Naw, man. If that's what I think it is, I ain't touching it."

She took his hand and held it on the rabbit droppings. "Still warm?" she asked.

"Naw," he answered after he'd gagged.

"You look. Where is good place to put trap?"

"Man, I dunno, how'm I supposed to know that?"

"Where are rabbits?"

Carver studied the rocks. "In the holes in the rocks, I guess."

"Where rabbits go when come out?"

"Well, they gotta come out to eat, right?"

"Good."

"What do rabbits eat?"

"Grass and seed."

Carver looked around. Behind them was the little stream they'd stepped over, lined with old brown grass that was just beginning to turn green again. Most of the seed heads were missing, but where the stream entered the trees, still half in shadow, there were some left. Pleased with himself, he pointed at them.

Rattlesnake nodded. "Find good place to set trap."

"You just set it right outside his hole. The minute he sticks his head out, zappo!, you got him."

"What hole?"

"The biggest one. It's gotta have the biggest rabbit, right?"

"No. Can't set trap for one animal. Catch nothing. Set trap for all rabbits on rock."

"Okay, then you gotta set it where all the rabbits go. Do you gotta hide it?"

"Better if hiding."

Carver looked around again. There was nothing on the face of the rock formation that would channel all the rabbits into one place. He looked at the stream again. The grasses stood near a big pine tree, but there was nothing on the ground to mask a trap.

"What if we put some dead wood in front of the grass?"

"Yes, but try not touch it. Rabbit smell you. Smell you some because you stand here."

"Okay." He pulled some leather thongs out of the backpack and dragged fallen aspen logs to the site to make a little fence with an opening. "Them rabbits can climb right over this, you know."

"Yes. Maybe lucky. One go through hole."

She had him cut a length of aspen about a foot long and three inches in diameter, notch it, and chop one end into a point. With the back of the hatchet, he hammered it into the ground with the notch at the top. She chopped a forked branch from the pine tree and shaped it so that it would hook into the notch. She tied a stout leather thong to a strong branch of the tree, then to the end of the hook.

Carver watched, so fascinated that he forgot about his cold feet.

She fashioned a noose, using the willow bark to hold the round shape and the thongs to pull and catch the rabbit. She tied the noose to the end of the hook with a thong about a foot long and pulled the pine branch down until she could set the hook in the notch. She set the noose on two little forked branches on the stream side of the fence. When an animal went through the opening, its head would catch in the noose and pull the hook out. The branch would swing up and the animal would dangle from the noose.

"Man," said Carver, "that's so simple. You don't even need no bait or nothing."

"Need luck, help from Mother Earth."

They left and set several more traps. Then the old woman start-ed telling him about plants. She knelt by a bunch of green leaves.

"This one grow so big," she said, holding her hand a couple of feet above the ground. "Have many red flower and long thin bean for seed. Seed have white hair and go far in wind. Can eat all part, even flower. Inside of stem sweet."

Carver looked down at the thing she was touching. Jeez, it coulda been any old weed. What was she telling him all this for anyhow?

"Come on, man, let's go back and check the first trap. I betcha we got a Big Mac of a rabbit in there by now."

"I show you how to find food. Can't eat just rabbit."

"What for? We gonna go back to Denver soon as we can get to the campground. All we do for food is hit the ol' Safeway. They don't sell no stuff you can't eat. And if you don't know what it is, all you gotta do is read the label."

"Maybe someday you live alone, need to know."

Carver knelt beside her. "Listen, Rat, that's real nice of you." He pinched off the top of the plant and nibbled at it. "But really, I ain't never gonna live like this. You been hiding out too long, and you just don't know. Nobody in the whole world live like this no more. You gonna see when we go down to Denver. Everything you could ever need, you just go out and buy it. It's gonna be so much easier for you. You ain't gonna have to work so hard just to stay alive."

"It is good to work."

"Maybe it is, but you gettin' old. Everybody else just quits and lets the social security take care of 'em."

She looked at him for a minute and then seemed to give some-thing up. Her shoulders drooped and she looked sad.

"Hey, man, I'm still learning to hunt. That's cool."

He helped her up and they started back. Before they reached the first trap they heard thrashing and gasping. Carver yelled, "We got one," and crashed through the trees to the trap, Rattlesnake limping behind him.

"Oh, shit," he gasped. "We got a dog, a fuckin' puppy. Come on, we gotta let it go." He started to rush forward.

Her skinny hand clamped his wrist like a door slamming on it. "No."

"Say wha'? We can't kill that. It's just a baby for Chrissakes." The gasping of the animal made him want to scream.

"Have to eat."

"You ain't telling me you could eat a dog. We was trapping rabbits."

"Coyote. Mother Earth give us coyote. You break his neck." She swung her arm to show him how to wring the neck. Her face froze in pain and she grabbed at her shoulder.

"Aw, no, not me. I ain't doin' that."

"You want eat today?"

"Not no dog, I don't. I rather go hungry."

"You want to hunt. This is hunt. You break neck. Coyote hurt."

"I know he hurt, man, I can hear that. But..."

"You afraid?"

That hit him in the gut. "Hey, man, don' never call me no coward, you hear?" The coyote was struggling less. Carver stepped over to it, watching its wild, terrified eyes, and took it around the neck. It thrashed again so hard that he lost his hold and the pine branch swung the puppy up and down in front of him. He looked back at Rattlesnake. She had her hand on her throat.

"Kill him!" she rasped. "He can't breathe."

Carver grabbed again and tore the knot that held the noose to the tree free with a force he didn't know he had. He held the coyote at arm's length to avoid the thrashing legs. The fur stuck through his fingers, the neck was warm under his hand, and he suddenly knew the feel of life. His breath was coming in sobs. He looked at the face, at the terrified eyes that pulled him in.

"Kill him!"

"Aaaah," he screamed and flipped his hand with all his might. The furry body circled in front of his eyes. He felt a snap under his fingers and let go. The tail caught on a branch of the tree then slid off. The coyote fell limp to the ground at his feet. He turned his back, staggered away and vomited.

CHAPTER 33

Red Moon stood at the stove and stirred the soup she'd made of the coyote's hind leg. Outside, under the silent stars, Carver sat where he'd been all afternoon—on the rock with his arms around his knees. He hadn't spoken after killing the coyote. He hadn't even watched as she skinned it, sliced the meat, soaked it in brine, and hung it to dry for jerky.

She chipped a little more salt from the old lick, and as she turned back, he came in with his head ducked away from her and sat on the bed. He put his hand in the fur, shook his head as if unable to stand the thought of the dead bear, and moved to the ledge behind the stove. He sat with his arms on his knees, his eyes pinched with pain. Above the crackle of the fire, she could hear his stomach growl.

Guilt gnawed at her heart. Whatever his reason for being here, her teaching him to hunt wasn't it. There must have been more to the sign that she hadn't seen. After waiting her whole life for the one thing she was supposed to do, she'd failed Mother Earth and she'd failed Carver. Her life had been one long winter of loneliness for nothing. And she'd made him miserable.

She offered him the only help she could think of. "You can take new name because you learn something today."

It was a long time before he answered. His voice was bitter. "You'd have to call me No Hunter." He shook his head. "Man, I had that puppy right in my hands and he was all warm. I could even feel a pulse racing someplace in his neck. It was his life in my hand, Rat, it was his life for Chrissakes." He leaned back against the rock, his eyes closed. "See, the only kind of killing I know is with a gun and you just pull one damn finger on a little trigger and somebody a long way off falls down. Like that woman I shot."

Horrified, Red Moon dropped her spoon and stepped backwards. "You shoot woman?"

He hung his head almost between his knees, and she hardly heard the words that came. "I didn't mean to, Rat. She ran at us and the gun just went off on its own 'cause I'd practiced so long and got so good at hittin' a movin' target. When I saw her fall, I didn't feel nothing but the kick of that gun and the blast in my ears and all scared o' the Bloods and the cops and the Crips, too, 'cause I'd gotten us all in a big ol' truckload o' shit. An' even when I thought she was dead, I didn't feel a thing. I didn't think she was connected to me at all, even by that bullet."

"You feel bad now?"

"Yeah, I feel like shit. I'm so fuckin' sorry I did that."

"Then that woman life part of your life now."

He nodded slowly. "You right. She gonna be with me forever. Now I know. I gotta make it right somehow. I gotta do better with my life. See, what I didn't know about killing was the dying. I just never was part of both right together in my hand like that."

She saw something heave inside him and feared he was going to vomit again. He swallowed hard and went on.

"You know what I saw when the coyote fell on the ground? Keeno. All dead and not moving no more, and the life running outta him in red puddles. He was my brother, Rat. My big brother."

He heaved again, and huge sobs racked him in wave after wave from deep inside.

Red Moon sat down next to him and put a hand on his shoulder. He turned and leaned into her breast and she rocked with her arms around him. She couldn't see his brother, but she could see the girl Red Moon trying to lift Rattlesnake by his legs in the dusty blue pants when he was a dead weight hanging from the tree. She could see herself crying for the invisible baby she'd buried in Rattlesnake's hand, and she rocked Carver for all the sorrow.

He cried until the heaving stopped then sat up looking ashamed and brushed away tears that ran down his face. When he could talk again, he said, "He was my hero and they shot him for nothing. That was his dying, but I didn' pull the trigger." He put his hands around his throat and squeezed. "But that coyote, I had him right in my hand, Rat, and he was warm, and then I made him dead."

Red Moon stroked her own arm where the feel of his body was still warm. "Sometime have to kill even if make you sad."

"Yeah, I know. I been thinking about that a lot, setting out there on the rock. I can understand you killing animals. You gotta eat. I'm talking about a different kind, and I ain't never gonna kill another thing as long as I live, 'cause I don't need to. And I ain't stealing no more cars. And I ain't doing no coke."

Red Moon returned to the fire and spooned some soup into the bowl, trying to hold the feel of the child in her arms, the strange child she'd waited for all her life. Was this why he was here? To learn the truth about killing? She put the soup next to him on the ledge. He set the bowl on his knee and stared into it. She went back to eat out of the pot.

It was a long time before he spoke and his voice was small.

"Rattlesnake, is it too late to thank the coyote?"

"Spirit gone from body now, but you should thank for you, so you can eat."

He lifted a piece of the meat in the spoon. "Thank you, coyote. I'm sorry I had to take your life. I'm sorry I let you suffer so long." He glanced at her and then said so softly she hardly heard him, "Thank you for what you taught me." He put it in his mouth and chewed it slowly. Then he looked up at her and grinned. "I guess you knew all along my stomach would get the best of me, didn' you?"

"No."

"Well, it tastes pretty good. I thought I'd just throw it right up."

CHAPTER 34

As Carver walked from the old woman's toilet back to her rock, he glanced at her cave. He grinned, shaking his head. "They'll never believe this," he said aloud. "Jeez, she's gonna be some kinda celebrity. We'll both be famous. Man, we'll prob'ly be on Arsenio Hall and all them talk shows." They should be able to leave soon; his ankle didn't hurt at all, and her limping had gotten better.

He climbed on the rock and sat down. Across the valley the sun was just touching the tops of the peaks, and the snow seemed to glow from inside with a gold-pink light. The forested slopes were still in the shadow of the mountain where he was sitting, and miles away his own shadow was darkening some tree or a rock. At home, he would'a been mad as hell if somebody woke him up this early. Funny, somehow it didn't matter when there wasn't no school and no schedule to keep.

The sun was good on his back, the air crisp and clean in his nose. His lungs welcomed deep breaths of it. He thought of the city coming to life, full of din and dust and millions of people rushing off to work. From here, it seemed to him like a dirty glass ant pile, nothing to the earth and he nothing to the city. When they were all gone the sun would still come up in the silence and light the peaks over there.

He remembered thinking there was something about time up here. Now he knew what it was. Time didn't belong to him. It wouldn't stop when his small part of it died. The thought made him panicky. I gotta leave a mark, he thought, a mark the sun can shine on.

He turned to go back to the shelter. The sun struck him full in the face and he stopped to let its warmth soak in. "Man, you something else," he said aloud. He glanced at the door in the wall of grass and made a small bow to the sun.

Back inside he found the old woman stuffing things into Dipstick's backpack.

"This mean we can leave today?"

"Yes. Your bag ready now."

"What about yours?"

"Not take anything."

Carver looked around. "Yeah, what's to take, huh, Rat? You don't need none of this stuff down there. They gonna give you all new stuff anyhow."

The old woman looked him in the eyes so long he began to fidget.

"I am Red Moon Rising," she said.

"Huh? I thought you said you was Rattlesnake."

"I am that, too. Have many name. Take Rattlesnake to scare the man who kill Rattlesnake."

"Uh-huh. Well my name's still just Carver. But you can call me something else if you want."

Red Moon nodded and stepped through the door.

Carver hung back and took a last look around. Nobody'd ever believe it. Too bad he didn't have a camera. Some "survival week-end" this turned out to be.

They walked a long time. Carver chattered for a while about how it was going to be in Denver and what all his bros would say about her. Finally, realizing that Red Moon Rising wasn't answering him, he fell silent. She probably just felt funny about leaving her home.

He tried to comfort her. "You can always come back here to see your place again, you know."

"Yes."

After that he just followed her, wondering if he'd come this way that night when he'd run away. Jeez, it seemed like months ago. How many days was it, anyway? Three, four? He tried to count the nights and couldn't keep them straight. No wonder Rattlesn...Red Moon Rising didn't know what year it was. He couldn't wait to set her down in front of a TV. And he couldn't wait to see the expressions on Lathrop's and Johnson's faces and all the guys when they got back to the campground.

Long before he expected it, she stopped and he ran into her. They were on a rock where they could see the campground from a distance. Several cars stood around, and light green pick-ups with yellow lights on top of them and people milling about. Even from here he could make out Mr. Lathrop. He nudged Red Moon with his elbow.

"See the man with the dark red jacket and the beard? That's my counselor. Holy shit, nobody else from the group's there, just him." He felt himself choke a little and had to stop talking.

"You can go there from here," said Red Moon.

"Okay, come on then." He started climb down, but she didn't move. Carver turned to her, surprised. "Hey, come on, man, you said you was gonna go, too."

"No, you said it."

"You can't stay up here alone anymore, Rattlesnake. You'll go crazy."

"Not already crazy?" She grinned at him and then her face turned serious. "Can't live in your world, Carver. Make me choke. Always want people to care for, but too late now. My root is here."

Carver wanted to protest, but no words came. Instead the sage-scented air surrounded him. He looked toward the big valley he could no longer see and felt a pang of loss. In his mind's eye he traced the line of snowcapped peaks beyond the green meadows, felt the sun warm him from the cloudless sky. He looked at the ground, at the pasque flower that was half crushed under his foot and knew that she was right. His world was too ugly for her. He fought back tears.

Her eyes were filling, too.

"Listen, man, you take care of yourself. I'm coming back and see you again. You think you can find me if I make enough noise?"

"Yes," she smiled, and a tear dripped out of her eye. "You tell no one about me, please."

"But..." he started. Then he knew they'd hunt her down out of curiosity if he gave away her hiding place. His short dream of fame burst.

"I won't, Rat...Red Moon Rising. I promise."

They stood looking at each other for a long moment.

"Well, I better get going."

"You go back and build house. It is a good thing."

"I promise you that, too." Still, he couldn't say good-bye.

"The coyote look out from your eye," she said.

"Yeah, I know. I feel him in there."

"When I find you, I don't like your eye. Full of hate. You hate everything."

Carver froze and stared at her. She'd blindsided him again. Hate. How did she know that? Yeah, he'd hated everything. It was what made him tough, a man, he'd thought.

She pulled the coyote skin from a rabbit-skin bag slung over her shoulder and held it toward him.

Carver backed away from it. "When'd you work on that? Last time I saw it, it was still all bloody and ugly."

"Work when you sleep. You take now."

"Naw, man, I can't touch that and not see his eyes all scared of me."

She shoved it into his hand. "You already thank coyote, he your brother now. Not scare any more."

As Carver's fingers slid into the fur, a breeze swept across the valley and ruffled the hair, swayed the tail. But there was another wind, like the wind of time rushing though him, and he heard Keeno's voice in it. His mind spun like a dust devil on the project playground, snatching up images of the past, spinning them into the future. Momma whirled in the dust, her face sagging with despair. LaRon and Odelle flashed by, their eyes clouded with the beginning of hate, their little hands already reaching for guns and knives. He had to go home. He had to stop them before the hate got them in the gang, too, in jail. He was the big brother now. "You right, man. About the hate. I'm sorry, Rat, I dissed you real bad when you rescued me."

Her face softened into a gentle smile. "Now I see no hate. This good. You go now. You keep coyote in your heart and he look out your eye."

"I will." He slid the backpack to the ground to put away the skin but changed his mind. He raised his shirt and flattened it against his chest with the tail around his waist. "I'm gonna call him Coyeeno."

He picked up the pack and started down the side of the rock. "Hey, Rat, ain't no reason why you couldn't have this stuff here." He dropped the pack again. "There's the good sleeping bag and the matches and the magnifying glass and stuff. You know how to use a magnifying glass to start a fire?"

She squinched her eyes all up. "No. Don't know that glass."

"Okay, let's get it out." He felt around in the bag for a minute, and drew the round glass out. He let the sun shine through it onto a couple of dead leaves and soon a little wisp of smoke rose from them.

Red Moon's eyes grew large. She took the glass in her hand and turned it over. She let the point of light shine on her other hand.

"Naw, man, you gonna burn yourself." He took it away and stepped on the smoking leaves. "Don't never do that, okay?"

She nodded.

"You wanna see something cool?" Shading it with his body, he put the glass over the zipper of the jacket he'd tied around his waist.

She shook her head as the teeth of the zipper appeared to double their size.

"Next best thing to TV," he said. "Here, this is for you, too." He handed her the bright blue down jacket and helped her slip it on. It came almost to her knees.

"Now don't you go cutting it into strips trying to weave no blanket or nothing. You gonna have tiny feathers all over the place." He pulled at one that was sticking through the fabric. "See, the whole thing's fulla that stuff."

Red Moon shook her head. Then she picked up the backpack and handed it to him. "This your bag?"

"Well, no, it's Mr. Lathrop's, but you need it more than him."

"I keep match, you give other thing back."

"Okay, you right." Carver shouldered the pack. "Well, I guess this is it," he said. His voice caught. "Man, I'm gonna miss you." He threw his arms around her, and she threw the big blue sleeves around him.

"I love you, Rattlesnake."

"I love you, too, Little Coyote." She handed him the jacket.

He started down the hill again.

"Carver," she called after him.

"Yeah?"

"Your head grow so square. All black man have square head like that?"

284

"Say wha'?! Naw, man, that ain't my head. It's just my hair." He came back up the rock and took her hand. He put it up on his head and pressed it in so she could feel that his head was round, just like hers.

She nodded seriously, feeling the stiff, tight hair.

Carver started back down the hill. He turned around at the bottom.

"So long, man."

"So long, *cher.*"

RED MOON

CHAPTER 35

Red Moon watched Carver approach the campground. The man with the red jacket and the beard saw him before any of the others and rushed toward him. They stopped short of each other, then Carver offered the man his hand. The man clapped him on the shoulder several times. The others gathered around them and soon they all headed for the green chuggies. Before he climbed into one of them, Carver turned and looked toward her. As he bent to get in, his white palm waved at her behind his back, flashing in the sun. The chuggies made their noise and moved away. All that was left to her of Carver was a cloud of swirling dust that drifted after the chuggies.

Red Moon waited until it settled, and then there was only silence. Solid, heavy silence, like the solid, heavy dark of the old winter cabin when she would come awake needing the sound of Rattlesnake's breath to give space to the night.

She started the long walk back, struggling through the silence. She looked at the sky to get above the weight of it. Against the blue, far above her, an eagle circled. From his eyes she saw the girl Red Moon lying in the sand of the nearly dry San Juan River. She did not want to see the lonely, aching girl. She did not want to see the old woman limping alone to an empty shelter, either. She focused instead on the rocks and sand and pasque flowers at her feet.

Red Moon faced the morning sun, letting its warmth seep into her old bones. But its comfort did nothing to fill the silence of Carver's absence. He had come and taken her over and then left her heart an empty place.

The sun was warm on her face, but Mother Earth pulled at her feet. It was time to go home. She scattered a few grass seeds to the wind before setting up the loom where she could work in the sun. She went back into the shelter, brought out the ancient sack of white wool and emptied the contents on the ground. She picked up a skein, intending to tie up a warp. There were breaks in the yarn where mice had chewed into it. She tried the rest of the skeins and found them all damaged. She pulled out the longest strands and tied them together to make her warp. The knots would not matter anymore.

She hadn't woven anything in a long time, and she hadn't used any of the white wool since bringing it from Taos. From Mr... She couldn't remember his name. She could still hear his strange speech, see the concern on his face when she told him about her mother's death. She could see the white blanket in the sand again, and under it the woman who had taught her how to weave and then died in the desert.

Her heart hurt and the pain ran down her left arm.

Red Moon sat at her loom with her back to the sun, feeling its warmth like that of her mother long ago. She wove a white border, removing dry mouse droppings from the yarn. Chewed and stained, the yarn would make a poor blanket, but it would not have to last long.

When the border was finished, she went into her shelter and brought out all of the small skins she could find. She spent the afternoon sitting on her rock overlooking her valley, cutting the skins into thin strips with the stubby knife, sharpening it again and again on the side of the rock.

For two days she wove with white wool and strips of fur, stopping often because the pain in her chest made it hard for her to breathe. She could hear the weaving song in the broken rhythm of her work. Again and again she started the song, "O Mother Earth, O Father Sky," but only a few of the words came.

The blanket was nearly finished. There was only the white border at the top, and as she wove, she chanted her own song:

> O Mother Earth, O Father Sky,
> Your child am I.
> With tired heart I bring you this finished life.
> Then weave for me a garment of light.
> Make the warp of my mother's teaching.
> Make the weft of Rattlesnake's loving.
> Make the border of Carver's changing.
> Make the fringes of sun rays from the clouds.
> Then weave for me a garment of peace,
> That I may walk fittingly where my people walk,
> That I may walk fittingly where there is love.
> O Mother Earth, O Father Sky.

Red Moon took the blanket from the loom and tied off the ends.

The sun was setting and already the moon was following it down from the top of the sky. She went to her rock, walking stiffly, her hip stiff and sore after two days at the loom. She laid the blanket next to the rock and then brought the bear skin and the old name blanket from her shelter. She laid the skin over the rock and painfully climbed up with the new blanket and the old. For a time she sat watching the lights come on in the town, but it was not her town and it was very, very far away.

She stroked the old blanket and allowed the memories to flood her. She saw other blankets, the many colors and designs she had woven with her mother, the one she had woven by herself, with the people standing in corn. She looked at her name blanket, washed gray on gray in the dusk, and knew that it was not only a picture of her name, but a picture of her life, a simple design badly woven by a hand too young to weave better. For the first time she remembered the child Red Moon's pride when the blanket was finished, and the promise that it had seemed to hold. She stroked the little lopsided Red Moon, holding the blanket across her breast.

The sun was behind the mountains leaving only a deep purple, jagged outline. The last rays brushed the underside of a long, thin cloud with a deep orange and that, too, faded to purple. There was peace. One of those flying machines was lit like a star, too high to hear, and it drew its long gold line away from her. The pain was great. She looked above the silhouette of the mountains at the sailing moon. It was lopsided on the wane but white and very bright, smiling at her.

She fingered the new blanket in the moonlight. At the bottom she'd woven the hogan of gray squirrel in a desert of rabbit and above it her laughing Rattlesnake, made of the belly of chipmunks, his brown eyes from strips of the back. The Rock with Wings was there, and a long rope that circled a gray cabin, and mountains with a valley she had colored green by rubbing the bleached skins with dandelion leaves. At the top she had used the darkest stripes of chipmunks to weave a black face, square at the top, with its mouth open, chattering like a squirrel.

She lay back, covered with the blankets. She felt herself on another rock, in another time, a cold cabin standing in shadow to her left. She had placed her hands on that rock, asking why she must live when her mother and Rattlesnake were dead. She'd thought Mother Earth refused to answer during all those winters and summers when the sign hadn't made sense.

But in the end the answer had come. Carver. The child Mother Earth had meant in all the black faces. He'd come hating everything. He'd gone saying he loved her. She had changed one child. Maybe he would change another.

A small cloud floated past the moon, its edges lit into a round, milky rainbow, so beautiful and so brief, like her time with each of the ones she'd loved.

The pain in her heart grew and the peace with it. A memory of dry grasses pulling at the life in her hands washed over her, and the moon smiled down.

She could not feel the line between her body and Mother Earth beneath her. Slowly her hands worked their way out from under the wool and fur blanket, stroked the rough surface of the familiar rock under the bear skin, and moved up to the black face over her heart. For one moment she had held a child in her arms, comforted his pain. The warmth of his body flowed into her heart. It was enough.

"I am White Moon Setting," she whispered. A breeze from the west eddied against the mountain and carried breath and spirit toward the waiting moon.

OTHER BOOKS
BY MARGARET BAILEY

Diamond in the Sky
In the silver mining town of Leadville, Colorado, in 1895, two lovers pin all their hopes for staying together on the success of the spectacular Ice Palace built to help the silver mining town through the bust that followed the establishment of the gold standard.

Waves of Amber, First Wave
A fictionalized memoir, this story reveals how Hong, a Vietnamese refugee, and Margaret, an American teacher, manage to become family to each other despite cultural and age differences.

Waves of Amber, Second Wave
Four more refugees join the fragile family life of Hong and Margaret and nearly tear them apart.

Waves of Amber, Third Wave
Another wave of refugees throw the now enlarged family into chaos again. Only love, loyalty, and determination can hold them all together.

Stephanie's Search

Stephanie Brenner has the personality of a hedgehog and a heart-load of anger over a deformed arm. Doug Lansing carries around a load of guilt heavier than all the gear in his Search and Rescue backpack. They both desperately need to find Floyd Bascomb, who has vanished in the Colorado mountains. Their paths will cross like two strands of barbed wire, but perhaps they will find something they weren't looking for.

Father President

Father Paul Greer bolts from the priesthood with no idea how to build a new life. A drunken brother, a natural disaster, and a serious flaw in the Constitution propel him in directions unseen in his worst nightmares. His traveling companion is Emma Light in the Lodge, a Native American and outspoken, radical Earth-rights activist. So how can two people who don't belong in Washington survive? And will Washington survive them?

A Little Witching at the Wall

What's a left-over hippie, would-be witch to do when her life crumbles around her? Why, marry a rich man, or course, and use her new position to put some good vibes out there. A love potion should serve nicely, if she can find the right ingredients.

Lily Marcuso entangles the lives of a bumbling hit man, a confirmed bachelor, a suicidal teacher, an East German guitarist, a West Berlin cop, and a self-serving secret service agent as they converge on the Berlin Wall on the night when it falls.

www.ingramcontent.com/pod-product-compliance
Lightning Source LLC
Chambersburg PA
CBHW061543170626
46811CB00001B/71